WAKING
DREAM

WAKING DREAM

Carol McD. Wallace

St. Martin's Press
New York

Design by Jessica Winer

Library of Congress Cataloging in Publication Data

Wallace, Carol, 1955–
    Waking dream.

    I. Title.
PS3573.A42563W39   1987   813'.54   87-15555
ISBN 0-312-01108-3

First Edition

10 9 8 7 6 5 4 3 2 1

To Rick and Willy, with love

Heartfelt thanks to Stanley Crane, for his years of vain attempts to elevate my tastes; Lynn Seligman, for taking all my efforts seriously; and Robin Desser, for helping this particular dream come true.

WAKING
DREAM

Chapter 1

He was much too good-looking for the library.

He had sleek straight blond hair and straight features that could have been called aristocratic. Gold signet ring. Blue blazer. Starched shirt. Definitely too good-looking. In the Local History and Genealogy Division of the New York Public Library, he was a distraction.

I couldn't see what color his eyes were. They were probably blue, with that hair, though his eyebrows were dark, so they could be brown. . . . He looked up and caught me staring at him. Blue eyes, a dark opaque blue. I felt myself blushing and looked at my watch. Come on, Sarah, you have more work to do. It was four o'clock and the genealogy room would be closed the next day and I wanted to finish with the book I was working on. It was very dull. *Genealogy of the Wright Family*, it was called. It wasn't indexed, and I was looking for Erastus, husband of Sophonisba, father of Lauretta. Lauretta was lucky to have been given such a comparatively normal name. In the 1870s—and especially, it seemed, in the western states—they went in for outlandish names. Benoni, Truax, Preserved. Preserved Wright. It was better than Preserved Fish, whose portrait I had seen somewhere. Imagine going through life with a name like Preserved Fish.

I was getting nowhere, so I got up to go for a little walk. I would go get a drink of water, get rid of the cobwebs. My route took me past the handsome blond and I couldn't help glancing sideways to see what he was reading. *Debrett's Peerage*—that was a coincidence. *Debrett's* was my escape reading when the genealogy books got too boring to bear. The whole system of aristocracy was such a strange survival, but I was completely entranced by its glamour; I would read endlessly about young duchesses or heirs to marquessates living at Monte Carlo addresses (tax exiles, I deduced). It was all completely unreal, of course, like something out of Trollope; but somewhere, these people lived and breathed and ate breakfast and had migraines. I wondered whom the blond man was looking up.

I wandered slowly out into the North Hall of the library, past the microfilm machines, stretching a little. A cluster of Japanese were taking pictures of the peeling painted ceiling. The little black bag lady sat, as usual, in front of a dictionary, lacing and unlacing her sneakers. The room echoed with muted voices and rustling pages and the occasional thud of a heavy volume dropped on a counter. There was, I noticed, still plenty of light coming in through the high windows. Winter was over.

As I bent over the water fountain I wondered if I should bother taking my heavy coat to England. I would leave in six days and be gone a month, which meant I would return the last week in March. On the other hand, I did have to go up to Scotland and it might be very cold there. And when I thought about the amount of luggage I was going to have—all my papers, index cards, notebooks, perhaps a typewriter—I wondered how other writers managed their research trips. Did they just take a pair of jeans or a little black suit? Was I really going to need the typewriter? And then there was the camera, and the lenses. I had made list after list and it all seemed organized—but I did not feel in control.

Wiping water from my chin, I ambled back to the genealogy room. London for the British Library; Bath for the costume museum and Mary Curzon's dresses; the Borders of Scotland to see Floors Castle, where May Roxburghe lived. . . . I wished I had heard from the Earl of Saltire, because I didn't know when I would fit in a trip to Ireland.

I slid back into my seat, and was immediately sleepy again. The handsome man was at the desk, asking for something. I strained to hear but he spoke softly; and with an English accent, it seemed. How very odd. He could read peerages in England. I realized that I was staring and forced my eyes back to the Wright family, flipping carelessly through the pages. Erastus's name leapt out at me, and I forgot, for the moment, the mysterious Englishman.

When I got home that night there was a letter from Saltire in my mailbox. I tore it open in the elevator. "Dear Miss Llewellyn," it began, on heavy cream-colored paper with a small engraved crest. (I got a little thrill out of that.) It was long, and typed, and I glanced down the page to see who had written it. "Yours sincerely, David Neville," in a neat near-italic hand. That would be Viscount Neville, *b.* 1953; ed. at Eton, at Ch. Ch., Oxford, and Roy. Agricultural Coll. (as *Debrett's* put it). "I'm sorry to have taken so long to answer your letter of the 15th of December. We would be happy to help you in any way we can in your research on American heiresses and their British husbands. Of course, as you must know, Countess Lauretta did not live very long and spent very little time here at Saltire. She died at Neville Park, in County Galway, shortly after her son was born.

"As a family we are not terribly well informed about our own history, and I'm afraid there are trunks of papers here that we haven't investigated thoroughly. (There are also trunks of Lauretta's dresses, if that would be of interest to you.) There may also be papers at Neville Park, which you may want to visit. Certainly you have our permission to do so, but it is currently let to a businessman who is using it as a country house. His name is Ludovic Walter. Perhaps if you write directly to him he would be willing to let you see the house.

"We would be very glad to see you at Saltire. Since the nearest hotel is a bit grim and we're not terribly near London, we hope you will stay with us. If you could call me when you get to London, we could arrange a convenient date for your visit."

It was an awfully nice letter. It was also just a little unusual. Of course, the Earl of Saltire wouldn't be as well organized as, say, the Duke of Marlborough, with librarians and archivists and so on. But surely there was someone besides the eldest son to write letters to importunate Americans? Didn't he have something better to do? And asking me to stay with them seemed almost overpoweringly cooperative. I would love it, of course, but it didn't quite make sense.

I moved a stack of index cards off my own copy of *Debrett's* to look up the family again. There it was: David Vernon Alexander Charlton, 17th Earl. Born 1927. Married 1952 to Cecilia Belinda Wrathmore, daughter of General Sir Hugh Wrathmore. Had issue: David, Henrietta, Hugh, Andrew, Cecilia. The current Earl had succeeded his brother in 1970, and their father had died only five years before that. I didn't know much about death duties, but perhaps with those two deaths in five years, the Saltires were broke and couldn't afford a secretary. And though the fourteenth Earl had married an American heiress, that was nearly a hundred years ago.

I moved some more papers to find my file of pictures. There was Lauretta, a dark-haired beauty in an elaborate white dress. She had come to New York from Ohio just when the fourteenth Earl had arrived from England. He was looking for a rich American wife; she was looking for a husband. Poor Lauretta; he had dumped her at Neville Park right after their honeymoon and gone off to the Continent, where he started to spend her dowry on horses and cards. And then she had a baby, the requisite heir to the earldom; and then she died.

And I was holding a letter from her great-grandson and I was going to see the home she had been taken to . . . and where she had died, if Mr. Ludovic Walter was amenable. I sat down to write him a letter. I hoped he would prove as helpful as his landlords.

On Friday the blond was back at the library. He had on a tweed suit this time. I didn't pay much attention to him because I was reading about Erastus Wright's will, in a funny circa-1910 publication that reproduced the last testaments of a number of very rich men. Though it was marvelous to have the complete text of the document, the language was awfully hard to plow through. As far as I could tell, Lauretta got everything, and her children after her. But if she died without children, the money reverted to remote Wright cousins, including the stock in Prairie Beach Railroad, which made up a large part of her dowry. That was strange; usually the husband's family kept the dowry, even in cases of divorce. Had Erastus not trusted his son-in-law?

"Excuse me," a voice said quietly. I looked up. It was the Englishman. I felt my face turning red. "I'm terribly sorry to interrupt you, but the man at the desk told me you had *Wills of the Millionaires*." He nodded toward the book I was reading. "Could you give me an idea how long you might be?"

I flipped through the sections I needed to read. "I might be done this afternoon," I said doubtfully. "But I'm not sure."

"I see. Well, thank you very much," he answered, and went back to his seat. Today he was at the same table as I, on the opposite side. He still had *Debrett's*. He wanted *Wills of the Millionaires*. And lying in front of him was *Genealogy of the Wright Family*.

I tend to be a little paranoid, and with this kind of book there is always a fear that someone else is working on the same subject that you are, but a jump ahead. I was uneasy when all the pictures of Jennie Jerome were missing from the Picture Collection, or when the best book on the couturier Worth was in use in the Art Division. And here, right in front of me, was a man reading *Debrett's* and the Wright family's genealogy, and he wanted the book on wills. Lauretta Wright had to be the link. He had to be writing a book on American heiresses and English aristocrats. There was no doubt in my mind that he was in the New York Public Library doing his research. Just as I was going to the British Library to do mine.

I glanced at him again. He didn't look like a writer. Not that writers look like anything in particular, but there was something too polished about him, the same quality that had made me notice him the first day. I didn't know anyone who would dress like that day after day at the long tables with the dusty books. Those shirt cuffs: who would wear a starched shirt to the library? And then, he didn't even have index cards or a legal pad for his notes, just a slender notebook fished from the inner pocket of his jacket.

The man was ruining my concentration. I turned back to Erastus's will and tried to understand the legal terms—and read the same sentence four times without taking it in. Could I just ask him what he was doing? I could not.

But he gave me the opening. He got up and came around to my side of the table, holding the Wright family book. "Could I trouble you again for a moment?" he asked, with a little smile.

I nodded dumbly, and he leaned a little closer. "I couldn't help noticing that you were working with this book yesterday. Is there any simple way to find the chap I'm looking for? Since there's no index, you know."

This time I shook my head. "No—they're divided up geographically, you realized that? Do you know where your fellow was?"

"Ohio somewhere, but he died in New York. I don't suppose you found him? Erastus? Made a pot of money in railroads?"

"Yes, I found him. May I?" I took the book from his hand and flipped to the place in the middle where Erastus was discussed. I gave the book back to the Englishman.

"Why, thank you very much! I didn't expect to be led to him by the hand." He glanced at my yellow pad covered with scribbled notes, and at *Wills of the Millionaires.* "Do you mind if I ask . . . I shouldn't want to pry, but we do seem to be using the same books. . . ." The elderly man across the table glared at us for the third time and made a loud sucking noise on his dentures. My eyes met the Englishman's, and I thought he was suppressing a grin. "Shall we . . ." he whispered, and motioned toward the door. I nodded and got up, pushing my chair back so that it squeaked loudly and trying to stare down the old man.

We sat on a marble bench in the main hall, and didn't say anything for a moment. I looked up at the gilded and coffered ceiling, pretending not to notice that he was sizing me up. The inventory had to be fairly neutral: a tall, thin frame, tawny hair inclined to wildness, green eyes, a checked flannel shirt and fawn corduroys. I hoped he was giving me credit for good skin and clean fingernails, at least. He broke the silence. "I'm Gerald Charlton, by the way," said my new friend.

"Sarah Llewellyn," I answered, hoping my face didn't register instant recognition. Charlton was the Saltire family name— could this be a cousin?

"You seem to be rather an expert with that business," he said, waving his hand in the direction of the Main Reading Room. Books, card catalogs, genealogies, wills; he might even have been referring to maps and photographs, so inclusive was the gesture.

"Hardly an expert," I demurred.

"Well, highly competent, then," he said charmingly. "Are you working on a book?"

I looked at him warily. If in fact we were writing the same book and he was related to one of the families involved, he had a great advantage over me. I might as well know the worst. "Yes, a book about the American heiresses who married into the English aristocracy at the turn of the century."

His face lit up, and he looked, if possible, handsomer than ever. "*Are* you! Isn't that marvelous! D'you know, I think we're probably looking up the same person, Lauretta Wright, the Countess of Saltire."

"Yes, I imagine so," I said dryly. "Is it Erastus Wright's will you wanted to look at?"

"Yes. You see, Lauretta was sort of a great-great-aunt of mine, and I just thought I'd poke around a bit and see what I could find out about her, since I was over here in the States for a while." His eyes drifted away from mine and he reached into his pocket for a cigarette case.

"Ummm . . ." I put my hand out.

"Oh, excuse me, would you like one?" He flipped open the case and offered it to me. "Americans so rarely seem to smoke." It was a pretty case, silver with a vermeil interior. A class act, Gerald Charlton.

"No, it's just that you can't in here."

"Oh, of course, how silly of me." He shut the case and put it back in his pocket. "I don't know what I was thinking of."

"Your great-great-aunt Lauretta," I suggested. I wondered idly if Viscount Neville was as good-looking as his more-or-less cousin Gerald.

"What a coincidence!" Gerald was saying. "I don't suppose . . . I mean, you haven't found anything as simple as a biography or anything obvious that I've missed?"

"No, I haven't. There's really not much about her," I said, sounding regretful and feeling disinclined to simply hand over what I knew anyway. "But—of course, I don't know what kind of thing you're looking for—have you done any of the microfilm stuff?"

He looked blank. "No."

I was suddenly brisk. "I haven't done much of it myself, but you know the *New York Times* and the other daily papers have been microfilmed. So have some of the magazines like *Vogue*, and Lauretta would be mentioned in the gossip columns, I would think. Certainly her wedding would have been covered." I felt in my bag for a pen and pulled out an old envelope.

My Con Edison bill. I wrote down the names of two publications and a date: February 14, 1898. "Try these. That's the date she got married." I handed the envelope to him and stood up. "And I'd better get back to work if you're going to get a shot at Erastus's will."

He stood up too. "I shall try these, thank you," he said, gesturing with the envelope. "Will you be here all day?"

"All day," I said, and went back to work.

Of course I hadn't seen the last of him. I went back to the wills with better concentration, and by the time he came back, at around five-thirty, I was reading William H. Vanderbilt's will and had decided how to deal with Gerald. It wasn't that I knew so much about Lauretta Wright. It was just that (I thought rather meanly) I didn't want to give it all away. I had had to dig to find out what I knew; and so would he.

He looked jaunty and pleased when he came back into the genealogy room, and he came and bent over where I was working. "That was marvelous," he said quietly. "They're about to close up, aren't they? Will you come and have a drink with me?"

I looked up into those blue eyes and the quizzical little smile and shut the book on W. H. Vanderbilt.

We went to a quiet, comfortable bar in a midtown hotel, a place with deep upholstery and a squashy carpet and knots of businesspeople "relaxing." I noted with interest that the waitress and I were the only women in the place who weren't wearing ties. Gerald and I chatted politely, exchanging a modicum of information. I ascertained that he was staying with friends in SoHo, that he liked New York, that he admired our American vitality. I had heard that it was rude to ask Europeans what they did for a living, so I didn't obtain the one bit of information I really wanted. He asked me about my book, and what stage it was in, and whether I would be going to England.

"Next week, in fact," I admitted.

"Really? And will you stay in London, or travel around?"

"I'll travel a bit. A few of the people I wrote to said they had papers they'll let me see, and of course I'm dying to visit the houses the girls lived in."

"Are you going to Saltire?" he asked, casually.

"Yes, I just got a letter from them. I don't really expect much from Saltire, since they said they don't have an archivist and the papers aren't even organized. It seems awfully odd."

Gerald looked amused, and poked an ice cube in his Scotch. "It might be odd in another family. I'm sure they can't afford an archivist, and I can't imagine anyone has cared about family papers for several generations."

"Have you ever been there?" I asked, trying desperately not to sound eager.

"No. I haven't spent a lot of time in England, actually. I was brought up in New Zealand, and after the university I went to Kenya." I wished he'd said which university, and supposed that, too, was vulgar curiosity. Gerald went on. "Cousin Hugh was up at the same time I was, but we barely knew each other. He read divinity."

"What did you do in Kenya?" I had to ask.

"Oh, this and that. Have you ever been there? Nairobi's marvelous. And of course after New Zealand I wasn't quite keen on the English climate. Nothing to compare to Ireland, though. Will you get to Ireland?"

"I don't know yet," I said, frowning. "I'd like to go to Neville Park, but apparently it's rented to some businessman and he may not want me poking around. I hope he doesn't object, because that is where Lauretta spent most of her time."

He signaled to the waitress, and leaned back in his chair, crossing his legs. "Would you . . ." He waved at my empty glass. I nodded, and he asked the waitress for another round. "I shouldn't think you'd have much trouble with a tenant if you have permission from Lord Saltire," he said sympathetically.

"Yes, well, you never know," I answered, thinking I sounded fretful. I suddenly wanted to go to Neville Park very much.

I escaped shortly after that. It was funny to think of it as an escape, because I liked him so much. But I didn't like to talk about the work I was doing, and he kept bringing it up. Of course, since he was related to Lauretta, I could understand why he was curious. And now that I knew he wasn't writing a competing book, I should have had no worry. Still, I wasn't comfortable telling him what I knew. All the same, when he asked for my phone number as we parted on the street corner, and suggested dinner on Saturday, I said yes.

When I got home that night I was sorry I had. There was so much to do before I left, and I shouldn't be wasting time going out to dinner. A feeble little voice told me that perhaps Gerald could tell me more about the Saltires and I could classify the date as "research." I knew that was just rationalizing, but I accepted it, even as I gazed around the piles of books, file folders, stacks of papers, and manila envelopes that littered my tiny living room. The first thing to do was to clean the place for my subtenant. So I opened a beer, put on a record, and started cleaning.

By the time Gerald called on Saturday afternoon, I was ready for company. He suggested meeting for a drink at the top of the World Trade Center; "touristy, I know, but it's a lovely night."

It was spectacular. The red streaks over New Jersey gave way to a blue darkness punctuated with twinkles. We were at a table facing north, and Gerald wanted to know what everything was. He was consummately charming, and we did not mention our common interest, Lauretta.

In fact, until we were sitting at dinner in an excruciatingly fashionable restaurant on West Broadway, we had mentioned nothing but generalities. But as I gingerly coaxed a mussel from its shell, I said, "What else do you know about the Saltire family?"

He smiled and took a sip of wine. "Not much. Just the usual gossip. What did you want to know?"

Our eyes met, and something passed between us that had nothing to do with our conversation. "Just the usual gossip," I said lightly, and poked an empty mussel shell.

"Well. It's an old family, of course; created under Henry the Eighth for the usual political maneuvering and given the land of one of the richest monasteries in Oxfordshire. There was a big Tudor pile there that burned, and was replaced under George the Third. The tenth Earl is supposed to have designed it, with a lot of help from Robert Adam, and of course the park is Capability Brown. They had thousands of acres, and did quite well agriculturally, but things started to fall apart in the nineteenth century. Somewhere along the line an earl married an Irish heiress and that brought Neville Park into the family, along with the Neville title. The money was a help, but the property is in the very bleakest part of Western Ireland, and good for nothing, I should think. Nonetheless, the thirteenth Earl took quite a liking to it; he turned Catholic and a bit potty to boot, and spent as much as he could on remodeling Neville Park under the influence of Pugin.

"As you can imagine, that made further dents in the Saltire fortune, and then came the fourteenth Earl—Lauretta's husband. His brother, by the way, was my great-grandfather. Anyway, though he was wise enough to marry American money, he was even more of a spendthrift than his father. He died quite young, crashed a carriage in a race of some sort. His son, little St. John, succeeded at the age of six. He was brought up by his uncle, my great-grandfather, who was a terrible prig from what I can gather. The priggishness seems to have rubbed off, since St. John married a very appropriate marquess's daughter and made a model earl. Do you mind if I have a cigarette? Are you finished?"

"Yes, I am; go ahead. No thanks." I shook my head as he offered the case.

"Right." He leaned back and lit the cigarette. "Well, St. John was exemplary in every way. He had four children, and, in marrying Henrietta, had brought some more money into the family. He was a magistrate and a J.P. and finally died in 1966. But the sixteenth Earl was a throwback, another reprobate like his grandfather. He was gay, for one thing." He looked to see how I would take that.

I nodded. I'd expected it. For an English earl to die childless argued a very strong disinclination toward women.

"And he liked gambling and racing a lot more than he liked being a good landowner. He was only earl for a short while but he managed to run through a fair amount of money before his death. He died in 1970, and his brother David succeeded him. Rather tough for old Uncle David, actually. He had married a very pretty girl and settled down to do something in the City and was leading a pleasant enough life when it gradually became apparent that brother St. John wasn't going to do the proper thing and produce an heir. But Uncle David was one of the correct Charltons, and when the time came, he put on the harness and he's been doing his damnedest to restore the fortunes of the family."

"So the death duties must have been a problem," I suggested.

"Enormous," agreed Gerald. "Not to mention what St. John ran through. He was part of that wild set in Kenya after the war."

"So what is the rest of the family like?" I pressed him.

Gerald exhaled, and smiled at me through the smoke. "You mean what can you expect when you get there?"

I shrugged. "I guess so."

"Well, as you no doubt know, the heir is David, Viscount Neville. He's an academic by vocation. Went through Oxford in a blaze of glory, got a First, and was all set to be a don when it became clear that he'd have to be an earl's son and heir instead. So off he went to the Royal Agricultural College at Cirencester to learn about being a farmer, and since then he's been doing his bit to make Saltire pay. They've opened it to the public, for instance, and I think there's some plan to turn the Irish property into a stud farm. Then there's the Lady Henrietta." He leaned forward to stub out his cigarette. "Nigel Dempster and the other gossip columnists love Lady Henrietta. She's a smashing red-head, and she designs clothes and wears them to parties and evidently does quite well with them. I believe the Princess of Wales has started to buy them, which could go far to restore the Charlton fortunes. Hugh, as I mentioned, did the classic youn-ger son bit and took orders; I imagine he's a curate in some fashionable parish now. There's another brother, Andrew, who I think is in the City, and then a sister who must just be out of school."

"No Lady Saltire?"

"She died a few years ago. And that is truly all I know about them. Are you tired?"

I couldn't help thinking about what I had to do the next day, and my resolution to get up at seven to get started on it all. And then I looked over at Gerald, lounging elegantly in his chair, with his eyes on mine, waiting for me to answer. He was playing with his lighter, turning it over and over on the table-cloth in his long fingers.

"No," I said, "I'm not tired."

"Good," he answered, and signaled for the check. I won-dered what he had in mind. He put on my coat for me at the door of the restaurant, settling it on my shoulders with a ges-ture that was almost possessive. I was very much aware of his hands lingering for a moment before he stepped forward to open the door.

He called a cab, and as it stopped in front of us he asked, "Do you like to dance?" I do, so he gave an address that was unfamiliar to me, up on the East Side.

It was an unmarked door, and it swung open when Gerald raised a hand to knock. The club was small, but a band at one end was playing rather bouncy music and the dance floor was surprisingly crowded for what was, after all, an early hour.

We sat down. We ordered drinks. Gerald told me a scandalous story about a distinguished-looking older man at a banquette across the room, involving a fake diamond necklace and an ex-senator's ex-wife. "Shall we dance?" he finished. Impeccable. Perfectly proper. Gerald seemed to believe in holding his partner closely and leading strongly. I had forgotten the heady feeling of not having to decide what to do with my feet. "You're a wonderful dancer," he murmured, very close to my ear.

"All a girl has to do," I managed to say, "is hold on tight and follow."

He did something with his arms which left me with my back toward him and his arms around me. Then he did something else which kept me spinning until I was dizzy, so that when I was finally facing him again I had to cling to stay upright.

"Should I change directions?" he asked, smiling.

"Did you know that in the eighteen-eighties a man who reversed directions with his dancing partner was thought a cad?" I asked. It sounded inane but was all I could think of.

He spun me for a moment in the opposite direction, and said, "I can see why." He touched my cheek. "Let's go."

He waited to kiss me until we were outside the door, and didn't stop until another taxi drew up, when we broke apart and hurried away. We walked to my apartment; it took a while. But when we got there I stopped in the shadow beyond the lighted canopy, out of the doorman's sight. "This is good night," I said.

He kissed me again. "I regret it," he said. "But only a cad would insist. When do you leave?"

"Tuesday."

"Do you have time . . ." I started to shake my head, thinking of my already-full calendar. "I'll call all the same. Where will you be staying in London?"

"Subletting a flat. I'll give you the phone number when you call. Thank you," I said, and kissed him on the cheek.

And that was that. The doorman, seeing me come in alone, gave me an avuncular wave. The first thing I did when I got upstairs was to look at myself in the mirror. I was flushed and my eyes looked greener than usual. All that spinning around the dance floor had made my normally wavy hair rather wild. I thought a leaf or two stuck in it wouldn't look misplaced. I tried to imagine what Gerald had seen in me, and gave up.

I wondered as I tried to go to sleep if I should have let him come upstairs, and thought that maybe next time I would. But as it happened, when he called I was out and I didn't see him again before I went to England. And the way things finally turned out, I was glad.

Chapter 2

I couldn't decide if it was raining or not. What I really couldn't decide was whether or not I needed my windshield wipers. There were drops on the windshield, but not a lot of them. Tentatively, I felt around with my left hand to test the controls. I took my eyes off the white line to my right for a second to see if I could fathom the little signals on them. I honked the horn and turned on the heat and gave up. The drops were drying anyway.

I had made it out of London in a state just shy of panic, caused by the confusion of the right-hand drive and the proliferation of rotaries or what they called "roundabouts," which went the wrong way. Several times drivers had squealed to sudden stops just short of my door. It was harrowing. But now that I was on the M40, things were a little calmer and all I would have to worry about was passing. I had no intention of it.

My week in London had gone very well. I loved being in England. I reveled in the voices in the streets, the watery changeable sunlight, the Queen's cipher on the mailboxes and the ridiculously heavy coins. I loved teatime. Twice I'd managed to get to Evensong at Westminster Abbey, where the choirboys' voices rising to the shadowy vaulting brought tears to my eyes. The flat was perfect, the top floor of a house in Kensington where an impoverished colonel and his wife lived. The arrangement was so genteel that money never passed from hand to hand but was left in an envelope on a salver in the front hall. They

(Mrs. Belton-Hogson in particular) were very interested in my research and were eagerly awaiting the results of my visits to Saltire and Neville Park. For Ludovic Walter had answered my letter, saying he'd be happy to see me, and naming a date. I had spoken to David Neville, and he had urged me to come and go at Saltire as was convenient. I had found lots of wonderful material in the British Library. I had spent a day in Bath at the costume museum looking at the trunks of dresses Worth had made for Mary Curzon when she was Vicereine of India. In fact, the only heiress about whom I'd found no information at all was Lauretta.

Nothing in the gossip columns I'd skimmed in the *Illustrated London News*. Not a mention in a list of American peeresses that the *Tatler* had published. Not a single photograph in the illustrated papers of the new Countess in her tiara and presentation feathers. I could have understood it if she'd been an obscure American marrying a younger son or a provincial baronet. But the Wright fortune and the Saltire title should have merited more attention from the press. I couldn't even find an obituary for her, which I found very puzzling. And when it came right down to it, I didn't know when she had died.

It wasn't particularly important. The book wouldn't stand or fall on this one tiny piece of information. She had died shortly after her son's birth, no doubt of the kind of complications that made childbearing risky in those days. The *Times*, which was meticulous about reporting births and deaths in the aristocracy, had a notice of St. John's birth on December 3, 1899. Though the obituary index didn't mention Lauretta, I had wasted half a day skimming the obits for the following few months just in case. Nothing. It was probably merely an oversight and I finally gave up. It didn't really make any difference when she had died, and, if I remembered, I would check the parish records when I went to Neville Park.

I stopped in Woodstock for lunch, and wandered around the town on foot, hating to get back into the car, for I still found driving mildly terrifying. Though there was something self-conscious about the neatness and prosperity of the shop-fronts, the pretty little town seemed idyllic. No amount of calculated quaintness, however, could erase the fact that it had seen hundreds of years of history. Finally my hands stopped shaking and my courage came back, so I zigzagged my way out of the village and drove the final hour on tiny hedged roads to Saltire.

I had expected something comparatively modest—after all, the family did still *live* in the house. But the gate into the park was an intimidating stone-and-wrought-iron affair, standing open at the end of a graveled drive. I turned in, noticing the entwined S's in the ironwork—and the potholes in the drive. An allée of enormous oaks lined the drive for several hundred yards, then the drive turned left, the allée went straight, and a lovely little brick house with a garden at the junction nestled next to a stone wall. But I didn't pay much attention to the little house, because the big house was in sight. It *was* big. Huge, in fact. Crowning a little rise of ground, it not only loomed over the drive, but spread, with its symmetrical wings, for what looked like acres. Hedges on both sides of the drive, even if they were rather shaggy, forced your eye up to the house. Dozens of blank, paned windows looked out over the drive and I suddenly felt very self-conscious in my rain-spotted rented Mini. I would have loved to turn and bolt.

But there was no way to turn around on the straight, narrow, and hedged drive. It broadened into a graveled terrace of sorts with a dry fountain in the middle, and an imposing flight of steps up to the door. There I was and there I would have to stay. But where, I wondered, should I park? There was so much space and my car was so small. I coasted to a stop somewhere to the right of the fountain. Then I decided I should pull the car closer to the building—not that I needed to leave room, heaven knows. I thought it would look neater. I put the car into reverse and stalled it, swearing. I hoped nobody was looking out any of the windows. I edged the car closer to the steps, remembering to leave myself room to get out. I didn't suppose I would need to lock it.

I climbed the steps and looked for a doorbell. There was a knocker; I knocked and a dog started barking far away. I looked again for a doorbell and found that the center of one of the flowers swagged around the door-frame produced a pealing bell. I heard the dog barking again, and this time the door opened.

I was partly gratified and partly horrified to find that it was a butler, but when I gave him my name he nodded and said, "This way, miss."

I followed him through a hallway with a checkered marble floor and a grand staircase, and glimpsed French doors at the other side of the house, opening onto sky and terrace. We went down a long hall that had astonishing plasterwork and eighteenth-century portraits, both in something less than perfect condition. There was a gilded French table with a sang-de-boeuf vase standing on a marble top. It was distinctly chilly. The butler stopped at a double door and knocked, then opened it. "Miss Llewellyn," he said.

I was very aware of the wrinkles in my pleated skirt, crunched up from the drive, and my hair, which was curling away from the combs I'd stuck in to control it, using my driving mirror. I had ascertained that there was no actual dirt on my face but I felt very crumpled. And the room was so very beautiful.

Most people have an idea of what good Georgian architecture looks like, and this was some of the best. I didn't notice until later the delicate rosette on the ceiling or the overmantel with its classical cornice or the tall windows with their long brocade curtains. I had an impression of light colors and airy proportions—and then there was a yellow Labrador sniffing at my feet and David Neville rising from a pretty French desk.

He was tall; much taller than I, and big-boned. He was welcoming me in a deep voice, rather gravely. "We are so glad you are here," he said, then bent down and snapped his fingers at the dog. "Cynthia! Leave the lady alone!" She leaned against his leg and looked up at him, panting, and her tail beat against my skirt. "She's shedding terribly," he said, and pulled gently on her ear. No dog ever looked so happy.

"Please, won't you sit down?" he said, gesturing at the pair of honey-colored silk couches facing each other on either side of the fireplace. "I thought perhaps I could just explain some things and we could walk around the house quickly before tea." He spoke slowly, and his speech caught a little on the hard consonants, hinting at a stutter.

"That would be fine," I answered, just as the butler came back into the room.

"If I might have Miss Llewellyn's keys, I will have her car moved around to the yard and her cases taken down to the dower house."

"Oh, of course," I said hurriedly, and bent down to fish them out of my purse. Cynthia got up from her place by the fire and poked her black nose in the bag. "Cynthia, darling, I think I can find them without you," I muttered, putting a hand on her solid shoulders. I heard a little splutter of laughter, and looked up at Lord Neville, who was smiling. He had one of those very sweet shy smiles. He snapped his fingers again and Cynthia went back to his side.

I gave the keys to the butler, who said, "Thank you, miss. And shall we unpack for you?"

"No, thank you," I said sweetly, trying to sound as if other people frequently unpacked my suitcase.

"We'll have tea in here, Figg," said Lord Neville.

"Very good, my lord," Figg answered, and left the room silently. I thought he looked like a butler out of the movies, with his black jacket and striped trousers and perfectly expressionless face. He was far more terrifying than the young viscount.

"I hope you don't mind," my host was saying, "that we've

put you in the dower house. We have room here, of course,"
with a hint of that diffident smile, "but we thought you might
like to be private. It's the brick house at the turning in the
drive."

"Oh, yes, it's very pretty."

"Yes. It's older than the big house, which burned in 1758
and was replaced by this one. But let me show you where the
main things are just to begin with. . . ."

"That would be wonderful," I said doubtfully, "but, you
know, I could wait and go with a tour when the house is open
to the public. I wouldn't want to trespass on your time."

"Not at all," he answered, holding the door open for me.
"And I can give you the guided tour, if you like, but it's a bit
dull."

I stared at him, trying not to be rude. "Do you give the
tours?"

He nodded. "We're only open by appointment out of season,
so it isn't terribly arduous. And we do have help in the summer." We were walking down the corridor to the front hall, and
I assessed him out of the corner of my eye. Dressed in a pair of
worn olive green corduroys and a beige V-neck sweater, he
looked more like an art history professor than like my idea of a
viscount. He had sandy hair, brushed back from a high forehead, and gold-rimmed glasses. If I had come to Saltire as a
tourist, I would have thought he was some young academic
earning a few pounds on the side. Which, when I thought about
Gerald's analysis of the family, wasn't so far from the truth.

"The most important thing," Neville was saying as we
reached the central hall, "is that you not get lost. Of course we
don't mind in the least your wandering around and you mustn't
worry about disturbing us, but you could spend a lot of time
trying to get from one place to another. Fortunately the plan is
simple, and in the central block the house is only two rooms
deep. I'll point out the main landmarks that you can steer by."

We had come out into the hall, and he started up the shallow marble stairs, followed by Cynthia. "We'll start in the library, which, unusually enough, is on the second floor. The tenth Earl was a bibliophile and an insomniac, so he wanted his books next door to his bedroom." At the top of the stairs a full-length window looked out over the terrace and fields, with a stream and a church spire visible in the distance. Neville turned right and pointed to a neoclassical painting of a hunting scene. "It's supposed to be a Poussin, but we have our doubts. Still, it's a perfectly adequate signpost because Diana is pointing toward the library." The corridor was similar to the one on the ground floor, but the paintings were mostly landscapes, and they were hung against dark green fabric.

"This is the library. We keep the doors closed to keep in the heat," he said, opening a door at the very end of the hall. "You see we're at the end of the wing; there's the dower house and the gardens, and over here you can see the home wood." I just had time to glance around at the long tables, the barrel-vaulted ceiling, the glass cases of books. "We'll come back," he promised, and we went back out into the corridor. He pointed out boudoirs and sitting rooms and state bedrooms—"This room was done over for the Prince Regent" or "The tapestries came from Schönbrunn." We reached the central hall, and he waved at the other wing. "Our bedrooms are down that way. We'll go back down to the ground floor; it's much more interesting."

As we went down the stairs Cynthia started to bark, and she left us at a gallop, skidding a bit on the marble floor of the hall. "Davey! Davey, where are you?" a female voice came from the east wing. Before he could answer, the owner of the voice came around the corner.

She was a vision. To begin with, she was remarkably beautiful, with brilliant auburn hair and brown eyes. She was clearly Neville's sister, with his cheekbones, his coloring intensified, his straight nose. But it was as if heredity, having practiced on him, produced in her the final statement. What made her startling, though, was that she had on a long black riding habit, with a top hat and veil. She had the full skirt looped up over her arm, and looked as if she could have stepped from a hundred-year-old photograph.

"Netta! Back already? Miss Llewellyn, this is my sister Henrietta. Netta, Miss Llewellyn."

"Please call me Henrietta," she said, as she took off her gloves and shook hands. "And call David David, in case you were wondering."

"Well, I was, thank you," I said, laughing.

He looked at me and nodded. "Please; we're too young to be stuffy about things like that." He turned to his sister. "You look splendid, but you weren't out very long. It wasn't a success?"

"You might say that," Henrietta answered. "I thought it might be rather fun to hunt sidesaddle," she told me, "so I've been trying it out. Today we went to meet the hunt when they drew the Little Spinney. Nash didn't like it at *all*." She turned back to David. "He was jumpy all the way down there, I could barely keep him to a trot, and once they found he was impossible. Of course I had to use one hand to keep this stupid hat on," she added.

"This was our great-grandmother Lauretta's habit," David explained. "Henrietta found it a few months ago and has been trying to train Nash to the sidesaddle ever since. But since he's the most high-strung horse in the stable, she's not been terribly successful. I still don't know why you don't use Hercules," he said to her.

"I will if I have to," she answered, "but Nash is a much better ride. Are we taking Sarah on a tour?"

"Yes, we just have time to swoop round the ground floor before tea. Don't you want to change?"

"No, of course not. I can't tell you how much fun this skirt is," Henrietta said, dropping it from her arm and letting it trail behind her as we walked down the hall. "I think this is what bothers Nash; I think it tickles him."

"Mother never had any trouble with Hercules," David said.

"Darling, Mummy's habit didn't have six yards of fabric in the skirt. And besides, Nash would look so much better." She explained to me, "The truth is that hounds are meeting here this week and I want to wear this habit. And Hercules is an elderly flea-bitten gray and I don't want to look as if I'm riding a retired circus horse. This is the music room. Do you play? All the instruments are out of tune." She lifted the lid of a lovely painted spinet and struck a chord.

"No, I don't," I answered, gazing around at the frescoes of nude gods.

"The eleventh Earl went to Venice and was much struck by Tiepolo," David commented dryly. "Fortunately the French boiseries he tore out of here weren't terribly damaged."

"Don't be such a snob, David," Henrietta scolded, running a finger over the strings of the harp. "Your grandchildren will probably think this is divine."

"No doubt," her brother answered, looking up at the fleshy deities.

We left the music room and opened the next door, onto a huge mirrored room.

"The twelfth Earl went to Versailles?" I suggested, then wished I hadn't been so flippant.

"Exactly," said David, with that smile. "It could be worse. An architectural historian at Oxford recently unearthed a local architect's plans to turn this into a Chinese gallery."

"Hideous," Henrietta shuddered. "All dragons and *faux* bamboo. And this is a lovely room for dancing, David. We had a combined party for his twenty-first and my coming-out and he loved it, though he'd never say so."

We looked quickly into the rest of the rooms in the east wing, which was closed off by a swinging door.

"The proverbial green baize door," said Henrietta. "Kitchen and pantry and so on, miles from the dining room, of course. Modernized in 1936 and untouched since."

"I told Figg we'd have tea in the Little Salon," David told

Henrietta as we turned back toward the hall. By the time we'd crossed the house my feet were beginning to hurt and, despite David's assurances, I was more or less lost. There was a little trolley set up in the room where I'd met David, and I was glad to sink down on one of the couches. Henrietta sat down to pour tea from a huge silver pot, and Cynthia promptly lay down on the long black skirt of her riding habit. David brought me a cup of tea and sat down at his desk.

"Sarah, would you mind terribly handing me the biscuits; I hate to disturb Cynthia," Henrietta said. "Now tell us what you've found out about our great-grandmamma. Such a romantic story!" She unpinned the veil over her eyes and took off the silk top hat.

"Yes, but very sad. I suspect she was rather naive when she married, and with all due respect, the fourteenth Earl . . ." I paused.

"Was a bad bargain," David finished for me, looking up from what he was writing.

"Well, yes. As far as I can gather, they went on a longish wedding trip in Europe, were in London for a month of the season, came here for a month, and then he sent her off to Neville Park alone. And never saw her again."

"Poor thing," said Henrietta. "Did you know that they went to Paris on their honeymoon? There are some clothes here that came from Worth, and some bills with them."

"Are there? That's wonderful! And you have the bills?"

Henrietta nodded. "Yes, and the dresses are in wonderful shape. There are all kinds of hats and gloves and parasols as well. I'd be happy to show them to you. Are you going to Neville Park? There might be some more things there, because there are bills for dresses we haven't got, like a white brocade ball-dress and lots of tea-gowns."

"Yes, I'm going there in a few days, so I'll see if I can find them." I paused to put a lump of sugar in my tea. "Do you know if there are any papers there? I mean as well as what's here?"

It was a simple enough question, innocently asked. Nothing to warrant Henrietta's reaction. Which, to be fair, I wouldn't have remarked had I not glanced up from my teacup just at that moment. What I saw was merely Henrietta looking over at her brother. But the expression on her face came as a shock; gone was the charm, the sparkling interest in her guest, the aristocratic assurance. The girl look frightened. And she was asking David, as clearly as if out loud, "What should I say now?"

It was only a moment, a second's break in the conversation. I looked away immediately, reflexively, embarrassed by the way she had exposed herself. David answered for her, smoothly covering up. "We don't honestly know what's at Neville," he said. "The family hasn't spent much time there. But then, we don't really know what's here either."

Henrietta added, "You can see why we were so glad to have you here. No one's looked at things in generations." She had recovered fast, I thought. Maybe I'd been imagining things. Maybe that silent fraternal exchange had been about something else. But now I was on edge.

"Why not?" I asked, perhaps a little sharply. "Some of the papers must be important."

David got up from his desk and brought his teacup over to the table between the sofas. He handed me a piece of paper. "This is a map of the house. It might be helpful." I looked at the precise little ink drawing while he sat down next to Henrietta, facing me. That was thoughtful of him, I had to admit. "The really important things are all kept by the solicitors: wills, letters patent, that sort of thing. And, in fact, up to the middle of the nineteenth century, even the less important documents are all neatly filed in the estate office. We do, for instance, have all the plans for the house in order, and the inventories of the paintings and so on. And even the most rakehelly of our ancestors had agents to keep rent-rolls straight. What's upstairs really just looks like the flotsam and jetsam collected by the recent generations who couldn't throw anything away." He smiled suddenly. "You know, things tend to collect when there's plenty of room. We did find, for instance, all tied up with baling twine, sixty years' worth of the *Spectator* which nobody could bear to jettison. We gave them to the local library."

"So you don't even know whether there are letters or diaries in those papers?" I said. It seemed impossible that nobody had ever taken enough of an interest to investigate a little.

"No, I've never even gotten to the bottom of any of the trunks."

"Every now and then," Henrietta added, "on a rainy day when there's no hunting, no tourists, and no major crisis, I have found David in the library staring into a trunk and sighing. But he always gives up after about an hour."

"I know I ought to try to sort the papers out, you see, but I've never had a block of time to do it. Something else more urgent always comes up, and they don't after all make a difference in the day-to-day running of the house. I have thought it would be a good idea to have some kind of Victorian expert come look at them. So you can imagine how glad I was to hear from you. At least you'll know what you're looking at. I didn't."

He met my look apologetically, as well he might, I thought. I was going to sort out the trunkfuls of Victoriana, was I? It was neat, I had to admit. For the price of a little hospitality they'd get a somewhat informed assessment of the papers. I had to be a lot cheaper than someone from the Victoria and Albert.

On the other hand, I was a lot less expert than someone from the V&A. It wasn't actually a bad arrangement. There might be real treasure in those trunks, and nobody else would have seen it. I wasn't being asked to catalog or inventory it, after all.

The diffident, scholarly Lord Neville had made a shrewd arrangement, but it was fair.

"We'd better give you a chance to unpack and get settled," he broke into my thoughts. "We'll walk you down to the dower house."

"Actually, if you'll excuse me," Henrietta said, "I think I will go put on modern clothes. This bodice is beginning to feel awfully tight." She gathered up her top hat and veil, and preceded us out the door, sweeping her skirt behind her. "I'll see you at dinner."

The sun was setting when we left the house by the French doors and walked around the west wing. The windows reflected the red glow from the sun as we went down a shallow flight of steps from the terrace to a formal flower garden. "The formal gardens of the old house were all torn up in the eighteenth century, when Capability Brown landscaped the park," David told me. "My grandmother's great project in life was restoring them in a form adapted to the new house, though they weren't, strictly speaking, correct. Here's the knot garden; it's lovely in the summer, since they're all aromatic plants. And these are roses on the arbor; another example of chronological jumble. Not very cheerful now." I looked around carefully, thinking that I would have to go back this way at night, and trying to remember where there were steps. We were walking now between two more high hedges. I couldn't help thinking that so much box (or was it yew?) must need one gardener to look after it full-time.

"It needs pruning in the worst way," commented David, echoing my thoughts.

I was also thinking that the path was narrow, and would be very dark at night. There was a little white gate in the hedge to our left, and an archway cut in the bushes.

"That's the maze," David said. "I wouldn't try it alone, since it's pretty fiendish, but the key is simple. Remind me to take you through sometime; there's a lovely fountain at the center."

I guessed that there must be another bed of flowers to our right, between the path and the drive, and asked David about it. "Yes, what grandmother did there is rather curious. There are successive little rooms, more or less, marked out by the hedges, each with a bit of lawn and different flowers. And here we are." The hedged walk came to an end and there, across a small lawn, was the side entrance of the brick house, with the stone wall at its back and the allée of oaks visible above its roof. French doors opened directly onto the grass; David opened them for me, shaking his head. "They should have turned on a light when they brought your bags down." He walked over to a table dimly visible in the dark room, and turned on a lamp. The room that jumped into sight was charming, much less formal than the rooms at the big house but nonetheless elegant. Here was linenfold paneling and a massive stone fireplace and the chintz that seemed necessary to complete the picture. There was a long refectory table behind the sofa with lamps, books, and a big vase of daffodils on it. I couldn't help smiling.

"Do you like it?" David asked seriously. I nodded. "I'm rather fond of it myself," he said, running a finger across one of the panels on the wall. "Let me show you where everything is. It's bigger than it looks."

Indeed, it was. There was a dining room, a library, a billiards room, a small formal drawing room by the front door. The kitchen was cavernous, and looked primitive. Upstairs there were six bedrooms and I guessed there must be quarters for servants tucked away somewhere.

"We've put you in here," David said, opening a heavy carved door. The switch by the door brought light to a pair of wall sconces, and showed a charming room with a window seat, a fireplace, and a canopied bed. It looked south to the big house, where the lighted windows glowed yellow. "There's a phone if you need anything," he said. "It goes directly to Mrs. Lowery but she can transfer it to us. Very modern stuff. You can also get an outside line on it, but Mrs. Lowery has to connect you. Let me show you." We went back out into the big hall, where David opened another door to reveal what looked like a Tudor version of a phone booth. "This used to be the linen press. Henrietta wanted to paint the door red and put a window in it, but we managed to persuade her not to." He looked at his watch and said, "Dinner's at seven-thirty; we usually have a drink at seven. If you don't care to walk through the garden in the dark, you can just walk up the drive. The traffic's not too heavy. Do you have everything you need?" I said I did, and he smiled shyly and left. I heard the side door shut behind him.

Drinks at seven. That gave me an hour and a half to unpack and make myself respectable for dinner. I went back into my bedroom, and looked out the window. The garden was so dark that I couldn't see David walking up to the house until finally his tall figure appeared silhouetted in the light from the windows.

Chapter 3

I turned back to the room. My 'cases,' as Figg had called them, were lined up next to the bed. They included a canvas duffel bag and a camera bag and one proper suitcase that my mother had taken on her honeymoon. The bed was huge and—I sat on it tentatively—soft. The mattress crunched, and I wondered what was in it: probably horsehair. The pillow cases were linen and, to my utter delight, embroidered with coronets.

I decided to explore a bit before I unpacked, with an eye to finding the bathroom. David was probably too shy to have pointed it out himself. I was glad to find it was next door. I thought it must have been converted from a bedroom, since the proportions of the room were gigantic. In addition to Victorian white-porcelain fixtures—no shower, of course—there was a free-standing towel rack made of white-painted cast iron, and a chaise longue. I couldn't quite imagine lounging in the bathroom, since it was chilly and ill-lit, but perhaps you laid out your clothes on the chaise. Or your maid did.

I went along the hall looking into the rest of the bedrooms, pushing open the heavy doors one by one. Some of the rooms were charming; one had a Victorian sleigh bed with a real Paisley coverlet, and one held pretty French provincial furniture. But in one there was only a brass bedstead that needed polishing, and one was completely empty. I supposed that the dower house had not been occupied to capacity for a while.

I went back to my bedroom to unpack. I didn't have many clothes, and stowing them in the big freestanding cupboard took very little time. But there wasn't a table in my room, or a place to spread out all my papers. So I shouldered my duffel bag and went back downstairs. There was a library; I would use it as a library.

I shivered as I walked across the flagstones of the hall. A good thing it was March and not January. Had there been a light switch in the library? I thought not; there was a standing lamp next to the big leather couch, and another lamp on the desk. I tripped over something (a stool?) as I groped my way toward the desk. I would have to remember to keep lights turned on at night because I didn't much like walking into dark rooms. Typical of the English to neglect light switches near the door—no doubt to save some priceless paneling—and force you to keep lights on when nobody was in the room. My hand found the corner of the desk, the base of the lamp—no, that was another vase of flowers. There. The library appeared. It had two small windows set into the walls of bookshelves, otherwise broken only by the door and a big fireplace. Beams in the ceiling that looked in the dimness as if they might have been painted long ago. I stepped over to one wall to see what the books were; with a library up at the big house, what would be relegated to this branch? I pulled out a handsome leather binding; something in Latin. A cloth binding farther down the shelf turned out to be an old biology textbook. No treasures here.

I turned back to the desk and hauled the duffel bag onto the desk chair. It was a sturdy mahogany partner's desk, so there was room to lay everything out on the top if I wanted to. File cards in one corner. File folders. I thought I could put the legal pads in a drawer, if there was one empty. The first drawer I pulled open contained the jack of spades and an old key. In went the pads, blank file cards, pens. A few crucial biographies I lined up on the desktop.

I thought the arrangement looked very nice in the mellow

light, with the striped tulips on the corner of the desk. Modern
Dutch still life. And it was time to do something about the way
I looked before dinner. I left the light on in the library.

Fifteen minutes later I came downstairs in a clean skirt, wondering if the family changed for dinner. They would have told
me, surely? And in the country, in the late twentieth century, it
hardly seemed possible. Moreover, there was not a single mirror in the dower house except the one in my powder compact,
so I couldn't even reassure myself that my hem was straight
and my slip didn't show.

I had decided that I would be brave and go back to the
house through the gardens. I noticed that the sitting room with
the French doors was quite cold, and then I saw that the
French doors themselves were open. I'd heard David shut
them, but I supposed in an old house doors drift open by themselves. I stepped out and pulled them carefully behind me,
making sure they latched. Thinking about my camera and
lenses upstairs, I wished for a moment that there was a lock. It
was a quiet night in the country, but New York habits go deep
and I hated to walk away from an unlocked house.

I pulled my jacket around me and headed toward the lights
of the big house. There were stars, even a moon overhead,
but the brick path between the hedges was exceedingly dark.
There was a breeze, and things rustled. Animals, probably.
Little moles or possibly rabbits. Cute, furry, harmless rabbits.
Definitely harmless. I passed the white gate to the maze. The
moonlight showed a narrow stretch of grass and then another
hedge. That would be my idea of a nightmare: a maze in the
dark.

I wished there were street lamps. Maybe I would come home
by the driveway. I was more than halfway there; here was the
arbor, and finally the high hedges gave way to the parterres.
The moonlight was bright and my steps slowed down. I passed
the side door and walked all the way around to the front so that
I could see the long view over the terraces and down to the

river. It looked like a fairy tale, or at least the land where fairy tales come from. I heard the door open behind me and two slow footsteps that brought David to my side. He didn't say anything for a moment, just stood there looking.

"I sometimes wonder," he finally said, almost reluctantly, "if I would have loved it more or less if I'd grown up here." There was another pause; I hardly knew how to answer him. "But it's chilly," he said, turning toward me. "We must get you inside. Did you find everything you need?"

So we went into the house and he took my jacket and gave it to Figg and sat me down in the Little Salon with a drink. "Henrietta always drinks wine, so we've a bottle open here, or would you like some Dubonnet or something?"

"Actually," I said, noticing a short glass of amber sitting on his desk, "I'd love whiskey." I was relieved to see that he had on the same corduroys and sweater, though he had put on a tie which bore no relation, colorwise, to anything else he was wearing. Cynthia was lying by the fire, and when I crouched to pat her she opened an eye and thumped her tail. "She's just the right color for the room," I commented as I straightened up to take the glass David was holding out. "Thank you."

"Yes. We had the pick of the litter and she was the only yellow one and Henrietta insisted we choose her even though she wasn't supposed to be a house dog."

"Do you hunt with her?" I asked, wondering if that was the right terminology.

"No, bless her heart, she's gun-shy," David answered with an amused look at the dog. She thumped her tail again.

"Which you were hugely relieved to find out," said Henrietta from the door. Clearly I need not have worried about dressing for dinner, since Henrietta had on a pair of pants and a loose top made from caramel-colored sweater fabric. She had a foulard scarf tied in a bow in her hair, which curled outward all around her head like a pre-Raphaelite aureole.

"Damn it, Netta, you've been in my drawers again," said David mildly, twitching the scarf.

"David, when was the last time you wore this? You hate scarves, you know you do." She sat down on the floor next to Cynthia.

"I was saving it for my old age, when I start to be a curmudgeon and smoke a pipe and say the country's going to the dogs." He poured his sister a glass of wine and handed it to her.

"In that case I'd better let you have it back now," she said, and pulled it off her head.

He laughed. "Oh, keep it, I'm not so desperate yet." I was fascinated to see how she re-tied the bow perfectly, at just the right angle, without any tentative pattings or pokings.

"Papa's up in town, so it will be just the three of us tonight," Henrietta said to me. "He promised Lord Delabarr that he would go up to vote on the drainage bill."

"Lord Delabarr is our neighbor and the master of the local pack of foxhounds. Drains are his other interest," David said dryly.

I was relieved that I wouldn't have to face the Earl quite yet. I imagined a rather austere and haughty figure whom I would have to call "my lord." (Or would that sound like a servant?) With that the door opened and Figg announced, "My lady is served."

I noticed that Henrietta and David left their glasses there, so I followed suit, and trailed behind Henrietta out the door. The proper dining room (proportioned like a roller skating rink) was just down the hall from the Little Salon, "miles from the kitchen," as Henrietta had said. But we sat at a small round table in the Rose Room, whose walls were lined with glass shelves full of Ming famille rose and Sèvres porcelain.

"We usually eat here if we're six or fewer," David explained as we sat down.

"It's so much closer to the kitchen that the food is still hot when it gets to you. You can imagine how hard it is to plan a big dinner party when you know all the food is going to be lukewarm," Henrietta added.

As I put my napkin in my lap I had to suppress a strong desire to pick up my plate and look at the name on the underside. The silver was heavy, very simple, and lustrous, and the plates were painted in a design similar to the ones in the cupboard. "Will you have some claret, Sarah?" David asked before pouring the wine.

"Uncle St. John's one constructive occupation was buying wine," Henrietta said. "Unfortunately, he also drank rather a bit."

"He put down more than he drank," David said reasonably, "and you can't begrudge him all that champagne. It doesn't improve with age, you know."

"Yes, I *do* know," Henrietta answered. "He was still pretty useless."

"Oh, yes. Definitely what Regency gentlemen would have called a 'loose fish.' Still, there are some in every family and we're lucky there are no remittance men in this generation."

"Unless you count Gerald Charlton," said Henrietta. A little shock went through me. She had to mean the Gerald I'd met in New York.

"What's he done now?" David asked. "This is a rather unsavory cousin of ours who has hovered on the brink of bankruptcy for years but can't seem to organize himself into a paying job. And plays on the family connection a little too freely."

I looked down at my plate. I had been on the verge of telling them that I'd met Gerald in New York, but it was obviously not a relationship they took pride in. Claiming acquaintance with him didn't seem exactly politic.

Figg came in then with soup, and Henrietta turned the conversation with an anecdote about the day's hunting; presumably one didn't gossip about family members, however remote, in front of the servants. The soup was followed by lamb with rather mushy beans, and strawberries, after which we went back to the Little Salon for coffee. I liked simply getting up from the table and leaving the dishes. When we got back to the other room the coffee tray was waiting, our drinks had been cleared away, there was a new log on the fire.

Henrietta poured the coffee and settled down next to the fire with Cynthia, where she'd sat before dinner. "Now how do you think you're going to proceed with the papers?" she asked, as if inviting me to tell a bedtime story.

"I guess I'll just open the trunks and see what's in them first," I answered. "It helps that I'm only working on a limited period of time; you know, I can safely ignore anything dated earlier than, say, 1890. And even then, whatever doesn't relate directly to Lauretta is only of marginal interest."

"Where have you done your research so far?" David asked.

"Libraries," I answered. "New York Public is pretty good, and there are several specialized collections in New York. And here, at the British Library in Bloomsbury and their newspaper collection in Colindale. The newspapers are a terrific source, especially the scandal sheets."

"Was Lauretta mentioned in them?" David asked.

"Not here. There was a lot of publicity in New York, the engagement and the wedding were covered in great detail. The New York papers weren't too keen on St. John; they kept saying she was selling herself. But there's not much about the pair of them in London."

"What is it, exactly, that you are trying to find out?" David said, looking intently down at his coffee cup.

"In her case, anything I can. I'm just hoping that seeing Saltire and Neville Park, and her dresses, and whatever else she left behind, will give me some information. You know, there may be a diary that you haven't found, if you really don't know what's in those trunks. Or there might be a scrapbook, or letters from home." I shrugged. "Or there may be nothing. One thing I've gotten a bit fixated on is finding out exactly when she died."

There was a little yelp from Cynthia. "Sorry. She must have a thorn in her paw," muttered Henrietta. But I was looking at David. And I had, again, the sense of having uncovered something. The sense that the chatter and the beautiful room and Henrietta's clothes and David's kindness were—a carapace, hiding something secret and painful. For a moment, his face showed something more than his usual expression of intelligent concern. It was as if he had receded into a world of his own, a world of tremendous responsibility. He took off his glasses and pinched the bridge of his nose. Migraine? I wondered. His shoulders seemed to sag and he looked, just for that moment, overwhelmed. And much to my surprise, I found myself wanting to ask him what was wrong, as if, somehow, I could help.

But it was only a moment. He looked up and caught my eyes on him and put his glasses back on and said, "But surely there's a death certificate somewhere."

I almost didn't know what he was talking about. It seemed as if so much time had passed between sentences of our conversation. I recollected myself. "I'm sure there is, but I was looking for an obituary, and didn't find one."

Henrietta exclaimed, and I turned to her. "It does seem peculiar, doesn't it? The *Times* was really very faithful about reporting deaths in the peerage in that era. But she wasn't in the index. I did find out that death certificates are filed in London at a place called St. Catherine's House. But they're filed by date, so it's not a help."

"I didn't know that," Henrietta said vaguely, reaching to put her coffee cup on the table. David took it from her hand and set it gently on the silver tray.

"Why would you? I don't know how they're managed in the States," I said. "Chronologically seems like a cumbersome way to do it, though."

David was smiling slightly. "Our brother Andrew would say that was a very American attitude."

"Oh? Why?" I wasn't sure it was a compliment.

"Efficiency. Always thinking of a better way to do things."

"Andrew's roommate works at the same bank, and he's always trying to figure out how the bank can get rid of the cashiers," Henrietta said. "They want to replace them with machines; it seems so odd."

I suddenly laughed, and stopped feeling defensive. "I'd much rather do my banking with a machine, it's so much faster!"

"Well, there you are then," David said. "Andrew has the greatest admiration for America and has begun to wonder how the English get anything done at all."

"Speaking of which, I have to catch an early train up to town tomorrow," said Henrietta as she stood up gracefully. "Andrew particularly disapproves of my taking days off from work to hunt. Can you run me to the station, David?"

He turned to me, smiling. "The world of fashion grinds to a halt while Henrietta careens around on horseback in her great-grandmother's clothes."

She seized a pillow and pretended to throw it at him. "I design dresses, Sarah, and naturally it's marvelous to have Lauretta's things to draw on as inspiration, particularly since I do mostly ball-dresses. But it is very helpful," she turned with mock severity to David, "to actually wear the clothes for the activities they were made for."

"I know, I know. The aerodynamic properties of the skirt while clearing a four-foot fence . . ." He stopped, smiling. I thought that he was actually very proud of her, and that she knew it. "What time shall we leave?"

"Eight?"

David nodded. "That's fine. Sarah, I'll walk you back down to the dower house, if you'd like."

"I would, thank you," I answered, glad that I wouldn't have to face the garden in the dark. David went to get my jacket from Figg and we parted in the central hall. Cynthia tried to follow Henrietta up the stairs, but David called her back. "Cynthia, come out with us. See you in the morning, Netta. Sleep well."

"Good night, Sarah. I hope the trunks are full of treasures," she said over the banister.

"So do I. Good night."

It was colder when we got outside, and I wished I had gloves. I tucked my hands under my arms and watched Cynthia run ahead of us, nose to the ground.

"Do you eat breakfast?" David asked. "Because if you do, you'd best come up to the big house for it. You can make coffee or tea at the dower house but I don't believe there's any food in the kitchen."

"Oh, that's fine. What time?"

"Is eight-thirty too early? If we all eat at once, it's easier for the staff."

That, I supposed, was the disadvantage of having servants: you had to think about their convenience as well as your own. "Eight-thirty will be fine."

We were silent as we went down the steps and under the arbor. David took my elbow at the steps, to help me down them, and then let it go. "I hope I didn't offend you with that remark about Americans," he said tentatively.

"No, really you didn't. I suppose the English must find our rushing around as exasperating as we find your . . ." I tried to think of a polite way to finish the sentence.

"Laziness?" he suggested.

"No, I would never have said that!" I protested as he laughed.

"No, of course you wouldn't, you're far too polite. But I'm sure you must have found the way we do things frustrating."

"Well . . . it does amaze me that you can never get anybody on the telephone at the first try."

"Yes, and I'm sure you found the British Library annoying," he encouraged me.

"Not a bit," I contradicted him. "I adored it."

"Well, then you are very unusual. Most Americans complain endlessly about how hard it is to get books and—" He broke off as Cynthia started to bark. She had gone ahead of us out of sight, and now it sounded as if she was off to our left somewhere. "Chasing rabbits," David said. He whistled, and called her name. We were at the white gate now and she sounded closer. David shook his head. "She's in the maze. She can't always find her way out. It sounds as if she's quite close. Are you very cold? Would you mind waiting while I look in and see if she's right here?"

"No, go ahead."

"If I don't find her right away, I'll come back after I've taken you home." He went through the arch in the dark bushes, and turned left, and disappeared. I could hear him calling the dog, and she barked once, then I didn't hear him anymore. The moon was directly overhead, and very bright now. I jumped up and down on the grass to keep warm. It was very quiet in the garden, no birds, no wind in the trees, no insects, no little rabbits in the undergrowth. Just the moon, with clouds floating across it—utter country quiet. And then I heard a rustling noise.

Not like the rustling I'd heard earlier, though. Not leaves and twigs, not sudden scrabblings made by small creatures with furry tails and beady black eyes. This was the distinctive sound of twigs on nylon fabric. And it was steady. As if someone in a ski parka were trying to squeeze through a gap in a hedge.

I stood stock-still. My heart was pounding like mad. It might be all right. It might be just a gardener out late. But why would a gardener be creeping through the hedge? The sound was plainly coming from the bushes opposite the maze, where there was a series of little rooms, as David had called them. It

couldn't be David, since he was behind me. It had to be someone who didn't want to be seen.

"David!" I called suddenly. "David!" If the creeping man
didn't want to be seen, I didn't want to see him. I quickly
stepped into the maze and a little to the left of the entrance.
"David!" I called again. My voice sounded a little hysterical,
even to me.

"Sarah! What is it?" He appeared around the corner, running. "Are you all right?"

"Yes, I'm fine," I gasped, and covered my face with my
hands. He put his hands gently on my arms. "I just thought I
heard a man. I'm sorry. I'm probably imagining it." I stood up
straight and took a deep but shaky breath.

He took his hands away. "Where? What did you hear?"

"Twigs on something nylon, like a parka. It sounded like he
was creeping through the bushes."

"In the maze?"

"No, on the other side. Opposite."

David stepped away from me and stood still in the arch of
the maze, listening. "Well, he's gone now," he said with deci-
sion, turning back to me. "Let's get you down to the house and
warmed up. You're shivering."

I was. We walked quickly the rest of the way to the dower
house, where the lights were burning as I had left them.

"It's chilly in here," David remarked as we stepped through
the French doors. It was. The daffodils on the table looked
pinched, as if they'd been caught by a late frost. "Is there a fire
laid in your bedroom?"

"I didn't notice."

"All right. Just a minute." There was a drinks tray set up
near the fireplace, with a few decanters and a soda siphon and
glasses. David went over and poured a drink into a glass and
handed it to me. I took it gratefully.

"Sovereign remedy," he said. "Let's see about that fire."

In the bedroom fireplace were logs neatly stacked on the and-
irons, surrounded by kindling, and David had only to put a
match to it. He pulled the wing chair next to it and sat me
down near the warmth of the flames.

"Now. Did you see anyone?"

"No. Just the noise. I couldn't hear you calling for Cynthia
anymore, and I was just noticing how quiet it was and how
bright the moon was and then I heard this—scraping noise."

"Did you call out right away?"

"Just about. I thought he probably didn't want to be seen
and if I called out that would give him a chance to get away.
And then I wanted to hide a little bit, so I ran into the maze." I
took a sip from the glass; it was brandy. I looked up at David,
who was rubbing his hands in front of the fire. "Did you find
Cynthia?" I asked.

"No. I'll look for her again on my way up to the house. If I
don't find her she'll just have to spend the night out. It's happened before." He turned to look at me. "Will you be all right
here, by yourself? Or would you rather come up to the house?
I'm sure it was just somebody poaching a few rabbits, but if
that bothers you . . ."

I could just imagine the scene: going back up to the house,
waking Henrietta, getting the housekeeper to make up a room,
explaining to Figg that I thought I'd heard a poacher in the
garden and so couldn't spend the night alone. "I'll be fine," I
said, and took another sip of brandy.

"It wouldn't be any trouble," David said.

"I'll be fine here. Is there any way to lock the doors?"

He shook his head. "The front door locks; the one facing onto
the drive. But the French doors facing the house don't. I'll
wedge them for you and you can let me out the front door and
lock it behind me. In any case, if you hear anything in the night
you have the phone and you can raise us in a moment, if you're
sure you want to stay here."

It was partly embarrassment and partly laziness, not courage at all, that persuaded me to stay in the dower house that night, but stay I did. David wedged the French doors with a chair and I locked the front door behind him. And I turned off the lights and climbed the stairs and went to bed.

I sat up for a while, propped on the pillows, looking at the fire, and sipping at the glass of brandy. I thought about the poacher. And I thought about the beautiful house, and Figg, and the coronets on the pillowcases at my back, and David's shy charm. I wondered what Henrietta had been about to say about Gerald Charlton; something about "what he's done now?" It was hard to see how sleek, elegant Gerald could be a discredit to the family. Interesting, though, that he didn't seem to work for a living. I remembered the silver cigarette case and the carefully tailored clothes and wondered how he paid his bills. But Gerald aside, what I kept coming back to was the sense I had gotten—twice—that there was something wrong. That there was some secret. Something that David and Henrietta shared, and hid. And that frightened them both. And it seemed to have something to do with Lauretta. What was it I had said the first time: something about the papers at Neville Park? And the second time, when David had looked so worried, was when I mentioned Lauretta's death certificate. What could be so worrisome about an ancestor who had died almost a hundred years earlier? I fell asleep before I figured it out.

Chapter 4

I woke up with a nasty taste in my mouth from the brandy, and with a vague sense of embarrassment. I had been making a mountain out of a molehill. If I had in fact heard a man in the bushes, he had probably been hunting rabbits, as David suggested, and been completely uninterested in me. I was glad I had stayed put in the dower house.

Sheepishly, I moved the chair that David had wedged under the handles of the French doors. But when I walked through the gardens to breakfast, I looked to see if there were any broken twigs opposite the gate into the maze. And there were.

"No more alarums and excursions in the night?" David asked briskly as Figg showed me into the breakfast room.

"Not a peep. Did you find Cynthia?" I sat down at the place that was laid next to David. "Yes, thank you," I said to Figg, who was holding a silver pot and murmuring something about coffee.

"She was waiting for me at the door when I got back to the house. But I didn't see another sign of your man."

"There were broken twigs in the hedge this morning," I told him, a little defensively.

"Yes. I did see them. And a footprint too. It wasn't your imagination."

"I don't know whether to be relieved or sorry. Did you get Henrietta to the train all right? How often does she go back and forth?"

"She has a flat in town and of course does her business there. Unfortunately, or rather fortunately, she's done so well lately that we don't see much of her. During the hunting season she tries to get down here at least once a week but often she can't. It must be a slow time just now. Do you ride? We could mount you," he suggested.

Figg put a plate of poached eggs and a silver toast rack in front of me. There were several mysterious dark objects on the plate with the eggs; I thought I diagnosed kidneys and sections of smoked fish. I poked them gently with my fork. "Kippers," David said. He was smiling slightly. "English delicacy. For many people, an acquired taste."

I pushed them clear of my eggs. "I haven't been on a horse in years, and I've never hunted. But I'd love to go out for a ride if you've something tame and trustworthy I could bounce around on."

"That's wonderful. Hercules would be the very thing for you. We'll find some riding things and perhaps we could go out this afternoon? Around three?"

I agreed, and finished my breakfast, thinking that this was more like staying in a fancy hotel than like any work I'd ever done. That impression, however, fled as soon as David opened the trunks in the library.

He hadn't exaggerated the disarray. There were three trunks, big round-topped, brassbound things. And they were all full. Full of paper dropped in any which way, folded, with corners creased, upside down. I couldn't help exclaiming.

"You can see how grateful we were to think that someone wanted to go through these things. I did try to warn you," David said apologetically.

I shrugged. "It wouldn't have made any difference. There may be priceless things in here, and there may not. May I spread everything out on the table? And the floor?"

"Anywhere you like," he said. I nodded, already thinking

about where to start. "I'll leave you now. Would you like to have lunch on a tray in here?"

"Please, that would be lovely."

"And what size are your feet?" I turned to him in surprise. "For riding boots," he explained.

"Eight." Impulsively, I touched his arm. "I really can't thank you enough. You're being so kind."

To my surprise, he blushed. But his eyes met mine, and he said formally, "The pleasure is all mine. I'll come fetch you a bit before three." Then he left me with the papers.

For a moment I stood there with my hands on my hips, looking down at the trunks. I could see how David had been discouraged. I knelt down in front of the trunk closest to me, and started lifting out sheaves and pamphlets and single sheets, laying them face up on the floor.

Before long, the library tables were covered with untidy stacks of the papers. A great deal of what was there could be dismissed without regret: catalogs from art galleries, race cards, programs from plays, the fixture cards of the local hunt. There were newspapers, bills, invitations, letters. It looked like someone had repeatedly emptied the contents of his desk into these trunks.

I would have been happy to read everything; surely all of these papers could give me a detailed picture of life in late Victorian England. But I didn't have time. I was concerned only with Lauretta. And so far, I could see nothing that pertained to her.

I was beginning to get discouraged around the middle of the second trunk when I found a sheaf of bills dated 1899. I flipped through them quickly, and set them aside for later reading; they seemed to be tradesmen's bills from the newlyweds' trip to London.

The third trunk was constructed a bit differently from the other two, which were perfectly matched. I hoped this was a good sign, but at first glance the contents looked even less promising. For it was the same kind of junk I'd found in the first two trunks, just more recent. I sat back on the floor to rest for a minute. Why would you save the program from Good-wood Races in 1966? Or an advertising brochure from a tailor on Jermyn Street? I picked up a ticket stub; the Beatles at White City. My distaste for the sixteenth Earl grew by leaps and bounds. I could imagine one of those stringy no-longer-young men with too-long hair and a medallion around his neck.

Someone knocked on the door and Figg came in with a tray. I scrambled to my feet.

"Ah. Miss. Where might I put this down?" he asked, impassive.

I pushed the stack of Royal Academy publications closer to the Covent Garden programs. "How's this?"

"Just so. Will that be all, miss?" He left. I wondered if he ever unbent. There was chicken salad and fresh tomatoes and some grapes, on china sprigged with butterflies. I lifted the grape dish to look underneath it; Limoges. No surprise. I ate slowly, staring out the window at the park. There was nothing ugly in sight; just the terraces, fields, woods, and, beyond, roll-ing hills. Very cultivated-looking; each tree looked premedi-tated. I wondered how Lauretta had liked it after the Midwest.

I fiddled with the grapes, delaying my return to work. Fi-nally, I had to sit back on the floor next to the trunk. I wasn't sifting carefully through the junk from the 1960s, but simply dumping it on the floor in piles. So it was a shock when the removal of a stack of *Tatlers* revealed a sheaf of heavy papers covered with script in brownish ink. I picked up the stack of magazines from the floor; stuck to the bottom of the last one was a heavy double page, ruled. Dated; July 1899. And care-fully written across the top of it was "Accounts, Neville Park." It was signed at the bottom, "(Mrs.) Jane Party."

I leaned over the trunk again, and carefully lifted out another layer of detritus from the sixteenth Earl. And another. Until it became apparent that the bottom quarter of the trunk was filled with older material. My eyes ran quickly over the headings of letters (New York, June 1899), of bills (Worth, rue de la Paix). Very gently, I reached down between piles to see what might be below them. My fingers met something more solid: the binding of a book. Possibly the ledgers from Neville Park?

Gingerly, I moved the pile of bills, letters, accounts. And on the bottom of the trunk were three big books. Leather-bound, stamped with gold on the cover, "Diary." My heart was racing as I picked up the center volume and opened it. On the flyleaf it read, "Diary of Lauretta Sophonisba Wright."

I flipped slowly through the pages, which were covered with a large, clear handwriting. I caught phrases and dates here and there: "Just a boy, for all that . . ." "October 27, 1897," "Mamma says Papa is eager to . . ." This was treasure.

I turned to the last page, to see how far the volume went: only to the end of 1897. I put the heavy book down in my lap and picked up the next one, flipping to the last page first. It ended in 1896. Lauretta was, it appeared, a methodical soul. She filled up one book per year. I turned to the first page of the 1896 volume: "I have resolved to write a diary," it said. I put the book down and sighed. There was one more volume in the trunk. If I could have chosen only one year of the diary to read, it would have been 1899. But I was somehow sure that the one volume I wanted was not there.

And I was right. It was for 1898. Not a complete loss. In 1898 Lauretta's family brought her to New York, she met the Earl of Saltire, they got engaged. It would certainly be interesting reading. But it wouldn't tell me anything about her life in England. And it wouldn't give me the one fact that was beginning to obsess me: the date of her death.

I put the heavy books aside and took up the letters, which were all signed "Your loving Mamma." Mamma had dated them faithfully, and I learned that the Wrights had gone to Newport, to Lenox, to White Sulphur Springs. The letters stopped in mid-October.

I was not exactly surprised; rueful was more like it. This seemed to be a principle of research—that precisely the book you want is never available. If you need a certain issue of a magazine, it is being microfilmed. The single volume of a reference book you want is the only one missing. You learn to adjust, make do, try to be resourceful. Maybe there's another source. Maybe, in this case, the missing matter would be at Neville Park. There should be at least another month's worth of letters from Mrs. Wright. I knew from the *Times* that the little Lord Neville had been born on December 3, 1899. So what had happened to November's correspondence?

Still. I was being silly, for what I had here was undeniably wonderful and much more than I had expected to find. I looked from the accounts to the letters to the diaries, unsure where to start. Finally, on the principle that you should save the best for last, I began leafing through the bills from the honeymoon.

They were satisfyingly staggering. Worth, Redfern, Doucet for dresses. Boucheron for jewels. I wondered what had happened to them; here was a bill for "an emerald and diamond stomacher, £40,000." That was roughly $200,000 in the currency of the time. No wonder the Earl had needed a rich wife. I was trying to envision an opera cloak of scarlet on blue voided velvet, with *galon d'argent* trimming and an olive green lining, when David knocked on the door.

"Any luck? You *have* turned them all out, haven't you?"

"Yes, I've found some interesting things," I answered as I stood up from the floor and stretched.

David had a pair of tall black boots in his hands. "These ought to fit you. Come into Henrietta's room and I'll see what Mrs. Lowery has managed to dig up." He led me past the painting of Diana pointing toward the library, across the upper hall, and down the bedroom corridor. Opposite a huge malachite vase, he opened a door.

Henrietta's bedroom was enormous, and very charming. It faced south, toward the terraces, and near the windows were a pair of armchairs and a table. The room also held a drop-front desk with a walnut veneer, a handsome Queen Anne highboy, and a canopied bed. Laid out on the bed were three pairs of breeches and two tweed jackets.

"That shouldn't be any problem. Something is bound to fit you. We'll meet in the hall, shall we, in a few minutes?"

The first pair of breeches I tried on fit, and so did the boots, to my surprise. Everything was exquisitely made, and well cared for, if worn. Both of the jackets were too small, however, so I left them there. I guessed that the clothes had to have been the Countess's, since Henrietta was so much smaller than I. It seemed rather poignant that her riding clothes should have been kept for years after she'd died.

I managed to find the hall without difficulty, and David was waiting for me with Cynthia. "We're going to have company," he said. "I think she can smell my riding clothes from any room in the house." He looked very dashing in brown field boots and a tweed jacket. "Neither of the coats fitted? You'll need a jacket, it's rather windy, but we'll find you something."

Sure enough, in the tack room at the stable David found a heavy wool jacket. "This was mine when I was about fifteen," he said, "and I've never been able to bring myself to give it away. Will it do?" The sleeves were too long, but I turned them up at the cuffs and said it was fine. After David had hunted out a pair of gloves and a crop and a velveteen hard hat, we went out into the yard, where a groom was walking a big calm gray horse and a handsome bay. The gray was Hercules, who stood patiently as David boosted me into the saddle. I felt very far from the ground, and tried to remember to sit up straight and keep my heels down. The groom held the bay, Cubitt, who kept sidling away as David tried to mount. Finally, he got a toe in the stirrup and vaulted neatly into the saddle just as Cubitt swung his hindquarters around in another nervous arc. The groom was grinning as we rode out of the stableyard.

It was a raw day, with a low gray sky that promised no change in weather. Most of the trees were still bare, and the grass was a wintry dun color. We walked sedately across the lawn, with Cynthia running ahead, and circled in front of the house. The yellowish stone looked bleak against the gray sky. I was beginning to get comfortable; Hercules was a sensible animal and paid no attention to Cubitt's startled reactions to leaves, gusts of wind, and birds. David sat very quietly in the saddle, undisturbed by the hundreds of pounds of horseflesh that looked awfully eager to unseat him.

"He's awfully fresh," David explained, after Cubitt danced in a full circle around Hercules. "We have too many horses since Mother died and Father's spending so much time up in town. But I can't bring myself to sell any of them and consequently I usually get a very bumpy ride. Shall we trot?" I felt capable of it, so I nudged Hercules with my heels. Obligingly, he started trotting.

"How many horses are there here?" I asked, as soon as I was used to the new gait.

"A dozen. Ridiculous, really. But I have an idea that I want to turn Neville Park into a stud when the current tenant leaves."

"Really? For race horses?" I remembered that Gerald had mentioned this.

"No. Quite frankly we haven't the money for that. But several of the horses here are very good jumpers, and there's an increasingly active market for show jumpers, especially in America."

"And Neville Park will be a good place for raising them?" I

was looking at David as I asked the question, and I thought there was a worried look on his face.

"It should be," he answered, looking straight ahead. "There's a lot of land and a big stable. I haven't been able to see it myself, so I don't know what kind of shape it's in . . . though of course historically Ireland has always been good country for horses. And the neighbors at Neville, the Pearsalls, train steeplechasers."

We had crossed in front of the big house, leaving the dower house to our right, and David turned left into the allée of oaks. There was a dirt road between the trees, and I cautiously urged Hercules into a slow canter. The trees moved past us like a pattern on film and we got closer and closer to the white gate at the end of the allée. Finally, we pulled up and David coaxed Cubitt close enough to the gate to bend down and reach the latch. His easy mastery of the high-strung horse impressed me. I knew just enough about riding to appreciate that his patient control required not just a calm temper but strength and stamina too. David Neville, for all his reserved manners, was clearly no wimp. Hercules and I went sedately through the gate first, and David pulled it closed behind him with the crook of his hunting whip.

We were at the edge of a large pond, with an island in the middle and clumps of trees around the edge. I waited for David to tell me which way to turn.

"We'll go along here," he said, turning left. "There's a dam, and then the river. How are you holding up? Is Hercules all right?"

"Hercules is a marvel, and I realize I needed the fresh air."

We were walking on the grassy bank, close to the edge of the pond, the horses breathing hard. The reeds waved and crackled as Cynthia nosed through them intently. "Yes, I would think your day's work would be a bit mind-boggling," David commented.

"What's mind-boggling," I answered a bit tartly, "is the amount of junk your uncle accumulated in a very short time. I think every piece of paper he ever picked up was in that trunk."

"Oh, dear," David said, comically. "Incriminating?"

"Well, not quite, but not exactly discriminating either."

"Discrimination was never his strong suit. Was there anything at all useful?"

"As a matter of fact, yes." I looked over at him. The raw air had flushed his cheeks and he'd left off his glasses, so he looked younger, less like a noble scholar and more—well, more red-blooded. He would always, I thought, be restrained. But it occurred to me for the first time that beneath the quiet surface, this was a man of considerable passion. He had already let me glimpse how deeply he cared about Saltire. Now I wondered what else—who else—he cared about. He turned toward me, as if he could feel my gaze, and there was something, a challenge perhaps, in the direct glance. I looked down and twitched a piece of Hercules' mane from one side of his neck to the other, and remembered that we were talking about the contents of the trunks. "I wish I had time to go through everything, but I won't, you know, and there's a great deal of material from the eighteen-seventies and eighties. It might be worth getting a proper expert to come look at it. The whole of it might be useful to a university or a museum."

"I suppose that's possible," he answered, considering. "But did you find anything about Lauretta?"

How thoughtful he was. I would have expected him to be eager to know about my progress through the family flotsam and jetsam. After all, that was, I assumed, what his hospitality was geared to achieving. But he kept turning the subject to my particular concern. I began to think that the Countess—or David's nanny—had done a wonderful job bringing him up. "Yes, in fact I found some letters from her mother, and a diary."

I was surprised at the way his face lit up. I had expected polite enthusiasm, but his delight seemed to be purely personal. As if finding Lauretta's diary would affect him in a tangible way. "That's marvelous!" he was saying. "That's really splendid. Have you had a chance to read much of it yet?"

"No," I answered. "It was the last thing I found. But what's odd is that there's a volume missing. She filled up one book a year, starting in 1896, and there are only three of them here. The last one, for 1899, is missing."

"No, really?" Our eyes met, and I knew he thought this was significant.

"And what's even odder is that the letters from her mother all end in October," I went on. "If the baby was born in December, which he was, there's at least a month of letters missing," I went on, rushing to get it all out.

"Well, assuming that Mother Wright didn't suddenly leave off writing to her daughter . . ."

"It seems unlikely," I broke in; "she's very faithful up until then."

"Then the diary and letters are probably all together under a bed or something at Neville Park."

We were riding past the little dam at the bottom of the pond now. There was a family of ducks swimming about near the edge, abruptly turning upside down from time to time, to feed. "How did these papers get here?" I asked, watching the ducks.

"My grandfather went through a new-broom phase when he succeeded and got married. He was always very efficient about keeping his things in order; there was probably nothing at all of his era in those trunks." There hadn't been. "All of the important papers—leases, contracts, passports, and so on—he filed in the estate room. And he didn't keep anything else at all. I suppose at one point he thought he was going to organize his father's life, in retrospect as it were. So he had those papers and some of Lauretta's clothes moved here from Neville Park. But then everything got caught up in the war and so he never got around to doing anything about them."

"So it is possible that he just *missed* the last volume of the diary, if it wasn't kept with the rest of the papers."

"I should think so. You'll probably find it when you go to Neville Park, if you look hard enough."

"God, I hope so," I said. But somehow I didn't feel optimistic. I could just imagine searching desperately through some huge drafty barracks of a house and never finding anything. Well, it was hardly likely that I'd be given carte blanche to search anyway.

"I say, Sarah, when are you going?" David broke into my thoughts.

"Saturday," I said. "That is, he's expecting me Sunday morning, but I'm going to spend Saturday night at an inn not far away."

David was staring straight ahead, idly tapping his whip against his boot. Cubitt didn't like it, and switched his ears back and forth in irritation. Suddenly David said with resolution, "I'll come with you."

I stared at him. "Why?"

"I've been trying to go over to Neville Park for almost a year now," he began to explain. "This Ludovic Walter has a very informal lease and it's up soon. I wanted to go and look over the place to see whether my idea about the stud is at all feasible, and what kind of changes are going to be necessary, so that when Walter leaves I can get started right away. I've written several times to arrange a visit, but he always says it would be inconvenient. But since you're going to be there it will be harder for him to find an excuse. And if I just send a telegram to announce my arrival, he won't be able to write back to put me off!" he finished. Cubitt broke into a trot, as if infected by David's sudden energy.

"Well, that's wonderful," I said, a little nonplussed. I didn't really want to be involved in a wrangle between David and his tenant, but on the other hand I liked the idea of having some moral support while I was there. And, being scrupulously honest, I admitted to myself that I very much liked the idea of spending more time with David.

We were on the grass next to the river, with the house on the high ground to our left. We started to canter along the path next to the river bank, and I kept my eyes on the fields and hahas, the gradually rising terraces of gardens up to the house. The sun was just breaking through the clouds in long melodramatic rays, so that the gray water was silvered as it flowed quickly over stones and sand. There was something eternal about the scene: the clouds pierced by the slanting sunlight, the house, the river, the two riders and a dog. I felt like a figure in a painting, and had a sudden feeling of deep thankfulness that I'd been able to share, however briefly, all this beauty and privilege.

It wasn't a long ride, but my legs almost collapsed when I slid off Hercules' back in the stableyard. David caught my elbow as I staggered a little. I laughed, shaking my head. "I probably won't be able to walk tomorrow!"

"Don't worry, there's an old wicker wheelchair around somewhere," he reassured me. "You did very well, you know."

"Thank you," I said, concentrating on putting one foot in front of the other as we walked back to the house.

"Would you like to hunt on Friday?"

"Well . . . could I?" I asked in surprise. "I mean, I'm not that good a rider. I think I'd be terrified." From what I knew of hunting it would require a lot of pounding across country and jumping huge fences and probably falling off and breaking a leg. Not what I had come to England for.

"We could put you on Hercules again. You know he's steady, and he has perfect manners on the hunting field. The country around here is mild stuff; in fact most people come to the Saltire meet for the look of it, not because the sport is good. And I'll show you the ropes."

"Well, of course I'd love to, then," I said. As long as I was living out all my fantasies . . .

"Good," David said as we reached the gravel terrace of the house. "Then perhaps tomorrow we should go out and pop over some fences to build your confidence."

We had a quick tea, still in our riding clothes. I was so anxious to read the diaries that I excused myself, explaining that I wanted to get back to work. But I had been settled in a chair in the library for only a few minutes when I started to be distracted by my aching legs. I sat still for a bit, trying to be stoic. I gave up in short order, though. A bath. I needed a long hot bath. So I gathered up the three volumes of the diary and the sheaves of letters from Mamma Wright, and took them back to the dower house.

I felt pretty wonderful as I strolled through the formal gardens. There I was, walking around the Saltire estate as if I owned it. I had in my arms the kind of material I had dreamed about finding. I was going fox-hunting. And David Neville was coming to Ireland with me. As I stepped onto the lawn of the dower house I saw that someone had been down to turn on the lights. They had also changed the flowers in the sitting room, I noticed, as I walked through the French doors. The pinched daffodils had given way to a glass bowl full of apple blossoms, which must have been forced indoors to be blooming so early.

I went into the library, feeling my way to the desk, where I put down my books and papers before turning on the light. I leafed through the pages of the diaries, hesitating, but finally decided to take all three volumes upstairs to my bedroom.

Of course, I realized when I got upstairs, I had been thinking in terms of American plumbing. It was cold on the second floor, and though I lit the fire in my bedroom, the bathroom was like an icebox. I turned on the hot tap in the tub all the way, and got a medium-size trickle. So much for a long hot soak. I left the water running—it would take the tub twenty minutes to fill at that rate—and sat on the edge of the bed to take off my boots. It was hard work, pulling at an uncomfortable angle, and I remembered as I got them off that I had left my other clothes in Henrietta's room at the big house. Well, I would get them after dinner. What mattered for the moment was getting clean.

To my great surprise, I found that the bath was completely satisfactory. My poor legs felt like they belonged to someone else, but stopped aching. With my alarm clock on the chaise longue so I would know when to get out of the tub and dress for dinner, I picked up Lauretta's diary and began to read.

The Wrights began the year 1898 in Chicago. Lauretta, it appeared, was twenty. There was a birthday for which her father gave her "the prettiest row of pearls, even larger than Mamma's and hers are thought to be very fine," and a number of swains sent her posies. I read quickly, planning to go back and take notes on the important passages. It became clear that Lauretta was rather simple. Kind, trusting, biddable, observant of details but unable to draw conclusions from them, she filled her diary with facts rather than speculations. She described minutely every dress she wore, the parties she went to, what she ate, whom she danced with, what her friends wore. The result was like the social column of a newspaper. And for my purposes, it couldn't have been more useful.

The year 1898 saw the Wrights' social assault upon New York and they made their attack, wisely, in stages. I was intrigued to find that it was Mr. Wright who plotted their strategy: "Papa is taking us to White Sulphur Springs, where he says we may have a chance to meet some new people." Then in May: "Papa says he has taken a house at Newport for the summer. It is supposed to be very fine, and in the best part of town. I hope I shall like being near the sea." The Wrights' success in

Newport seemed mixed; I knew from my research that the parties they went to were not the first-rate parties, and though they did go once to Bailey's Beach, they were not invited back.

Lauretta enjoyed it, though; she didn't have the same acute social perceptions as her father. ("Papa says we are not invited to the best parties, and indeed I know that Mrs. Belmont had a ball last night to which there were six hundred invited. But as we have not met Mrs. Belmont, I do not know how we could be invited to her house. Mamma tells me that Papa has decided we must go to Lenox in September, before we go to New York.") Lenox was a clever move; the little town in the Berkshires was less pretentious than Newport, and Lauretta made a few friends who would be in New York for the season. Moreover, Mrs. Wright became acquainted with one of the old Knickerbocker matrons. ("She is so odd-looking, in her funny black dresses, but she is very kind to Mamma and me and says we must come to her house in Washington Square. Louisa told me that this is a great honor as she is very exclusive.")

And then one night in New York, when Lauretta was at the opera with Louisa's family, she met her future husband. I glanced at the clock on the chaise longue and realized that I was running late. Damn! David had told me that we would be eating alone, and I didn't want to keep him waiting. I carefully shut the diary and heaved myself out of the tub. When I had dried myself I took the book into the bedroom and skimmed over the pages as I dressed myself. Standing on one leg, pulling on my stockings, I read, "He is a very pleasant young man, not perhaps handsome but possessed of great charm. He told me of his home in Oxfordshire, which is one of the grandest of the old estates there. His family were made earls under Henry VIII and have a great position in England. He asked if he might call on me at home and of course I said he might." It was ten after seven. I had to go. So I dashed downstairs and ran through the garden, arriving at the house out of breath.

"I'm sorry I'm late," I puffed when I walked into the Little Salon, where David was reading by the fire. "But I was reading Lauretta's diary and it was so gripping that I couldn't put it down."

"Don't worry," said David, getting up to greet me. "I just got down myself. Whiskey?"

"Yes, thank you," I answered. As I sat down Cynthia came and placed her head on my knee.

"So the diary is interesting?" David handed me my drink and sat down opposite me.

"It's so marvelous. She's just met Saltire, and she repeats their conversation practically word for word. Poor thing, she was awfully naive."

"What did he say?"

"Apparently he fed her the stately-homes-of-England line. She seems to have loved it."

"And then what happened?"

"I don't know! That's why I was late. They met in the opera box of a mutual friend, and he asked if he could call on her parents. Her father was the one with all the social ambition, so I'm sure he egged Saltire on."

"How far does the diary go?"

"Well, remember she filled one book a year, and started a new one each New Year's Day. So it will only go through 1898. But I'm sure they were engaged before the end of the year."

"She's frank, is she?"

"Very. I'm not sure she understands everything, but she writes it all down. What Mamma said, what Papa said, what she said, verbatim."

Figg came in to announce dinner, which we had in the same small room as the night before. David told me he had sent a telegram to Ludovic Walter, announcing that we'd arrive together on Sunday morning. "And where did he tell you to stay? I should call and book a room there for myself."

"There's an inn at a village called Ballyhannock, which is about forty-five minutes away, I think. I can get you the number after dinner, if you like; it's with my notes."

"Good. You can call up on the house phone."

David entertained me with hunting anecdotes and irreverent stories about his ancestors for the rest of dinner, but I was only half-listening. I wanted to get back to the diary, to find out what happened next. So after coffee I went back to the dower house, promising to call David with the number of the inn near Neville Park. Or fairly near—it did seem a bit odd that the nearest empty bed was nearly an hour's journey away. But I supposed in the rural West of Ireland outposts of civilization were bound to be few and far between.

As I walked in the door of the dower house I remembered that I hadn't gotten my clothes from Henrietta's room. I supposed one of the servants could bring them down, but I hated to put them to the trouble. I would just have to get them to-morrow.

My files were in the desk in the library, and the number of the Irish inn was in the Neville Park file; so after pausing to light the fire in the sitting room, I went to the library to get the file. It was dark.

That was strange. I clearly remembered having turned on the light earlier, and having left it on. The room seemed very black suddenly, and I braced myself, listening. I heard nothing, and forced myself to walk forward to the desk.

My hand went automatically to where I knew the lamp was. But I must have been wrong; I reached a little farther, and lost my balance. I put down my outstretched hand to prop myself up, and knocked over the vase of flowers. Still in the dark, I groped to right the vase. And thinking of the letters I'd left lying on the desktop, I felt all over the surface of the desk to move them from the spilled water. I felt flowers, a pen tray, and the wet leather writing-surface. I finally felt the base of the lamp, and turned it on. There were no letters on the desk.

I ran into the kitchen to get rags to wipe off the desk, as the water was already seeping into the leather. I found dishtowels in the first drawer I opened, and ran back. I stuffed the flowers back into the vase, and hastily mopped up the spilled water. Under the pen tray, under the base of the lamp. It didn't take long, and though there were faint marks on the leather, I was satisfied that they wouldn't show when it dried.

But where were the letters? I stood there with the wet cloths in my hand, staring at the desk. Cautiously, I opened the top drawer. My index cards, where I had put them. In the second drawer, my files. In the third drawer, there were the letters. I dropped the dishtowels on the floor and wiped my damp hands on my skirt. I lifted the packet and leafed through it. The letters seemed to be complete, and in order, as I'd found them.

How had they gotten there? And why was the light turned off?

No doubt a servant had come in while I was at dinner, I decided. That had to be the reason. And he or she had tidied up. The house around me suddenly felt enormous. I found I was standing as stiff as a sentry, listening again for strange noises. I took a deep breath and scooped up the file and the letters and fled into the sitting room, dropping the damp towels into the kitchen sink on the way. The fire was burning brightly, the apple blossoms glowed pale pink. The very picture of a cozy English sitting room. My imagination must simply have been getting the better of me. I was being silly.

Feeling chastened, I went upstairs to call David from the linen closet/phone booth. I picked up the receiver and a phone on the other end began to ring. "Yes, Miss Llewellyn?" a female voice answered.

"Could I speak to Lord Neville, please?"

"Just a moment, please."

David's deep voice came over the line. "Ingenious system, isn't it?"

"Very. What happens when Mrs. Lowery goes to bed?"

"It rings through directly to me, and I pretend I'm Figg. I do it quite well."

"I'm sure," I answered. No doubt he did imitate Figg well. Figg had a very distinctive manner to imitate. I gave David the number of the Ballyhannock Inn, and we agreed to ride at three the next afternoon.

"Don't work too hard," David said, and rang off.

Maybe I *had* been working too hard and that was why I was imagining things, I thought a little skeptically. I got the last volume of the diary from my bedroom and went back down to the sitting room, where I settled in front of the fire with a stool under my feet. I turned to where I had left off: Lauretta's meeting Saltire at the opera.

He called on her mother in their rented house near Madison Square. He took a box for the opera and invited the whole family. He dined with them, at home. He and Lauretta went bicycling. He proposed; she accepted. I was struck by the fact that nowhere did she make mention of her feelings in the matter. She was not, it seemed, in love with him; there were no raptures about his character, no repetition of tender passages between them. Nor was there any discussion of how she felt about being engaged. She was as dispassionate as she had been about her dancing classes back in Chicago.

I closed the book and picked up the letters. These, since they had all been sent after the wedding, should at least give me some more exact information about Lauretta's married life. But I gathered, after reading a few of them, that Mrs. Wright was not very curious about her daughter's new way of life. The letters were full of minutiae: "At the Opera last night a clumsy gentleman stepped on my train and left a great rent in the fabric. I should not be surprised to learn that he had on hobnailed boots. It was the purple satin with cabbage-roses and Bertha is not confident that she will be able to mend it so we may have to add some trimming which is not precisely the fashion but as the dress is a Worth and very costly I feel we must do what we can to make it wearable, if only for dinner at home." There were occasional references to Lauretta: "We are so glad you are enjoying Italy; Papa says you must not go into the Roman Coliseum at night" and "While you are at Worth's I wish you would order a reception toilette for me."

I was able to piece together a chronology. Early in April Lauretta discovered she was pregnant. She and Saltire went to London for a bit of the season, and late in June Lauretta was deposited at Neville Park. Saltire, apparently, did not stay with her and it seemed that rumors about him reached even the Wrights in New York: "We have heard that Saltire is seen in undesirable company and has been betting too much on horses. I hope this is not true." And in the meanwhile Lauretta stayed at Neville Park, apparently content. The neighbors on the next estate, the Pearsalls, appeared at the end of the summer: "So glad to hear you have some company tho' I cannot think it wise that you drive around the country in your condition." And then the letters stopped.

I felt a little groggy from having pored over Mrs. Wright's handwriting for so long, and I realized it was after midnight. My legs were beginning to ache again from the afternoon's ride. I stretched, and gathered the letters back into their pile. I put a screen in front of the fire, and then hesitated for a moment. Feeling foolish, I propped a chair under the lock of the French doors as David had done. Nobody would know, I reasoned, and I would sleep more soundly knowing it was there. I turned off the light in the library, checked the lock on the front door, and went upstairs, clutching the letters and the diaries to my chest. For some reason, I wanted them in the room with me while I slept, like a security blanket. And in fact, after I'd lit the fire in my room and put on my nightgown, I got in bed with the books and the letters. There was room, certainly, for all of us, and I told myself that I merely wanted to read in bed. I was asleep very shortly, though.

I was dreaming about driving in an open carriage, jolting over a rough road and feeling seasick. There was a gate approaching and we weren't slowing down; I suddenly realized that there was no driver. I couldn't get to the reins and the gate was coming closer and closer and then I heard the crash . . .

My eyes flew open and my heart was thudding uncomfortably in my chest. I lay there, rigid, listening. Yes, I had heard a crash; the sound had come from downstairs. I turned my head carefully on my pillow—it seemed necessary to make as little noise as possible—to look at my alarm clock. Ten after one. I had been asleep for only half an hour or so.

I leaned up on one elbow to see if there was light coming from under my door. There wasn't. I heard no more noise, but I was terrified. Should I get up and go look? Or stay where I was? All my instincts told me to stay put, to pull my pillow over my head and play possum. I tried to think of logical reasons for the noise. Something had fallen over; it was an old house, and maybe as it settled a shelf in the library had fallen. I didn't believe it. The noise had sounded like somebody tripping over something, and I could not escape the fact that I had carefully locked the front door and wedged the French doors. That meant there was somebody in the house with me; and that person had been there since I came back from dinner.

I wanted to crawl under the bed, or into the closet, anywhere I wouldn't be discovered. I was shaking now. I remembered that you shake because your body is so full of adrenaline and your muscles need to be moved. I wriggled my fingers and toes under the blanket, not daring to move more. It didn't stop the quivering, and when something popped in the fireplace I jumped. That did it. I got out of bed, as silently as I could. I had to move around; I couldn't just lie there in bed shaking. I swung my arms around my head, feeling ridiculous but hoping that the movement might calm my body. And I looked around the room to see if there was anything that might serve as a weapon. I had a collapsible tripod for my camera; at full length, a tripod could keep someone at bay, or even bash them on the head. I had a Swiss Army knife in my purse. I could do some damage with that, if I got close enough. Then I heard a creak.

I don't suppose three minutes had elapsed since I'd been wakened by the crash, even though it felt like ages. And the creak explained the first noise; it was the sound of the French doors being opened. I stood stock-still, listening again. The complaint of the hinges evidently frightened the person at the doors, because the sound stopped immediately. But then it began again, as if the intruder were trying to open the doors as slowly and quietly as possible.

Oddly, I was relieved. It, he, whoever, was trying to get out, not in. And trying not to be caught at it. And not doing a very good job, I thought. It seemed somehow amateurish to crash into my little barricade. Surely a professional housebreaker would carry a flashlight? And surely a pro would know how to manage squeaky doors? The noise stopped. I went to the window, which, since it was placed high in the wall, didn't allow me to lean out. And even when I pulled up a chair, opened the casement (which resisted but did not squeak), and stuck my head out, I saw nothing. It was a dark night because of the clouds, and my bedroom looked over the allée of oaks and the fields. The French doors were on the other side of the house. I stood there on the chair for a few minutes, straining to see any movement in the dark, or to hear twigs snapping or bushes rustling. Nothing.

I got down from the chair and sat on my bed. I was calmer, but still agitated. Should I go downstairs, armed with my tripod? What if he was still there? *Why* should I go downstairs?

Why shouldn't I just go back to bed and lie there in the dark until I was relaxed enough to sleep? Why risk it? My feet were cold, and I realized I'd left the window open, so I got up to close it. The doors were probably still open downstairs, I thought, letting in cold air. Should I go down and close them? Would I be able to sleep knowing that the doors were still open? I wondered if I would be able to sleep in any case.

Finally, just to have something to do, I began quietly to assemble the tripod. I pulled the legs out to their full length, and locked them into position. Then I took the Swiss Army knife, and opened the biggest blade. I held it to the top of the tripod, and wondered how to fasten it. Adhesive tape; there was a roll in my cosmetic kit, for blisters. The cosmetic kit was in the bathroom. I was at my door, listening, about to creep out into the hall, when I froze. I could have sworn I'd heard a man's voice.

Chapter 5

I flew back to bed and was huddled under the covers in a twinkling. He had a friend. There were two of them out there. They were going to come back. Maybe they were armed. Whatever they had planned, I wasn't going to stop it. I planned to lie there, feigning sleep, even if I heard them removing every stick of furniture in the house. I was going to pretend I was asleep until one of them shone a flashlight in my face.

My head was under the pillow in the age-old ostrich gesture. But I listened tensely. And I heard something. I heard the man's voice again, coming this time from under my window. He was trying, it seemed, to shout in a whisper. Trying to get something across urgently with the minimum of volume. But it wasn't another man answering him; the other sound was barking. Cynthia?

Quietly, but no longer in a panic, I got out of bed and opened the window again. I clambered up on the chair and leaned out. I could see, to my left, a shadow against the grass; a man's shadow. And Cynthia's tail, a lighter streak in the darkness. She seemed to have grabbed the man's ankle, from what I could see. And he was trying to talk her into releasing it. Her tail wagged. She thought it was a thrilling game. Those were barks of delight.

Then, suddenly, the man broke away. Cynthia was thrown off balance, and lost a few seconds as she got back to her feet and took off after him. How fast did a Labrador run? How fast did that man run? Two unknown quantities. I had no idea.

I shut the window and climbed down from the chair. Now what? What if the man had left an accomplice in the house? Should I call up to the big house? I could just imagine myself waking them all up to tell them what I'd seen. But even if there were only one man, what had he been doing here? Should I call David before the man had time to get away?

Cynthia solved the problem for me. I heard her barking again, but this time it was language I understood. This was, "I am outside and I want you to let me in," the universal communication to dog lovers everywhere. Friendly, but imperative. "I am prepared to sit here all night but soon I will start howling." I picked up the tripod and held it like a javelin on my shoulder, just in case. As I tiptoed down the stairs, feeling foolish, she embarked on the first howl.

The sitting room was chilly, but the intruder had closed the French doors behind him; odd, I thought, for a man in haste. There was Cynthia, a silhouette planted in front of the glass panes, prepared to give voice all night. Dark as the rest of the room was, my eyes were used to it and I could just see a patch of darker darkness, the chair tumbled by the French doors. I turned on the light and, blinking, righted the chair. Still grasping my silly weapon, I unlatched the door for the dog.

With her whole body wagging she pushed her way in the doors before I had them fully open. I have to admit I was equally glad to see her. I put down the tripod and knelt to hug her, letting her lick my face. Her fur was cold to the touch from the night air, and her paws, which she kept placing on my shoulders like a dancing partner, left muddy smears on my nightgown. I didn't think David would have approved of her abandoned behavior, but I didn't care.

I calmed down before she did; it was quite a night she was having, what with rough games and unlimited face-licking. I stood up unsteadily and picked up the chair to prop it as David had showed me. And I noticed, glancing around the room, that the apple blossoms looked wilted, as the daffodils had been the night before. I remembered that when David had brought me down after dinner, the room had been chilly like this.

I picked up my tripod, poured myself a glass of brandy, and with Cynthia behind me, went back upstairs. I left the light on as a tiny measure of comfort. My momentary relief at seeing the dog had obscured the basic problem. Who had been in the house? And why?

I tried to think about it rationally, without leaping to wild conclusions. But I remembered immediately the sound of someone creeping through the hedge. And the letters, moved from their place on top of the desk; the light in the library turned off in my absence. The servants, I told myself, climbing into bed. The servants must have been moving things around. Cynthia stood beside the bed looking up at me wistfully. "I bet David doesn't let you sleep in his bed," I told her. It was a relief to hear my own voice, somehow. I patted the place beside me, and Cynthia bounded up and settled against my hip. It was reassuring to have her there, I admitted to myself. Especially if I couldn't explain away the intruder.

Maybe it was all coincidence; maybe the person in the garden was a poacher and maybe a servant had moved the letters and maybe the sitting room was cold because the French doors let in a draft.

It seemed equally possible, though, that they were all connected. What if the person creeping through the garden had just come from the dower house? And had left the doors open by mistake, causing the chill we'd felt? What if he had come back tonight while I was at dinner? I had surprised him, I thought, by returning so early. So he hid somewhere in the house until I was asleep, then tried to leave and knocked over the chair barricade. I swallowed some brandy nervously. It couldn't be true. Why would somebody be prowling around the dower house when he knew it was inhabited? Surely the house stood empty for most of the year, and it would be easier to break in when nobody was staying in it? If there was anything valuable here, there must have been better opportunities to burglarize.

I was getting sleepy, probably from the liquor. I turned out the light and sat for a moment propped up in bed, looking at the fire and stroking Cynthia. She was asleep already, her feet twitching as she chased something in a dream. I was missing some logical point, I thought; something about this intruder. But I couldn't think straight anymore, so, utterly exhausted, I slid down between the sheets and fell asleep.

When I woke the next morning, I remembered it all. I knew why Cynthia was on the bed beside me and why I felt gritty-eyed. I also remembered the point I couldn't figure out last night. Of course a burglar would have better opportunities to rob the dower house when it was unoccupied. So, what he wanted was something I had.

I lay in bed looking at the ceiling and trying not to accept the thought. It was silly. What did I have? Nothing! My camera—not very sophisticated—wasn't worth housebreaking for. I wore my father's old gold watch but I had no other jewelry. Just a selection of worn clothes and miscellaneous writing materials. If one were a burglar, wouldn't it be more profitable to break into the big house and swipe any old Chinese vase?

On that thought I got out of bed and got dressed. I would talk to David about this. He would know what the servants might have done, and whether or not the dower house contained anything valuable, and how often poachers were actually seen around Saltire.

It was early, before eight, when Cynthia and I walked up through the garden. I wondered, for that matter, how Cynthia had happened to be out at one in the morning; had she run away from David on another nocturnal stroll? When we got to the house she ran off in the direction of the kitchen, presumably to get breakfast. Remembering my clothes left in Henrietta's room, I went straight upstairs.

My corduroys and loafers weren't lying on the floor where I'd left them, and the riding clothes had been tidied away too. I opened what I hoped was a closet door near the bed and peered in; it was a small dressing room, and my clothes were neatly folded on a bench against a mirrored door. Evidently the dressing room adjoined another bedroom, and had been closed off. I walked in to pick up my clothes, and stopped. Because in the next room, I heard David's voice. And he was talking about me.

"She hasn't found anything conclusive yet, but there is a diary . . ." He was talking on the phone. I knew I shouldn't listen but I couldn't have moved. Who was he talking to?

"No, there's a volume missing. Yes, the last year . . . I know that's no help but at least we know there *was* a diary . . . no, I haven't seen it and in any case . . ." There was a long pause. "Look, Netta, please listen to me for a moment. We think the last volume of the diary is at Neville Park, and she's going there in a couple of days. I'm going with her, it works out very neatly . . . yes, I can look the place over and then if she finds the diary . . . no, I haven't told her anything, though I'm beginning to feel I should . . . no, all right, *please,* Netta. I won't. I'm sure she's trustworthy, but if that's how you feel . . . no," he sounded thoughtful now, "I think she's telling me everything. She has no reason not to. There were some letters as well. . . ." Another pause. "Netta, let me handle this, won't you? So far it's going even better than we hoped. Right. Nine-twelve tonight? Shall we hold dinner for you? Fine, someone will be there."

I had stood frozen through this conversation, but as I heard David hang up I sped from the room, clutching my clothes, and ran down the hall into the library. Fortunately I didn't run into anyone in the long corridor. I must have looked like a ghost. What did it mean? I couldn't figure it out; my mind objected, refused to face it.

David was telling his sister about my progress with the papers. That was innocuous, I tried to tell myself. She might be interested. Lauretta was, after all, her great-grandmother. She wore Lauretta's clothes. It was natural that she take an interest in the traces of Lauretta that I might find. But two phrases stuck in my mind: "I'm going with her" and "No, I haven't told her anything."

There was a secret. I had been right in thinking that there was a strain behind Henrietta's charm and David's affable concern. That first night at dinner Henrietta had been visibly tense when I mentioned the papers at Neville Park and the date of Lauretta's death.

I'd left the diaries and letters back at the dower house, and suddenly I wanted them with me. It was only eight; I still had time to go back and get them, and if anyone saw me I would say I was just taking my clothes back to the house.

I trotted down to the dower house, and walked slowly back up through the garden, thinking hard. There was a mystery. David and Henrietta were in it. It had to do with Lauretta and the diaries. Was it connected to the prowler at the dower house? As I walked past the maze I stepped inside it for a moment. Green hedge, mustard-colored grass. You could go left or right. I walked to the opening of the hedge on my left and peered around it. More hedge, with another opening in it. If I went and looked at that opening, would I remember where I had come from? Probably not. I stood still for a moment. There I was, surrounded by hundred-year-old hedges, and if I looked up I could see milky clouds threaded with blue. It was neither sunny nor cloudy. I held out a hand to see if I cast a shadow on the grass. No shadow. The hedges were much taller than I was, eight feet, ten feet, and dense. It was very alien. I didn't understand the appeal of a maze; that was not my idea of fun.

I left the maze and made my way up to the big house. I didn't understand what was going on at Saltire, and suddenly it felt alien too. The gracious house looked ominous in the watery light. I realized that I didn't even know where my car was; for that matter, Figg still had the keys. There were prowlers. And somehow I was being used, in a different way than I had guessed.

Should I tell David about the prowler? What if—oh, what if the prowler *was* David? I stood still, arrested by the idea. The day suddenly seemed grayer and colder. Was it possible that a man who seemed as . . . principled as David could be creeping around in the dark like a second-rate burglar? Why did I think he was principled, anyway? Just because he wore gold-rimmed glasses and stuttered a bit and was kind to a dog?

Then, as I stood there, I realized what the prowler had been looking for. It was obvious: he wanted to see the documents I had found. That had to be it. That was why the letters had been moved from the top of the desk; somebody had been reading them.

But why? Why would anyone care that much about Lauretta? And who would know that these documents even existed, let alone what I might be expected to do with them? And why was the sneaking around necessary? Who could there be who knew enough about the family to know that I might be privy to interesting (for whatever reason) material, and yet who wouldn't in the ordinary way of things have access to that material?

Not someone in the immediate family, that was clear. Because they owned the papers, and could read them at will. That let David off the hook, I realized with relief. He had only to say, "Would you mind my taking a look . . ." and of course I would turn everything over to him. And besides, I had spoken to him on the phone at the big house, I realized. Good heavens, I was getting confused! David couldn't have entered the dower house without my knowledge after our phone conversation and before the crash that woke me. He might be using me somehow, in fact I knew he was, from his conversation with Henrietta. But he hadn't been my nocturnal visitor.

As I climbed the steps to the terrace Cynthia came around the corner to meet me, barking. I was unreasonably touched by her warm welcome, and knelt down to put an arm around her. From that level I saw David's feet and shins follow Cynthia. "She's starved for company. She spent the night out again last night."

"No, she didn't. She spent the night with me. Does she usually sleep on your bed?"

To my surprise, he blushed. I burst out laughing in spite of myself. "Your guilty secret! It's safe with me, I promise."

"If Henrietta knew, I'd never hear the end of it. Do you know," he looked around as if afraid someone would hear, "I even brush my blanket every morning so Mrs. Lowery doesn't find her hair."

I was momentarily disarmed. But then David asked how Cynthia had gotten into the dower house, and my dilemma flooded back. Without thinking, I answered, "I heard her barking under my window, and went down to let her in."

"Clever girl," David said, scratching her head. I stood up, awkwardly, one arm around the three diaries.

"Did you get through those last night?" David asked as we turned toward the house.

"Yes, through the letters at least," I answered, thinking of the conversation I'd overheard. *Let me handle this* . . . he'd said. I was angry now. He wanted to handle me, did he? All that superior English charm that he and Henrietta were so carefully exerting for me really had a purpose. They wanted something from me. Purely contrary, I didn't want to oblige. The problem was, I didn't know what it was they wanted, so I didn't know what to withhold.

"Were they helpful?" David asked, holding open the door into the house.

"Not terribly," I said. "More concerned with what Mrs. Wright had for dinner and the weather in White Sulphur Springs. They don't give much information about Lauretta at all."

We dropped the subject over breakfast, and made plans for another ride that afternoon. David told me he would get Mrs. Lowery to find a jacket I could hunt in, "if necessary, one of mine," he said. And then we separated for the day.

I sat in the library staring into space for a while. I had a very strong impulse to leave, simply to bail out. The situation was getting odd, and I was apprehensive. "Fight or flight," I found myself thinking. I'd learned about that in Psychology 101; the old fight or flight response. Experienced, as I remembered, by trapped animals. Of course, flight wasn't really an option; I would never forgive myself. In spite of the peculiarities here, I had been lucky enough to find original documents that no one else had pored over yet. It was a tremendous opportunity and I would always regret not exploiting it to the fullest.

Fighting wasn't an option either. But I did feel angry, principally at myself. I'm cautious by nature, slow to trust. But I'd been taken in. The gullible American, fooled by European deviousness. Right out of Henry James. Things at Saltire were not what they seemed and I, with my literal mind, had been completely taken in by appearances. I was particularly annoyed to think that I had been ready to run to David with my prowler tale, sure that he would be able to clear it up. St. George and the dragon, rescuing the maiden. Wasn't St. George the patron saint of England? Instead it turned out that St. George, in this case, *was* the dragon. Precisely the kind of reversal the English considered vastly amusing.

I found I was tapping my pen in an irritated little rhythm on the tabletop. I was wasting time. The only practical answer to my dilemma was to get my work done as quickly as possible, and then leave. A question of five days at the most, if I included the trip to Neville Park with David. And as for David . . . I would worry about David later.

I spent that morning puzzling over the accounts I'd found, trying to decide how useful they really were. I read through the itemized list of expenditures: butcher, wine merchant, Farmer Tynan's potatoes. Neville Park didn't produce much of its own. I decided to copy the lists onto one piece of paper; it wouldn't take long, and if there was information to be gathered from the figures, I could puzzle it out later. Then I turned to the early volumes of the diary and read them carefully, taking notes. It was slow going, and I wished I had decided to bring my typewriter after all. When Figg came in with my lunch on a tray, I asked him if there was one in the house.

"Yes, Miss Llewellyn, there are several. Would you like me to bring you one?"

I was momentarily amused. Circumstances might be complicated but the service was a lot better than at the New York Public Library. "Yes, please."

He came back a few minutes later with a portable typewriter in each hand; a rather battered antique Underwood and a Smith-Corona. "If you care to use the electric model, I believe there is an outlet near the door," he said, and pulled an extension cord from his pocket. I almost said yes for the sheer pleasure of seeing him crawl on the floor and drag the extension cord behind him, but I told him the Underwood would do, and went back to work taking notes.

David came at three to take me riding, and I managed to keep the conversation off Lauretta by asking about the hunt. I rode Hercules again, and David mounted Nash, Henrietta's striking chestnut.

"I thought I'd take some of the mischief out of him," he said, "and Netta will get a quieter ride tomorrow."

"Who will you ride tomorrow?" I asked.

"I need a pretty big horse for a day's hunting, so I'll ride a stallion we have called Abracadabra. Stupid name, isn't it? He's quite young, but we have great hopes for him as a stud. He can jump anything, and he has a wonderful disposition. Very matter-of-fact, you know, stands around at the meet half-asleep, but when you ask him for speed it's right there. It's as if he turns it off and on with a switch. Now, would you like to just pop over these to get used to the feeling again?"

"These" were a few low fences set up in the paddock, and David cantered over them first. I suspected he was being tactful, so that I wouldn't feel he was watching me. We went around the paddock several times, until I felt comfortable with the rhythm of jumping, and then went out toward the river on a wide trail that was punctuated with jumps: a stone wall, a brush fence or two, a gate, several timber fences. Most of them were larger than anything I had ever jumped before, and my stomach felt hollow when they loomed into sight. But I grabbed a healthy handful of Hercules' mane, and managed to stay on. When we slowed to a walk to cross the river on a wooden bridge, David said, "You won't jump anything tomorrow that's bigger than those fences, so you'll be all right. And I'll stay near you in any case, to see you through the crowd."

He was so sweet, I thought regretfully, when I went back to work on the diaries. He might be a latter-day Gilbert Osmond but he was very kind—I remembered the little map of the house he'd made for me. And sensitive. And entertaining, and intelligent (of course Gilbert Osmond would have to be that). Even though his sandy hair and gold-rimmed glasses didn't make for matinee-idol material, I was even beginning to find him handsome. Something about his voice, his height, the deliberate way he moved, the warmth in his brown eyes . . . I shook my head and sighed. It was too bad.

Chapter 6

As I was dressing the next morning, the phone rang. It was Henrietta, whom I hadn't seen the night before, since I shut myself in the library directly after dinner.

"Hello, Sarah. I didn't get a chance to ask you last night, since David said I shouldn't disturb you. But are you all set for today? David said he'd made sure you had everything but he doesn't always pay attention."

I was at that moment standing in the hall wearing breeches and boots and a shirt that came almost to my knees. "The shirt is a little big, and I'm afraid I don't know how to tie the stock," I said.

"Fine. Why don't you just wear a sweater to breakfast and we'll fix you up afterward," she said briskly. "Bye." Click. Maybe there was something a little high-handed about the aristocracy.

As I walked through the garden carrying the shirt and the black jacket David had found for me, I could hear the sound of vans crunching up the drive, and voices in the distance shouting. When I got to the house Cynthia was at the door whining to get out. I edged by her, pulling her back as I shut the door behind me.

"Poor dear, she would so love to be out barking at everyone, but the huntsman would probably shoot her," Henrietta said. I couldn't help smiling when I saw her standing next to David. He had on his scarlet coat, and had left off his glasses again.

Henrietta was wearing the long black habit, and her hair was swept into a net. Standing together framed in the doorway, with the long hall behind them, they looked like a Sargent portrait: dashing, aristocratic, impossibly beautiful.

I was so nervous that I didn't want to eat much for breakfast, but Henrietta remonstrated. "I always have butterflies," she said, "but they go away after the first fence and then I'm *starving*. Really, you'll be better off if you have an egg or two." Then she took me upstairs to her bedroom while David went out to the stable to make himself helpful. Figg was in the front hall supervising the pouring out of the stirrup cups and the arrangements for the breakfast that would follow the hunt. The whole house buzzed with the energies of dozens of people working at full capacity.

Even Henrietta, for all her nonchalance, was excited. She chattered nonstop as she handed me a smaller shirt to try on, and tied my stock standing behind me in front of the mirror. "You're awfully tall, aren't you?" she said. "I can't quite . . . Here." She pulled up a stool and knelt on it, and her head appeared above my shoulders. "I always think that this must have been just what it was like years ago, you know; so little has changed about hunting, except for the people following in cars, of course, and women riding astride. Breeches aren't really becoming unless you're thin enough; *you* are, but lots of women . . ." She slid off the stool and plucked something from the dressing table. "Don't move now." She pinned my stock with a gold safety pin. "I always wondered if Lauretta actually wore this habit; so many of her clothes seem unworn. And then she had that baby so quickly, right after they were married. Well, nine months after, of course, but she didn't waste any time. And a good thing, too, since she died so soon afterward. Shall I braid your hair? Good. With your high cheekbones you should always pull it off your face. See how it brings out your eyes?" I nodded. She was right. The severity of the crisp white shirt and the chignon she was braiding made me look, well, elegant, in a way I wasn't used to. "Let me know if I pull." I tried to see her face in the mirror but she stood directly behind me. I didn't think the chatter was as artless as she wanted it to seem, though; she sounded brittle as she went on, "I mean, if she hadn't gotten pregnant so soon, or had that baby, we wouldn't even have *been*. But all of this would have been here just the same. Somebody else running it, that's all. It'd have been Gerald, actually, our ne'er-do-well cousin. Imagine that . . ." Watching my own face in the mirror, I was glad that Henrietta didn't see the very obvious wave of scarlet pass over my cheeks. I had almost forgotten about Gerald Charlton, but now Henrietta's words reminded me that the longer I kept my acquaintance with Gerald a secret, the more embarrassing it would be if it came to light.

Henrietta stuck in a last hairpin and stood back. "Very good. Now here's a waistcoat, and is this the coat David found for you?" She held it up as I put on the yellow vest. "He should at least have had Mrs. Lowery brush it; it's got Cynthia all over it. Or rather, it's not Cynthia, since it was David's when he was younger and we didn't have Cynthia then, so," she pulled a pale hair from the sleeve, "it must be Gladstone."

"You had a dog named Gladstone?"

"David named him. Out of profoundest respect, he said, and actually he did become one of those elder-statesman dogs, very dignified, you know. But he was just as silly as Cynthia, and David let *him* sleep on his bed, too."

I laughed. "David doesn't think you know about that."

She looked tolerant. "Positive *drifts* of dog hair all over his room, and he thinks nobody catches on. Here." She held the coat and helped me into it and tweaked the collar into place. Shaking her head, she pulled at the back of the jacket to make the front look tighter. "You're swimming in it, and the sleeves are down to your knuckles!"

"I'll be fine," I said, trying to sound decisive. "As long as it's not outlandish-looking."

"All right," Henrietta said, looking at her watch. "Let's go. Hat, gloves, whip," she muttered, taking them off her bed. "Right, then."

Twenty minutes later I was seated on Hercules in front of the house, watching. I wanted to remember everything. Near the stableyard, where the horse vans had lined up, controlled chaos reigned. Saddles tipped endways against tires; buckets and blankets and wooden boxes crammed with hoof-picks, brushes, currycombs, and mysterious dark bottles—everywhere you looked the arcana of the stable littered the ground. And scurrying under necks and around hindquarters were grooms and riders, bundled up in sweatshirts and scarves and distinguishable only by the latter's clean breeches and glossy boots. They checked the girth of a saddle, gave a last polish to a bit, finished the braids of a horse's mane. They all knew each other, of course; they hunted together, sometimes driving hundreds of miles for a particularly good meet or for a horse show during the summer. They trotted back and forth from van to van, chatting and exchanging gossip, borrowing a saddle pad or a pair of gloves; I heard one man tease a matronly woman about the red bow she was tying on her horse's tail, to signify that it kicked, while a pair of grooms stood concentrating on the bandaged leg of a delicate-looking chestnut mare.

Out in front of the house, it was like looking at the right side of the tapestry. Olive green windbreakers had yielded to impeccable hunting habits, and not a horse was less than perfectly groomed. Riders greeted each other and lit cigarettes and chatted, or walked their horses in circles on the edge of the crowd. The lady with the red-bowed horse was given a wide berth. Grooms held horses that sidestepped away from riders trying to mount them. Red-faced men in scarlet coats sat astride their big horses with a magisterial air. Figg and his helpers went through the crowd with trays of the stirrup cup. Leather creaked and bits jingled and the smell of horse and saddle soap hung in the damp air. The crowd kept forming and re-forming, waiting to fall into

the order of the hunt, with hounds in front and the field following. Henrietta stayed on the edge of the crowd, where Nash
sidled and switched his tail. The horse's gleaming coat was just
the color of her hair, which I thought (unkindly) probably
hadn't escaped her. I noticed that she remained close to the
handful of photographers in the crowd of onlookers even when—
as often happened—men came up to try to talk to her. There
was David now, on a rawboned giant of a bay that seemed to be
in another world as it walked through the crowd. Then Abracadabra stood still, ears flopped in utter relaxation as Nash
pranced around it in nervous circles. Henrietta, laughing with
her veil over her face and her silk top hat perched rakishly, said
something. David shrugged and smiled, and reached out to
touch her elbow as Nash brought her near. The photographers
loved it.

I watched them curiously for a moment, wondering how
many of them were professionals, and where the photographs
would end up; in the pages of the *Tatler,* I guessed. "Viscount
Neville and his sister Lady Henrietta Charlton, at the Saltire
meet of the Delabarr Fox Hounds." Then, as one of the photographers lowered his camera and looked at the lens, I saw that it
was Gerald Charlton.

I glanced away quickly, and nudged Hercules around so that
my back was to the photographers. Gerald Charlton, the "ne'er-
do-well cousin." For some reason I didn't want him to see me, and
I didn't want to acknowledge him.

But what was he doing there? Why was he there in the guise
of a photographer at the meet, someone who was anonymous
and guaranteed not to be noticed? Why not simply present himself at the front door as Cousin Gerald Charlton?

Because he knew he was unpopular with them? Because he
was ashamed of himself? But why be here at all? Was he simply
torturing himself by taking this opportunity to watch his glamorous cousins? Thinking that, if only things had been different,
he would be Earl? I hadn't checked Henrietta's statement in

Debrett's genealogical listings, but I was sure she was right. If only Lauretta hadn't had her son, Gerald Charlton would be Earl of Saltire. Was that why he'd been researching Lauretta in New York? I felt as if I were groping for something that I knew was there, and if I just had the power and the concentration to figure it out . . .

"Sarah? Are you all right?" I looked up from Hercules' tightly braided mane to see David in front of me on the somnolent Abracadabra.

"I'm fine," I said, smiling.

"I'm sorry, I just wondered if . . . you looked as if you might be regretting having decided to come out."

"No, not at all." I couldn't help wanting to reassure him. "I see what you meant about Abracadabra. Are you sure he'll wake up?" The horse swiveled one ear back to hear David's answer.

"Yes, he's like a bird. You'll see. Now, if you don't mind, I thought I'd stay with you; it's sometimes harrowing to ride in a big crowd like this."

"I'm very glad, but don't you have some official duties?"

"Not until later, when the vultures have to be fed. I may have to drop out a bit early to be back here, but you'll be confident enough by then to stay with the hunt."

"More likely glad to go home," I answered, and turned around as I heard the huntsman blowing his horn. The hounds, a small sea of brown and black and white, flowed around his feet. He moved off, and the crowd on horseback followed at a slow trot. We stayed toward the back of the group, with plenty of room on all sides. But we could see Henrietta ahead, in the thick of it. Evidently Nash had settled down.

We trotted for nearly half an hour, then stood round while the huntsman sent the hounds into a little clump of woods. "They always draw here first," David explained, "because it's the most successful bit of wood near Saltire and they find about half the time. Then there's a nice cross-country run of about forty-five minutes that the adult foxes usually take."

"I'm surprised it's so systematic," I said.

"Even the foxes have their traditions," David answered, deadpan. Then we heard one of the hounds begin to cry. "Violet," David said. "She's very reliable. Some of the younger hounds give voice at rabbits or even birds, but Violet never speaks unless she's sure." In a moment everyone had straightened up, thrown cigarettes away, thrust hands into gloves, jammed hats on heads. All the hounds were baying now, and the huntsman and whips were encouraging them. The horn sounded, and suddenly we were off.

It was amazing. I was unprepared for the wild exhilaration of it. I was terrified, clutching poor Hercules' mane again as we cantered across a field and over a stone wall and across the next field. It took me that long to settle down and realize that I was probably not going to fall off and our headlong flight was actually a reasonably controlled gait. I found myself grinning and looking around for the first time. Hercules didn't need any help from me. Next to me, David grinned back. Abracadabra was loping along, ears pricked forward, practically smiling. The horses' strides matched, but as we came to the next wall, Abracadabra pulled out in front, jumping much farther than Hercules. David stayed a little bit ahead of me as we crossed the next field. Ahead of us, I saw Henrietta and Nash jumping a timber fence while a large crowd waited to go through a gate. David glanced back at me and pointed to the fence. I nodded, and slowed Hercules a little. I didn't want to jump directly on Abracadabra's tail, and the fence was too narrow for us to jump side by side. We were at the back of the field, and the crowd at the gate had almost all gone through and cantered on. A man on a gray jumped the fence in front of David, ducking to avoid the tree branches that were a little close. I decided to try to take the fence a little farther away from the tree, and headed Hercules in that direction. I watched as David and Abracadabra cantered toward the fence. There was a split-second pause as Abracadabra set himself at the fence, feet together. Then I saw his head rise, and his hind hoofs leave the ground, and there was air between them and the fence, and then he landed. Then, suddenly, I could see his head rising again, as if he were jumping another fence that wasn't there. Then his hindquarters rose, like a bucking bronco's.

I was at the fence. Two strides, and Hercules would lift himself to clear it. There, on the other side, not five yards from where we would land, Abracadabra was rearing and bucking like a horse in a rodeo ring and David . . . I could see that David was not going to stay on much longer. He had lost a stirrup and the saddle was sliding around; his hat was on the ground somewhere and he'd dropped his whip. I hauled on Hercules' mouth, pulling him around to the right to circle away from the fence. Bless the horse, veteran that he was, he simply cantered smoothly around in a circle, as if he were always pulled away from jumps. I slowed him to a trot and we went through the gate and stopped. David was on the ground. Abracadabra, a few yards away, was still bucking. As I jumped off Hercules and looped his reins about the gate, I saw Abracadabra lie down and roll over on his back, as if he were violently scratching an itch.

David was breathing, at least. I knelt on the muddy grass and took my gloves off, I didn't know why. Someone who had been behind us in the field had led his horse across the fence so that nobody else would jump it and land on David. Somebody else dismounted and fetched David's hat from the mud, and came and knelt next to us. David opened his eyes and tried to sit up, but when he put his right elbow on the ground, he winced and fell back.

"Hold on, old man," the man kneeling with us said. "Frank's gone for the doctor. All right, are you? What did you hit?"

"Not my head," David said, "and my legs are all right. It's

probably ribs and collarbone." He wriggled his feet and bent his knees as if to prove it. "What about Abracadabra?"

We all looked over at the bay, which was now standing quietly, looking bedraggled and exhausted.

"He's all right now. Broken your saddletree, I shouldn't wonder," the man said. "Looked like he was trying to get it off. New saddle? Or do you usually use a pad?"

David just shut his eyes for a moment and shook his head. Wanting to do something, I said, "Should I catch him and take the saddle off?"

To my surprise, he clasped my hand. "Would you? Careful."

I got up and walked cautiously over to Abracadabra, trying to look calm and authoritative. They say horses always know when you're scared. He was apathetically nosing the grass, and I caught hold of the bridle without trouble. "Come on," I said to him, and clucked. He lifted his head and followed me over to the gate, where I fastened his reins next to Hercules'. I patted his neck by reflex, as if the horse had been a child that needed comfort. "It's all right," I crooned, pushing up the stirrups in their leathers, "everything's all right." I lifted the flap of the saddle and pulled upward on the two girth buckles at once. To my shock, Abracadabra's ears went back and he swung his head around toward me, showing his teeth. But as the girth fell to the ground he lapsed back into his daze. I ducked under his neck, not wanting to walk behind him even if he was calm again. I threw the girth over the horse's back and dragged the saddle off. It did seem that the solid part of it was broken, and I remembered the horse rolling on the ground. Trying to scrape off the saddle?

There was a dark mark where it had been on Abracadabra's back. Holding the heavy, sweaty piece of leather against my hip, I stood on tiptoe to see over Abracadabra's backbone. Nothing that shouldn't have been there. Unless . . . I ducked under his neck again, awkward with the weight of the saddle against my side. I looked at his left side. And there, near the edge of the sweat stain, was a small patch of raw, bleeding skin. Small, not even the size of a postage stamp. But ugly.

I hung the saddle on the top rail of the gate and mechanically ran my fingers over the underside of it. I flinched when I found them; little spikes. I looked at my fingers. Blood on them. Could that be part of the saddle, worn through? I thought stupidly. No, it was impossible. There was something wrong.

I stood there between the two horses for just a moment, looking at the blood on my fingers. The gray sky was lightening and a flock of crows in a nearby tree rose in noisy flight. Something wrong. David was hurt, and not by accident. Somebody had fixed his saddle so that the horse would go wild and throw him. That was a lot more serious than just people tripping over chairs in the night. I could feel the damp from the mud I'd knelt in, extra cold at my knees, and a gust of wind whipped at my fingers. I wiped them on the sleeve of the black coat, and went back to where David was lying.

He was sitting up, propped against the man who'd stayed with him; recovered enough to introduce us. "Sarah, this is Will Erskine," David said. "Will, Sarah Llewellyn. How's Abracadbra?"

I just looked at him bleakly. "Fine," I said, "calm as ever." I didn't want to mention the spikes in front of this stranger, whoever he was.

"Sarah, if you'd prop David up," he was saying, "I'll get my flask. I think we could all use it." So I sat where he'd been sitting, and let David lean against me.

"This is the part of hunting you're not supposed to find out about your first time," he said feebly.

Trying to match his attitude, I answered, "Better you than me," and was rewarded with a wan smile. "You probably shouldn't be talking," I added.

"It's all right. Ribs and collarbone aren't terribly serious."

Will Erskine knelt by us and held his flask to David's mouth. "Still, Sarah's right. Save your energy." David grimaced at the effort to swallow, and shook his head when Will proffered the flask again. So we sat there on the muddy ground in silence. The horses' bits clinked as they mouthed them, and the birds called out at random. Will, tired of squatting next to us, got up and walked the horses around, to cool them off. The ground was very cold and the damp had soaked through to my skin.

"Sorry, Sarah, to be such a bore," David said without opening his eyes.

"That's all right. You couldn't help it."

He shook his head. "I can't understand it. Perfectly simple fence, and Abracadabra's completely reliable . . ." He opened his eyes and looked up at me. "Was there anything wrong with the saddle?"

"I didn't see anything," I said. My voice sounded completely right, casual, with a note of puzzlement. I hadn't even taken the time to think about telling the truth. The lie had come out automatically. Why? David would examine the saddle later and would find the spikes. He would know that somehow his fall had been planned. Was it even plausible that I might not have noticed them? I couldn't tell.

And I regretted my answer immediately. It was clear, now, that there was some kind of trouble at Saltire. If I had told David about the spikes in the saddle, he might have been able to explain part of it. Who would want to hurt him, for instance? I might find out the reason for his phone call to Henrietta, and I could have explained about the nocturnal visitor at the dower house.

But it was too late, for over the horizon came a Land Rover, and Will brought the horses back to the gate, and there was suddenly a little bustle. The doctor was a big taciturn man, who prodded gently at David's shoulders, watched him wince, and nodded. "Ribs too?" he asked.

"I think so," David said.

"Did you get kicked?"

"No, I fell clear, and hit with my shoulder."

"Well, we'll take you along to check for internal injuries, and tape you up."

The back of the Land Rover was outfitted with a stretcher that locked into place as a cot. David protested at being loaded onto it, but Will and the doctor strapped him in without listening.

"Thank you, Sarah," he said, with a gesture of his hand, as they slid him into the Land Rover. "Will is going to take you home; would you see that Riley looks over Abracadabra?"

I nodded, and Will shut the door. We got back on our horses and began to trot home, silently, Will leading Abracadabra. The doctor had picked up the saddle and loaded it into the front of the car.

It was a long ride home, well over an hour. I went over and over what had happened, trying to fit it all together. Did David's fall have anything to do with the prowler? Was it connected to his conversation with Henrietta? What were they expecting me to find out that they wanted to know? What could be so important about Lauretta that they would be affected by it? What earthly difference could her life make?

And then, of course, I realized. I must have stiffened, for Hercules broke into a canter. Automatically, I slowed him back to a trot. Henrietta had told me that morning, in her nervous chatter while she braided my hair. "We wouldn't even have *been* . . ."

The date of Lauretta's death. I couldn't find it. Her son had been born early in December and she had died shortly thereafter. But if she had died before he was born; if she had had no son, then indeed Gerald would have been the current Earl of Saltire. Did Gerald know something about Lauretta that I didn't know? Something that made this more than pure fantasy?

I looked around me for a moment, trying to clear my mind. It seemed ridiculous. Substitutions of babies; that was the stuff of Stuart melodrama, or those Ruritanian romances so popular in the Edwardian era. The baby St. John's birth had been announced in the *Times* as occurring on December 3, and even though Lauretta's death hadn't been in the paper, there would be a death certificate filed in London at St. Catherine's House. Simple to find, if time-consuming; there was no need to go hunting about through diaries and letters for proof that would be circumstantial at best. Even if the diary did break off earlier than the third of December, that wasn't proof of Lauretta's death.

And yet David and Henrietta—and at least one other person—were interested in what the diaries had to say. Could it be . . . ? It was Gerald who would be most nearly affected. Gerald, I knew, had been in the vicinity. Gerald would have no legitimate access to those papers, particularly since he seemed to have offended his cousins somehow. I had difficulty imagining the refined, correct Gerald I'd met in New York creeping around in the bushes and tripping over my makeshift barricade. But I had felt, that night, that the prowler was an amateur. It could well have been Gerald. I accepted the thought grimly. Little though I welcomed the notion, astounding though it seemed, it fit.

Why had this fall been engineered, then? Was it an attempt at—not at murder? As soon as the thought crossed my mind I felt foolish. That was overheated paranoia. It just wasn't possible. For one thing, it was too uncertain a way to kill someone. There was no way to guarantee that a fall in the hunting field would prove that serious, particularly for an experienced horseman like David, who would know how to minimize the effects of a fall. Moreover, what good would killing David do? Gerald might not be perfectly innocent but he couldn't be planning to kill off, one by one, David and his brothers. There; I had assumed Gerald was responsible for the fall. And why not?

But *why?* I was completely at a loss. Perhaps the goal had been simply to put David out of commission, to keep him from doing something—to keep him from going to Ireland? The tenant, Ludovic Walter, had put him off repeatedly. Could this accident have been staged to prevent David from seeing something untoward at Neville?

A wave of disappointment swept over me as I took this in. David wouldn't be going to Ireland with me, of course. If that was the point of the accident, it had been successful. And I was sorry. Everything would have been easier: the drive, the crossing, finding Neville Park, dealing with Ludovic Walter. I had been counting on David to smooth the way. To act as St. George, in fact. And I had, despite my doubts, been looking forward to more time spent with him, perhaps even to clearing those very doubts away. . . .

I suddenly recognized where we were; there was Saltire off in the distance, with the river in front of it, and the crowds of vans and cars barely visible off to the left. In a few minutes we were riding into the stableyard, and Riley was running out of the tack room to take Abracadabra's reins from Will.

"What happened to his lordship?" he asked, with worry plain on his face.

"Abracadabra bucked him off. You know the narrow timber fence by the gate into Edgar Tristram's farm? It was right there."

"This horse never bucked anybody off," Riley said, affronted, feeling Abracadabra's front legs. "He's not got the temperament for it, and never had, not even before he was broken."

"But he did. Miss Llewellyn was right behind him."

"And where's his lordship now? He's not hurt then?"

"Collarbone and ribs, most likely. Dr. Fox came."

Riley was obviously still puzzled, shaking his head as he felt Abracadabra's hind legs. "MacIntyre!" he bellowed. "Damn the man, he's never where he should be. The new undergroom," he explained to Will. "He's only been here for a matter of weeks, but you'd think he'd know better than to go running off on a hunting day. Miss Llewellyn, perhaps you'd not mind unsaddling Hercules yourself? I'll rub him down, but if you could put him in his box . . ."

"Of course," I said, and slid down.

"I'll go put Stevedore away and see you at the house, then, shall I?" said Will, and rode out of the stableyard. I turned and led Hercules into his stall, where I began to take off his saddle. Riley would find Abracadabra's injury, and I knew he would ask me about it.

Sure enough, I had no sooner unbuckled Hercules' girth than Riley appeared at the door of the stall, holding a halter and a light horse-blanket.

"I'll take that, Miss Llewellyn. Could you just take off his bridle now? And if you could put this on . . ." He held out the halter. He leaned the saddle against the wall of the box, and unfolded the blanket. I took the other side without being asked, and pulled it straight, waiting for the question.

"You saw the fall, then?" Riley's voice was muffled, as he was leaning down to buckle the blanket under Hercules' belly.

"Yes, I was right behind him. Abracadabra was going smoothly, cleared the fence, and then, right after he landed, began to buck and rear. Like a horse in a rodeo," I added.

"And would you happen to know who took the saddle off? Or where it is?" Riley asked, coming around to face me.

"Yes, it's in Dr. Fox's Land Rover. I took it off; the saddletree seemed to be broken."

"Ah. And how would that have happened?" Riley's face was impassive.

"Abracadabra rolled around on his back," I said. "Like a dog scratching an itch. Has he done that before?" I was counting on a show of ignorance to protect me from the hostility I sensed in the groom.

"No, that he has not. You wouldn't have noticed anything else about that saddle, now?"

"Not besides the saddletree. Will did ask if it was a new one, but it wasn't, was it?"

"No, it was not," Riley said. "You'll be wanting to get up to the house, then, miss. I can manage the two horses."

I walked up to the house, relieved at my dismissal. Riley clearly thought I was too ignorant (or too stupid) to have noticed foul play. But now, I was going to have to face everyone else. More questions, more explanations. I was tired, aching, and longing to curl up somewhere and forget the last few hours.

The anticipatory bustle of the morning was gone. The sky was a bleak unforgiving gray and the grass was a muddy mess, tracked with hoof marks and deep tire-treads from the horse vans, and sucking at my boots as I tried to pick my way around the worst of the muck. The spectators had all gone home, the photographers to their next assignments. It made me wonder where Gerald was now. Did I have to worry about another clandestine visit? Had he perhaps broken into the dower house while we were out hunting?

Maybe that wasn't fair, I told myself, hesitating before a particularly soupy stretch of mud. I had no proof against Gerald. I hadn't caught him in the act. It was possible that the prowler and the author of David's accident were two separate people and that Gerald had been there today simply as a spectator. And besides—what did Gerald have to do with Neville Park? Why should he care whether David went there or not? For that matter, what did any peculiarities at Neville Park have to do with Saltire? And if David had been injured to keep him from going to Ireland, didn't that mean he wasn't involved in anything underhanded? I liked that idea. But there was a huge flaw in it—I had completely invented those sinister goings-on at Neville Park. As I walked into the house I told myself there must be a rational explanation for the whole thing. My imagination was getting the better of me, and I felt like Winnie the Pooh, a bear of very little brain. For the moment, though, all I had to do was act ignorant (an easy task), be casually sociable, and keep my overheated suspicions to myself.

I managed. People were beginning to straggle back, and though word got around about David's spill, nobody seemed to think much of it. I drank tea, and chatted with the neighbors and the people I was introduced to. They asked polite questions about my research, I asked polite questions about the rest of the run. Finally, well after it was dark, I was kneeling in front of the fire with Cynthia when Henrietta came up.

"Sarah, you needn't stay if you don't want to. You must be dying for a bath."

"I am. I'd love to sneak away."

"Good. You'll be glad to know I just spoke to David. He's fine, no internal injuries, and they've taped him up. They're keeping him in hospital overnight but he'll be back tomorrow. He said to be sure to thank you."

I shook my head. "It's him I should be thanking, and you, for being so kind. I was sorry the hunt ended so badly; I was enjoying it."

There was a flash of pleasure on her face. "It didn't end badly for everyone. We had a tremendous run, went on for miles, and finally killed our fox." The serious look came back to her face. "But tell me, you were right behind him; was there anything wrong? Abracadabra just doesn't . . ." She trailed off.

"I suppose he must not, everyone has been so surprised. I didn't notice anything wrong. But I think Riley went over him with a fine-tooth comb, so if there is I'm sure he'll find it." Should I even have said that? Would Riley want to tell her about the sore spot? It was all so complicated, I didn't know whom to tell what, and how I should act. But at least I would be gone the next day. I reminded Henrietta, "I'm leaving for Neville Park tomorrow, and I'd like to get an early start. Figg still has my car keys, I suppose?"

"I expect so. But you'll be coming back here, won't you?

Because if you'd like to leave anything at the dower house or in the library, we'd be happy . . ."

I looked up at Henrietta's face in the glow of the firelight. She seemed honestly eager to have me come back, and I couldn't help remembering that I was supposed to be finding something out. She hoped I would come back from Neville Park with the key to the Charltons' problem, whatever it was.

Well, so did I. Squatting by the fire with Cynthia, looking up at the strain on Henrietta's face, thinking of David strapped up on a hospital bed, I wanted to do what I could. I would have liked to put the whole thing out of their minds.

I almost broached the subject then. I was on the verge of telling Henrietta that I had deduced what she was worrying about. But Figg came up with a message for her, and the moment passed. The three of us arranged for my early departure and I said I'd be back on Tuesday by dinnertime. Henrietta was going to the hospital that night to see David, so I said good-bye and went down to the dower house. Too exhausted even to worry about who might have been there in my absence, I tumbled into bed and slept dreamlessly.

Chapter 7

It was foggy when I left. It was foggy when I got there. The whole day had that dreamlike quality of traveling alone. The roads were nearly empty when I started, close to seven. The traffic swelled around Birmingham, and dropped away when I crossed into Wales. The cloud cover lightened, then got heavy again. I stopped and bought gas and could barely understand the man at the pumps. I drove into Holyhead with half an hour to kill before the ferry left.

It was dreary, and I was worried, which gave the dreariness a threatening air. There was no one in the streets, and when I got out of my car at the ferry dock, there were only three people waiting. The Channel was gray, just plain gray, with no light showing on the water, and a heavy chop. You couldn't see far, certainly not to Ireland. The ferry itself was streaked with rust.

There were so few of us that we seemed to be spying on each other; when I climbed the stairs to the upper level and found a fellow passenger there, I felt like apologizing. I tried to read indoors, and started to feel seasick, so I went back out and stood at the rail and stared into the fog. I sat for a while on a damp bench and glanced at the newspaper. There was a vituperative editorial about American nuclear stockpiles in Europe; a report on a serial killer in Yorkshire; an investigative piece on the prevalence of drug use in the horse world. It seemed that the paraphernalia of getting horses from one place to another, and the constant travel from race course to race course, made an ideal distribution network for drug dealers. Remembering the scenes at Saltire yesterday, I could well believe it. Any one of those grooming trunks could have been lined, I supposed, with expensive white powder. But how sordid. I hated the idea of it. The trip seemed endless.

And then when we got to Dun Laoghaire, I had to drive clear across Ireland. I wanted very badly to get to the Ballyhannock Inn before dark, since I had an idea that the roads in rural Galway might be tricky. So I was grateful when, near five o'clock, I saw a road sign for Ballyhannock. The inn, however, gave me pause. It looked damp and very seedy. The village, for that matter, was unprepossessing; whitewashed cottages with doors opening directly onto the street, and thatched roofs that looked mildewed. In the middle of the village (it was really just a crossroads) there was another road sign, and one arm of it read "Neville." Rather than spend more hours than necessary at the musty Ballyhannock Inn, I decided to go and take a look at Neville Park, so I turned at the sign and kept going.

Twenty minutes later, I was still driving. I could not have missed a turn—there had been no turn—and yet there was no village in sight. The narrow road looped up and down over little hills, between tumbledown stone walls with rocky irregular fields on either side. It was green; that I could appreciate. But pretty soon the sun would set and it wouldn't be green anymore, just dark. Half an hour. Forty-five minutes. And finally I drove into the village of Neville.

It looked better than Ballyhannock. There was a flat area in the middle, more or less a village green. The cottages looked more prosperous—the whitewash was fresher, the thatch newer, there were more of them. I wondered if the relative wealth here came from contact with Neville Park. A hundred years ago the villagers probably supplied the big house with farm labor, and I remembered "Farmer Tynan's potatoes" listed in the accounts I'd seen back at Saltire. There was probably still a Tynan here in Neville.

It was a long drive back to Ballyhannock, but I was curious, and having come so far, I wanted to get a glimpse of the big house. Though the lights were showing yellow from the cottages, I drove on through the village. There was only the one road, and Neville Park had to be on it.

Half an hour later, I saw it. It came as a shock.

The tumbledown stone walls still lined the road; the fields rolled scrubby and desolate on either side. To my left, the land rose and to my right, it fell away. There was the sea, below uneven bluffs. And there was the house.

It was preposterous. I'd done enough research to know that after the Irish famine in the 1850s, the West of Ireland was so poor that nobody built anything. Except the thirteenth Earl of Saltire, who'd converted to Catholicism and built himself a gothicized castle on the edge of the sea.

I couldn't see very clearly, since there was a mist coming off the water and thickening the twilight. But I could make out that there were a pair of towers (one square and one round), battlements, banks of casement windows. One of the towers seemed to have a mansard roof and, of all things, a clock on it. Out here at the back of beyond, where probably no more than a dozen people drove by in a day, there was a huge clock. I was tickled by that, and I wondered if it kept time. I was just too far away to see, even squinting. But on an impulse, I pulled the car off the road next to the stone wall (which didn't look any less dilapidated for its proximity to a nobleman's house). My camera bag was on the seat next to me. I fished out the camera body and attached a 200-mm lens. The top of the tower, the mansard, was roofed with scalloped slate in red and blue, and there was lacy cast iron running along the peak of the roof. I moved the lens down to focus on the clock, which had large and elaborate Roman numerals. It said ten to six. My watch said six-twenty. It might be slow, or it might have stopped. I ranged the camera over the front of the house, and wondered idly where all the cold gray stone had come from. It looked like granite, a little the worse for a hundred years of sea air. Between the road and the house was a low block of buildings in the same style, with a roof that was even more elaborately tiled, and broad-arched windows like a monk's cloister. A stable, I thought, though it was awfully close to the house. The horses lived well in those days.

I stiffened. A man had walked out of the stable entrance. Even in the dusk, his blond hair showed quite clearly. He was walking jauntily, with his hands in his pockets. I sharpened the focus. Yes, it was Gerald Charlton.

I kept the lens trained on him as he walked up the drive to the house. He disappeared into the shadow under a vast porte cochere, but I saw a crack of light appear, increase, and shrink to nothing as he opened the door and went in.

I tried to dismantle the camera and put it away but my hands were shaking. Gerald here? What did it mean? During the day's long drive I had almost succeeded in convincing myself that neither David nor Gerald could be connected with anything suspicious at Saltire. I'd made excuses for that telephone conversation of David's I'd overheard; I had found reasons why Gerald might have been at the hunt meet.

Yet here was Gerald, at Neville Park, looking perfectly at home. And all my anxieties came flooding back.

I started the car again, and gave my mind for a moment to the problem of turning it around. It was a narrow road, and a sharp curve to the left made it blind. It would take forever to work myself around to head back to the village of Neville; I would have to turn in the Neville Park drive. I didn't like to do it. In fact I didn't want to have much to do with the place for the moment, until I figured out Gerald. But I carefully swung the car into the drive, and backed out. I hadn't turned my lights on, for which I was grateful; somehow I felt as if the house, or someone in the house, could see up the drive to my little rented Mini and see me cowering inside it. I didn't turn on my headlights until I was well out of sight.

I slowed the car as I drove into Neville village, and looked around again. It was really rather charming. The street was damp with mist, and glistened in the lights from the cottages. On one side of the village green was a long low building with a sign for Watney's Ale outside it. The door was open, and I could see a corner of a bar lined with glasses, and a television. Then I noticed a sandwich board propped out in front. It said "Pub menu. Bed and Breakfast. Sandwiches." I braked and sat for a moment looking at the building and the green and thinking about the long drive back to Ballyhannock.

No contest. I would stay here if I could get a room. It was so much closer, and so much more appealing, that I wondered why Ludovic Walter had suggested the Ballyhannock Inn in the first place.

They didn't exactly receive me with open arms, but they were polite. Reserved, I would call it. Yes, there was a room for the lady. Two or three nights? Certainly. The car could stay on the street, yes, and Tommy would bring in the bags.

I felt funny about going down to the bar for dinner, but the stern woman who had assigned me the room had instructed me. I didn't dare do otherwise.

I felt very much of an intruder. I had a book and planned to sit in a corner and creep back upstairs as soon as I could. And indeed I was placed at a table in the corner, and Tommy— young, silent, and jug-eared—brought me soup and some tough meat and gray-green beans. I pretended to read and tried to understand the conversation, which seemed to center on the soccer game on TV. Bit by bit I got more words; the accent was very strong, and the inflections were so unexpected. Tommy brought a slab of dry pound cake; I turned a few pages of the book, chewing valiantly. Then Tommy stood in front of me again.

"Excuse me, miss, but I've brought this with Mr. Flannery's compliments." "This" was a short glass full of dark liquid. I glanced over at the bar; a tall dark-haired man with a gap between his front teeth was smiling at me.

Now what? I wished I knew what the convention was. Mr. Flannery looked nice. I wanted to do what was proper. Tommy was still standing there, having put down the glass. I looked up at him and said, a little tentatively, "Thank you. Perhaps Mr. Flannery would like to join me?" Tommy nodded, impassive, and turned to convey the message to my new friend. Mr. Flannery looked delighted, and I hoped devoutly that he didn't think I was a woman of loose morals (or something even worse) driving around by myself and eating dinner in pubs.

It became rapidly apparent that my feminine attributes were secondary to my novelty value. Not much happened in Neville, it seemed. I was the greatest entertainment he'd had in weeks.

It didn't happen right away—there was no sudden flood of eager gentlemen crowding around to chat—but in the course of an hour or so the groups in the pub had coalesced, the television abandoned, and the conversation was general. Everyone had a cousin in America; did I know him? He was a police officer in Brooklyn, a fireman in Queens. I expressed admiration for the police force and the fire department. More Irish whiskey (that was the dark liquid, and plenty potent, too) appeared. America was a grand place, and what did I think of Ireland? Beautiful, I said. I explained that I had arrived only that morning; more whiskey was drunk as a toast to the young lady's first night in Ireland. Might they know what my name was? Llewellyn? Was I Welsh, then? Yes, but several generations back. Both of my parents were teachers. Ah, an education was a fine thing, and I must be very educated myself. I said I hoped so but there was always more to learn. This sentiment warranted more whiskey.

And what might I be doing in the village of Neville, if they might be so bold as to ask? (It was Mr. Flannery who asked the question; I realized immediately that the whole previous hour of talk had been the prelude to this interesting question, and that Flannery, having been bold enough to approach me first, got to ask it.)

I was prepared for this. I said I was driving around the West Country taking pictures for a book, and was there anything around here worth taking pictures of? Well, there was old Mrs. Tiverton, the BBC took her picture some ten years ago when they came to do a TV show. They took her picture then because she was so old, and now she was ten years older, so she was certainly worth photographing. And then Farmer O'Malley's black-faced ewe that won first prize at the agricultural fair was due to lamb in a week or two; how long could I stay? I was afraid I couldn't wait that long.

"There's always the big house," said a young man who hadn't spoken much.

"That there is, but I do not imagine that they would be glad to see this young lady there," answered an older man with a pipe.

"Are they very private then?" I asked. "Who lives there?"

"A gentleman who calls himself 'Ludovic Walter,' and if that's his actual name then mine is Margaret Thatcher." Waves of laughter were followed by several appreciative repetitions of the witticism.

"What does he do, living out here?" I asked, furrowing my brow.

"Ah." There was a lot of nodding and glances exchanged.

Flannery leapt into the breach. "We wouldn't want to guess, miss, but there's a lot of coming and going after dark there. Aeroplanes, even."

"He said when he came that he was training horses, but there's only the three horses there and he doesn't do much schooling of them."

"He's a roly-poly man for riding, too; fourteen stone he must weigh, at the least."

I found none of this reassuring, but was shocked by the next statement. Out of a lull, Tommy spoke from where he'd been hovering near the group of men. "And then there's the blond man who's staying there too. Just like he lives there, comes and goes . . ."

His statement silenced everyone, and there were sharp glances exchanged. But a wink or two and a smothered smile made me wonder; did they think Gerald was Walter's lover? It was possible, after all. I remembered with chagrin my evening with Gerald in New York—was that why he hadn't insisted . . . Never mind. "Is it pretty, this place?" I asked, to break the smirking silence.

"O'Malley's lamb will be prettier by far, but as houses go it's grand enough."

"Set there right next to the sea, it is; a foolish place to build a house so big, the wind there is something terrible."

"It belongs to an earl, though we've never seen him. I don't suppose you've ever seen an earl either, there in America?" the man with the pipe said. And the conversation came back to America, and the police force, and the fire department, and . . .

I got away half an hour later, though it was difficult and I had to plead exhaustion from my drive. I was offered more whiskey to make me sleep, and Mr. Flannery called out to the stern lady to make me some hot milk to take up to bed, which I declined. They all wished me good night and said they looked forward to seeing me in the village. I heard the voices rumbling downstairs for an hour more after I went upstairs, until the men were kicked out at closing time, and scattered to their cottages.

Now what? Gerald Charlton came and went at Neville Park, and was evidently on terms of intimacy (even if it wasn't the kind of intimacy the village assumed) with Ludovic Walter. What in the world did it mean? I padded around the room, getting ready for bed, trying to think it out. Trying also—performing these routine little rituals, brushing my teeth, brushing my hair—to dispel the sense I had of being caught in some horrible sticky web. Gerald in America, researching Lauretta.

David and Henrietta, worried about the legitimacy of their grandfather. Gerald, possibly the real earl, at Neville Park. The prowler—Gerald?—at Saltire, reading letters and putting them away in the wrong drawer.

But what was he doing at Neville Park? What was going on at Neville Park, for that matter? I hadn't liked the reference to planes coming and going at night; it sounded sinister. Maybe this was why David had been prevented from coming with me. What could Ludovic Walter be up to? More to the point, why was Gerald practically living there?

Looking for more information. Trying to find the *proof* that he was, in the phrase of the old romances, the rightful heir. Maybe he had appeared, charmed Walter, weaseled himself into being a semipermanent guest. This I could imagine. And while he was staying at Neville Park, he could look around for proof that Lauretta had died before December 3, before the birth of the putative heir. He could look for that old standby of genealogists, the parish register.

I got into bed and turned out the light. I didn't like the situation one bit, and I couldn't imagine what I was going to say to Gerald Charlton when I saw him the next day.

Chapter 8

But when I arrived at Neville Park, Gerald didn't seem to be there. I was greeted at the door by a big man who looked—it came as a little shock after the quintessentially Irish faces in the pub—extremely Germanic. He had on tweed trousers and a shirt with the sleeves rolled up, a noncommittal costume that gave me no hint as to what he might be in the household. He showed me into a long room off the hall and left me waiting there, reflecting that whatever he was he had good circulation. It was the coldest, dampest room I'd ever been in.

The air had that moist salty smell you never escape at the seaside, and the long row of windows looked over the ocean, like a screened porch in an old shingled house on, say, the New Jersey shore. But the windows were wide-pointed arches, and rather than being screened, they were made of leaded glass, with occasional colored panes and a few that were artfully "cracked." Very literal, the Gothic revival. And rather than slightly mildewy wicker furniture painted green, with chintz cushions, the room held heavy, ecclesiastical-looking oak and crimson velvet. Any of the chairs could easily have served as a church pew. There were huge fireplaces at either end, topped by heroic mantels blazoned with the Charlton arms. And in the empty hearths were brass bowls filled with, of all things, dusty fronds of pampas grass. How in the world, I wondered, did one get pampas grass on the west coast of Ireland? It must have been carefully imported and cherished for dozens—scores, I supposed—of years. I moved to a window to look out at the water. The house wasn't built right at the edge of the bluff; a hundred yards of very scrubby grass, flat and dreary, intervened and then dropped off in an irregular coastline to the water.

I heard footsteps approaching on the flagstone floor (it would be flagstone), and turned around. This had to be Ludovic Walter.

He was, as I'd been warned, heavy, one of those big barrel-shaped men who always seem to wear sweaters that accentuate their girth. He had dark hair, cut in a fringe around his forehead to disguise a receding hairline—what I thought of as a Julius Caesar haircut. Dark eyes that didn't move much. Nothing in his face moved much; he barely opened his mouth to talk. True to his physical type, he wore a pale yellow sweater—cashmere, I thought—and a starched white shirt that reminded me, jarringly, of a Chinese laundry in New York. He had one of those soft handshakes.

"Miss Llewellyn," he stated. "I am Ludovic Walter." Contrary to what the man in the pub had said, I thought it probably was his real name. His English seemed a little foreign; just a slight softness in the consonants gave it away.

"You're so kind to let me take up your time," I said. "I really do appreciate it enormously."

"Not at all. I would like to show you around the house and grounds; then, if you will excuse me, I will leave you to your researches while I attend to some business of my own. We shall have luncheon together at one o'clock, if that will be all right." He gestured that I was to precede him out the door. Doesn't waste much time on civilities, I thought.

"Of course I do not know anything about the history of this place, since I am only renting it, but I will show you where everything is. This is the hall." So it was. Two stories high, drafty, dark, despite diamond-paned clerestory windows. It needed a couple of suits of armor, I thought; there wasn't much else in it besides an enormous table smack in the center, bearing a huge faience vase full of peacock feathers. They looked even older than the pampas grass.

We walked quickly around the ground floor; Walter showed me the dining room, the study (in the base of the round tower), a smaller drawing room, a room with a covered billiards table. I could see that the legs of the table were inlaid and elaborately carved; it looked as if the thirteenth Earl had even had Gothic-revival taste in indoor sports.

"You will not need to come up here except for the trunks," my guide was saying as we climbed the stairs (dark creaky wood, with another stained glass window on the landing that looked like it might be a Burne-Jones). "Here they are."

He opened the door to the room that was just above his study in the round tower. It was bare, except for the trunks and boxes on the floor. "I myself do not know what is in them, being only a tenant. But I suppose you have the Earl's permission to examine the contents?" I assured him I did.

"Now if you will come downstairs with me; you will need a coat, as we are going to the chapel." So I put my jacket on and followed as he walked out through the porte cochere and around in front of the house. The wind was strong, and I could see that the water was very rough. It boiled and broke over rocks dotting the little coves. I knew from maps that there were little islands directly west of us, but you couldn't see for more than a hundred yards.

"I will give you the key to the chapel, if you like. There might be some records there."

The church was tiny, tucked behind a few runty trees right on a headland, and even more Gothic than the house. A doll-house version of a cathedral, with lacy stonework and flying buttresses and a crocketed spire. Walter opened the wooden door for me with an old-fashioned key, and let me go in first. I stood silent, looking around. The building itself was actually quite lovely; the proportions somehow worked, and the details were beautiful. The thirteenth Earl had hired some very skilled stonemasons. I was amazed, too, that the windows were intact after exposure to a hundred years' worth of storms.

Walter broke into my thoughts by saying, "If you don't mind, I will be getting back to my work now. Would you like to stay here? Here is the key; please lock up after you go. I will see you at luncheon." And he was gone, barely waiting for my answer.

I sat down in one of the pews, relieved that he was gone. His lack of expression masked, I thought, some kind of hostility. Maybe he just resented being interrupted in what he referred to as "his work," which hardly seemed to be schooling horses. I wouldn't have been surprised to see a computer somewhere with listings of the latest stock prices in London and New York. And he'd said nothing about Gerald. I wondered whether Gerald had examined the chapel. The place was surprisingly clean. I would have expected at least a few needles from the wind-twisted pines outside, but there wasn't even any dust. I got up and walked toward the altar. There had to be a sacristy somewhere, for storing the priests' vestments, the chalices, the vases for altar flowers.

Sure enough, there was a door hidden behind a big pillar, just beyond the first pew on the right. It was wood, with a little diamond-shaped window in it at eye level, like a kitchen door. I pushed and it opened easily, swinging smoothly on its hinges. I stood on the threshold to look at the room before I stepped in.

It was tiny, and dark. There was a small wardrobe against one wall, a small table with a chair, and a low bookshelf. The furniture all matched; plain heavy oak with a bit of Gothic detail. Clean, but spooky. There was a solitary black cassock hanging in the wardrobe, and a tidy row of beautifully bound missals in the bookshelf. But as soon as I picked one up and opened it, the leather spine cracked, and I could see that the pages, elaborately printed in red and black, were spotted with mildew. There was a large Bible, too, bound to match the missals, and on top of the bookshelf stood a pair of candlesticks that still had wax clinging to them.

I wondered if the villagers in Neville had come to Mass here in the thirteenth Earl's time, and whether the fourteenth Earl had been a Catholic. I couldn't really imagine him caring much about religion one way or another. Had Lauretta had to convert to marry him? I couldn't imagine her having strong religious convictions either. Their son had probably been urged back to the Anglican faith of his fathers, and the chapel deconsecrated under the aegis of the stuffy uncle who'd brought him up. There was a deep drawer at the bottom of the wardrobe. I pulled it open. There was a book lying in it. The parish register.

I opened it to the first page, partly out of curiosity, partly because I was stalling. This heavy old book open on the table in front of me held the answer I was looking for. But I didn't want the answer quite yet. The entries started in 1876, with the consecration of the chapel by the Bishop of Galway. The Earl had no doubt pulled a few strings to achieve that. Records of Masses and saints' days followed; here was a marriage, witnessed by the thirteenth Earl. I couldn't stall anymore. I turned over the pages until I got to 1899. My hands were shaking a little and my stomach felt hollow, which I was ashamed of.

On December 4, 1899, the service of Burial of the Dead was performed for the Countess of Saltire and her newborn son. I stared at it. Worried as I had been on David and Henrietta's behalf, I hadn't expected this. I had honestly thought that the parish records would provide reassurance, telling us that Lauretta had died a month after her son's birth. Sad, but nothing to affect future generations.

Instead, here was proof of something far worse. Lauretta's death paled next to the death of her son. For if the heir to Saltire had died, some other child had been brought up in his place. And then the Charltons I had met were not the legitimate occupants of Saltire.

St. John, the fourteenth Earl, must have managed the whole

thing. Summoned back to Neville from the Continent, perhaps, expecting the birth of an heir, arriving to find the death of his wife and their child, he must have come up with a scheme to salvage his hopes. I suddenly remembered something else; by the terms of Erastus Wright's will, Lauretta's money reverted to her father if she died without children. So St. John had a lot at stake. But where had the other child come from?

I looked back down at the register. The next entry, for December 5, was the baptism of a baby boy, witnessed by the Earl.

Could it possibly be? Was it credible that on the eve of the twentieth century a man had successfully substituted a living child of other parents for his own dead child, so that he would have an heir? I remembered that at royal births it had been the rule to have a member of the Home Office present to ensure there was no opportunity for foul play. That had been stopped only in the nineteenth century. Maybe in a backwater like Neville the idea of droit du seigneur had remained current. Maybe the feudal lord could still dispose of lives as recently as 1899. Would a mother object to having her baby raised as heir to an earl? Having seen the village, I thought not. It could have been seen as a splendid chance for a child.

But how had the secret been kept? Servants, the doctor, the priest—all must have been aware of the noble baby's death. It seemed impossible that so many people could share complicity without any betrayal. There had to be traces somewhere— maybe in the village a lingering tale of trickery, rumors about the family at the big house.

Nevertheless, it had happened almost a hundred years ago. And there was no point in fretting over ancient gossip. I looked again at the page, hoping, I suppose, to find that I'd been mistaken. It told me again that the Countess and her baby had been buried together. I clapped the book shut and put it back in its drawer and shoved the drawer in, then left the little chapel, locking the door. The wind met me as I moved out of the shelter of the building, cutting through my khaki trousers and whipping my hands. I jammed them into the pockets of my jacket and walked around the back of the chapel to look at the shore. There was a little stone bench there, facing the water, carved by the same hand as the church but softened, blurred by the weather. I sat down on the cold stone, idly thinking that the thirteenth Earl must have dearly loved the sea.

I felt sick. I folded my arms over my stomach and stretched out my legs stiffly and bowed my shoulders. This was working out all wrong. It was supposed to be a research trip. I was supposed to come over here, find out facts about people who were dead, and go home and write a book. I wasn't supposed to get swept up with anybody and start to like them and then dig up skeletons that would ruin their lives.

In my mind's eye I could see the family tree sketched out. Lauretta's husband, St. John, the fourteenth Earl, had died without a legitimate heir. The title automatically passed to his brother, Gerald Charlton's great-grandfather. Gerald was the eldest son of eldest sons. His father was dead. So he was the real Earl.

What would happen now? Would Gerald have to make a formal claim that he was the true heir? I dimly remembered reading of other cases where a title had lapsed or become extinct and a claimant had appeared from the wilds of Canada or Australia. The result was a lengthy investigation by the College of Heralds, accompanied by endless legal wrangling. But this was different. David and Henrietta and their family were actually impostors. The shame of it! Even though their share in the deception was unwitting, the exposure would be mortifying. It wouldn't help that Henrietta, at least, got so much publicity. I could just imagine the front-page headlines in the *Daily Mail:* "Earl a Fraud" or "Fake Peer Exposed." How could they ever live it down?

The bench I was sitting on faced a little cove where the cliff was not very steep; there was even a path down to the water, half-worn and half-carved into the rocky ground. Why would anyone want to go down to the water there, I wondered with half of my mind. Maybe the thirteenth Earl liked to swim, though it looked much too rough for safety.

There was a big rock a little way out from the shore, a huge round boulder that the waves broke against. The rock was covered with barnacles to the very top, so it must have been submerged at high tide. A big seabird—a cormorant?—lit on it now, and perched for a moment. It took off again, and its strong wings carried it unhesitatingly through the wind.

I watched the bird dive for fish in the rough water, and saw in my mind's eye the crowd of photographers at the Saltire hunt meet. Lady Henrietta Charlton was wonderful material for the gossip columnists, with her dramatic looks, her glamorous business, and her title. Being stripped of the title was even more interesting. The poor girl would be hounded by reporters.

It would be different for David. He hadn't been raised to be a peer's heir, as Gerald had explained. He'd spent his childhood as the son of a banker, and he could go back to academia. But he loved Saltire. I thought of his oblique comment that night on the terrace: "I wonder if I'd have loved it more or less if I'd grown up here." Leaving it would be so painful for him.

God, it was depressing. I looked at the big rock with the waves thrashing against it and felt disgusted with myself. Because I'd fallen for David. I sighed and rubbed my face, which felt damp and a little salty. My hair probably looked like Medusa's from being blown around so much. What a fool I was.

The cormorant was standing on the rock now with some poor fish flapping in its beak. I didn't want to watch what happened next. I might as well go on doing what I'd come here to do, instead of sitting here making myself miserable over the sorry fate of an ill-founded crush. In a month's time, when I was back in New York, I'd be dining out on these stories: ". . . and I found proof that their family was illegitimate!" But what, for now, was I going to do about it?

I supposed, walking back to the house over the patchy brown

grass, that this was why the Charltons had been so kind. Some-how, they suspected what I had just found to be true. Henrietta's seemingly artless chatter made that clear. And that telephone call; David reassuring Henrietta that he would han-dle everything, including me, I guessed. I must have been a godsend, actually; someone who could ferret about in their past, find the facts about Lauretta's death and the birth of her child. They wouldn't have to do the research themselves, possi-bly arousing suspicion. But what had they expected me to do? David was handling everything. He'd asked all kinds of leading questions (which I had taken as flattering signs of interest). He had decided to come to Neville Park. If everything had gone as planned, he would have been with me, might even have seen the parish register.

Had the whole thing been set up to keep me quiet? Was he going to exert the diffident charm to which I was so suscepti-ble? And talk me into keeping this a secret?

Surely not, he couldn't be capable of that kind of duplicity. But I felt very small and stupid. Just because David had seemed so sensitive. I thought of all the little kindnesses: the map he'd drawn of the house, his taking me riding. I remem-bered the way he'd held my hands, lying there in the mud after his fall, and my heart turned over. I squashed the voice inside me that said, "But don't you think he's fond of you. . . ?" I remembered the worried look that came over his face and how he took his glasses off and rubbed his eyes. And how I'd felt a little surge of tenderness for him. Could I be that wrong about somebody? Could that instinct of sympathy be so misplaced?

Evidently. I stood at the corner of the house, looking back at the chapel. What a bleak landscape. Gray water, stunted trees, blasted grass. The chapel looked like a very feeble attempt to impose some human order on this apocalyptic place.

I went inside, and climbed the stone stairs to the tower room. I didn't have to decide just yet what to do about the parish register. Out of decency, I had to tell David what I'd found before I told anyone else. Then I could decide whether to keep the secret if he asked me to. And there was still a chance—though it seemed a slight one—that the records stored in London, birth and death certificates, might not agree with the parish register. There was, of course, no reason why they shouldn't.

The trunks cheered me a bit. As I lifted their lids one by one, I found gloves and hats, carefully wrapped to keep the trimmings in place, and stockings embroidered with flowers or lacy patterns. One trunk contained thirty-six pairs of shoes—stuffed with shoe trees—in pink satin pockets. They were magnificent, buckled or covered with lace or rosettes, row after row of them. And there were dresses of every description. The first one I saw had a bright green satin bodice embroidered with a ribbon pattern, and a Worth label neatly stitched into the waistband. I lifted the bodice gently by the bows that would sit just off the shoulder, and thought how wonderful it would look on Henrietta. I moved the tissue paper aside, to glimpse what else might be in the trunk; there was a layer of pink satin, and farther down, what looked like heavy tobacco-colored silk ottoman; probably a walking dress.

I wished I'd asked Henrietta for her list of Lauretta's Worth dresses; it would have been interesting to see if they all matched up. Another trunk had a loose-fitting tea-gown on top, a soft dark blue velvet with sable at the neckline and the edges of the sleeves. I spent a moment blowing on the sable to puff it up, and held a sleeve up to stroke my face with the fur. What an alluring piece of clothing! I tucked the sleeves back in and looked to see what was underneath: bright red-and-bronze-striped silk and stiff plum-colored brocade. One trunk was full of underwear, all neatly ironed and starched, with ruffles and lace and ribbons threaded through, yellow with age.

The next trunk, surprisingly, wasn't as neat; the dress on top was the palest cream brocade, another evening dress, but it wasn't wrapped in tissue paper. I looked around, counting. There were still six trunks I hadn't opened, and Walter had said lunch was at one. I wondered if they were all clothes; shouldn't there be one trunk of papers, with the last volume of the diary in it? I closed the lid on the white dress and went around the room, opening the lids of the other trunks; dresses. All dresses. Under other circumstances I would have been ecstatic, but I wanted to find the diary. The parish register said Lauretta and her son had been buried on December 4, but I didn't want to believe it. Not that I expected the diary to refute what I'd learned. The blank pages left in the volume would only serve to confirm it.

I began gently pushing dresses aside, to see if there might be something underneath them. I was lifting a moonstone-colored satin dress, sliding my right hand down the side of the trunk, when I felt it: paper. I craned my head down to look under the satin and saw a stiff parchment corner. I pulled it out slowly, and looked at it. Two sheets, folded together. I unfolded them. Black Gothic script at the head of the page read "Certificate of Death." My eyes flew over it, looking for the name and the date. And there they were. Lauretta Sophonisba Wright Charlton, Countess of Saltire. December 3, 1899. Cause of death: Haemorrhage during childbirth. Signed, Dr. Theodore Bannon. Witnessed, (Mrs.) Jane Party. I looked at the second certificate: Baby Charlton. December 3, 1899. They hadn't even had a chance to name him.

I sat down on the bare floor, staring at the certificates. That was that, then. Official proof, signed and witnessed. It was a funny place to keep something this important, and if I'd been the fourteenth Earl, trying to pull a fast one, I would have burned these documents. I frowned, remembering that the certificates should have been filed in London. Did they keep duplicates in those days? I held one of the certificates up to the light; it certainly looked genuine. I licked a finger and rubbed a tiny corner of Dr. Bannon's signature. It smudged, the way it was supposed to. This was the real thing. Did that mean that the documents in London were fakes? Or was the proof of Gerald Charlton's claim sitting quietly filed away on a shelf at St. Catherine's House?

I would find out. For now, I wanted to hide these certificates. I couldn't leave them lying around where anybody could find them. I slipped them into the inner pocket of my jacket, and ran downstairs. My camera bag was in my car, parked just beyond the porte cochere. I opened the car door and, with my back to the house in case anyone was looking, tucked the certificates into the side of the bag. It was probably robbery; it was certainly irresponsible. I couldn't have cared less.

To make the sudden trip to the car look plausible, I sat in the passenger seat with the car door open and put a zoom lens on the camera, then loaded it with film. I stuck a spare canister of film in my pocket, and shut the car door. This time I locked it, though I hadn't felt I needed to lock the car since arriving at Saltire. I walked back around to the ocean side of the house, and began to take pictures. The chapel, the bench, the facade, some of the details. I shot almost an entire roll, ranging the viewfinder over the house and changing the length of the zoom lens, zeroing in on one of the windows in the tower, pulling back to get a section of the bifurcated battlements at the second-floor level. I glanced at my watch and saw that it was one o'clock. I took one last shot, of the cormorant sitting on his rock again. I pulled the lens out to its full length, and the bird filled the viewfinder. I thought his beady eyes were looking right at me. There was a section of fish-tail at the edge of his beak. He looked mean as hell.

I walked into the dark hall, brushing my hair out of my eyes and unhitching my camera from around my neck. Ludovic Walter was standing there by the central table. And standing next to him, shaking his hand, as impossibly handsome as ever, was Gerald Charlton, saying, "Terribly kind of you, sir. I know it's a bit pushy of me to barge in like this but I was in the neighborhood and thought I'd pop in to take a look at the old family home."

Chapter 9

I was glad it was shadowy in the hall, and that my skin could plausibly have been flushed from the wind outside. Because Gerald turned to me and said, "Sarah! What a pleasant surprise! Actually I was hoping I might run into you somewhere; I suppose it's not so surprising that it's here."

And I know I blushed, and in my confusion could only manage to say, "Yes, it is a surprise," and turn away to take off my jacket. Gerald stepped forward to help me, and his solicitude, which I'd found so disarming in New York, seemed out of taste in this gloomy spot with only Ludovic Walter to witness it.

"Miss Llewellyn and I were about to have luncheon," Walter said. "I suppose you might as well join us."

"Why, thank you so much. Awfully good of you. I'd be delighted," Gerald answered, ignoring Walter's rudeness.

It was all I could do not to stare at them openmouthed. What was going on? I was beginning to feel like Alice in Wonderland, as if I'd strayed into a world where everything was topsy-turvy. I had seen Gerald strolling casually from the stable to the house. The gossip in the village said he was Ludovic Walter's lover. And yet here they were, pretending that they'd never seen each other, and it had to be for my benefit. But why?

We went into the dining room, where the table was set for two. The shirtsleeved man who had let me in that morning backed through a swinging door, carrying a water pitcher and a bottle of wine.

"Sam, lay another place, we'll be three," Walter instructed him. "Mr. Charlton, would you sit here." Gerald pulled out my chair for me before going around the table to the seat Walter indicated.

There was a sticky little silence as Sam laid another place for Gerald. I stared at the tabletop in front of me, making a great business of unfolding my napkin to avoid having to look at Gerald. I was afraid that my face would give away my suspicions of him. Then Walter, as if reluctantly taking up a burden, asked if I would drink wine and how my morning's work had gone.

"Wonderfully. There are splendid things in those trunks upstairs."

"And in the chapel?" Walter asked, filling Gerald's glass.

"I didn't find much there. It's a funny place. When was it deconsecrated, do you know?"

"No. I know nothing about it," he said dismissively.

"Is the family still Catholic?" I asked. "Or did they go back to being Protestants?" I was prepared to lie about what I'd found, but I have never been very good at it, so I wanted to keep the conversation away from my discoveries.

"Oh, all Anglican now," stated Gerald, "and very proper, too. Remember I told you that Cousin Hugh is a clergyman?"

"Oh, of course," I answered brightly, and cast about for something else to say.

"How has the research been going since I saw you last? Have you been having luck in England?" Gerald asked.

"Oh, yes, it's been splendid," I answered. "I found wonderful material at the British Library and in the back files of the *Illustrated London News*. And then the costume museum in Bath was tremendous. They were very good about letting me look at the clothes very closely, and there are some dresses there that are particularly important. . . ." I went on at length about Mary Curzon and Worth and India; I sounded to my own ears like a fatuous fashion columnist. Sam took away our soup plates and brought in salmon and asparagus. I wasn't paying attention to what I was saying, and neither were Gerald and Ludovic Walter. They seemed to be waiting for something else, and finally when I paused to take a bite of fish, Gerald broke in.

"But tell me, Sarah, what you've found out about Lauretta. I don't know if I made myself quite clear when I came in," he explained to our host, "but the woman Sarah's researching was a kind of great-great-aunt of mine, and actually Sarah and I met in New York while I was looking her up in the library."

"I see," Walter said, his face a blank. I would have said he looked bored, but he kept fidgeting with the saltcellar in front of him, aligning it exactly with his knife, and adjusting it by millimeters.

"I haven't been so lucky on her," I said, trying to sound frank and open. "I've been at Saltire for the past few days, and they had some papers there. I guess the fifteenth Earl made a vague attempt to sort things out and then got forestalled by the war. Apparently he came over here and took away several trunks of papers and nobody ever got around to looking into them. Seems surprising to me, but there was a lot of junk there."

"Was there anything useful?" Gerald asked, and looked directly at me. There was just a hint of change in the tone of his voice. The light, affected P. G. Wodehouse tone was suddenly a little steely.

"Yes, in fact. Could I have some more water?" I asked Walter. "There was a lot of background material, you know, late Victoriana, race cards and opera programs and so on. But there were some letters from Lauretta's parents which were priceless." Sam filled my water glass and I drank. "And there was also a diary, which you can imagine is the most exciting discovery I could have made."

I happened to glance at Gerald as I said this. And he gave himself away completely. For just a moment his expression of charming interest fell away, and he turned instinctively to Walter. He looked shocked.

I bent over my plate, and concentrated on separating a tiny bone from the flesh of the fish. I sneaked a look at Walter, who was gazing steadily at Gerald. His face was expressionless, but I sensed displeasure.

He hadn't known about the diary. I was suddenly sure, from the naked look on Gerald's face, that he had been the prowler at Saltire. He knew about the letters. But the night I had surprised him, the diaries had been up in my bedroom and he evidently hadn't found them. And Walter, for some reason, wasn't happy about it.

All of this raced through my mind as I carefully dissected another mouthful of fish. In another moment, Gerald had regained his composure, and said to me, "That really is marvelous! What kind of diary?"

The less I had to tell him, the better. "Oh, very charming," I answered. "And from my point of view ideal, because she wasn't very introverted. It seems odd, doesn't it, that someone who isn't much given to self-examination would keep a diary?"

"I suppose so," Gerald answered, giving a brave pretense of considering this inanity carefully. "But it was the sort of thing they did in those days, wasn't it? After all, they had so much more free time than we do."

"That's true, and of course they wrote so much more, letters too. Her mother wrote to her every day while they were on their honeymoon," I said, and would have gone on about the letters. But Walter interrupted.

"Does the diary go up to her death?"

The sixty-four-thousand-dollar question.

Gerald wanted to know. Walter wanted to know. They were both looking at me. And a thought drifted into the frozen blankness of my mind.

Walter had been living at Neville Park for over a year. Gerald came and went as if he, too, lived here. If Gerald was eagerly seeking proof that he was the rightful heir to the earldom, he *must* have checked the parish register. It was an obvious source of information. It wasn't hard to find. And it supported his claim.

But rather than openly acknowledge that he was familiar with Walter and Neville Park, Gerald was pretending to have "barged in," to use his disingenuous phrase. *I* was supposed to discover the parish register, and Gerald was supposed to hear about it from me. That was why I had been led to the chapel, and why Walter's first question had been about it.

They had been waiting to hear me tell about my discovery in the church, and I had told them instead about a diary they weren't aware of. And they wanted to know what that document said about the date of Lauretta's death.

"I don't know. I didn't get to the end of it," I said, and turned back to my fish. If they believed that, they might believe that I was simply too dim to have found the parish register. I regretted that I had been so eager to show off my competence to Gerald when we'd met at the library in New York.

We got through lunch somehow. I continued to play dumb and they continued to ask me questions, Gerald oozing debonair charm (wearing a little thin, however) and Walter with all the finesse of an inquisitor. All I knew was that I wanted to leave as soon as I respectably could, and to have nothing more to do with either one of them.

I had to spend the afternoon there, though. Much as I longed to, I couldn't just drive away after lunch, or they would realize that I knew something was wrong. So I went upstairs to the tower room to look more carefully at the trunks of clothes, accompanied, inevitably, by Gerald.

"What are you looking for?" he asked brightly as I knelt down by a trunk.

"I really just want to look carefully at the dresses. You see, Lauretta had most of her clothes made in Paris by the man who dressed most of the American heiresses. It's rare to have a chance to examine Worth's dresses so closely, since they're mostly in museums. I think some of these are even unworn, and they're in perfect condition from having been packed so carefully in tissue paper all these years. I just glanced at them before lunch, but it will be so helpful to have you here, if you don't mind. Because the two of us can unfold the dresses and wrap them up again."

"Good," he said, and smiled. "Lord, it's cold in here."

It was. Before we'd been there twenty minutes I unfolded a heavy Paisley shawl and draped it around my shoulders.

"It looks marvelous on you," Gerald said, and pulled a fold of the fabric closer to my neck.

"Thank you," I answered, all politeness, and loosened it again. Great. He was going to try to romance me too. I reflected savagely that it was going to be a little more difficult for him than it had been for his cousin David. I might be a sucker, but only for one guy at a time.

My project for the afternoon, I had decided, would be an inventory of the trunks, with the most detailed descriptions possible. And I hoped it would bore Gerald to tears. "Would you mind terribly holding it up straight, so I can get an idea of how it hangs?" He had the green dress in his hands. Obligingly, he lifted it from the trunk, and I drew a little sketch. I couldn't resist running the brocade between my fingers, to feel the weight and smoothness of it. I twitched the train to its full length, noticing how it was finished with a band of the same fabric cut on the bias and lined with pink. "See, the underside is as pretty as the right side, because it shows when you carry it over your arm." I arranged the train over my arm to show Gerald, whose interest seemed to be flagging.

We went on like this. We went through the trunks, taking everything out and folding it back up. All the time, as I chattered to Gerald about dresses and the late nineteenth century and Edward VII's taste in women, I was thinking about leaving. I would not come back. I would drive out the gate and put as much distance as possible between myself and Neville Park. I could probably get to Ballinasloe before dinnertime. And when I got there I would call David and tell him that there was something very odd going on at Neville Park.

Gerald, meanwhile, was getting restless, casually lifting the lids of trunks we hadn't opened and looking blankly at their contents. He sneaked several glances at his watch. It was almost as if he were waiting for something to happen.

I knelt in front of the next trunk, the one with the cream dress that had not been as carefully packed as the rest of them. I remembered Henrietta had mentioned a white brocade gown on a bill at Saltire. This must be it. From behind me, Gerald said, "How many more are there to do?"

"I don't know. One trunk is shoes, and one is hats and things; I don't care so much about them. Do you want to count? I think we can finish this afternoon," I answered, lifting the dress and draping the bodice over the raised lid of the trunk. It was nougat-colored satin, figured with a pattern of roses and ribbons in the same color. There was a deep ruffle of lace embroidered with pearls over the bosom, gathered into puffs on the shoulders. Even in the dim light in that tower room, the dress seemed to glow. And as I picked up the full skirt to lift it out of the trunk, something fell onto my knees. Something light; a little piece of thin cardboard, folded in half, with a tasseled silk cord threaded through. Instinctively, I looked over my shoulder to where Gerald was opening another trunk. Holding the cardboard in front of me, out of his sight, I looked at it. On the front, engraved in silver script, it said "Pearsall House 15 December 1899." A dance card! I opened it for a moment, to see that there were names written down for every dance. And as quickly as I could, I lifted a corner of the trunk and slid the dance card underneath it.

My heart was racing as I stared at the dress, noticing half-consciously the wrinkles left by the careless packing, and a small tear in the bertha of lace. What on earth could this mean?

There was no solid proof that the dance card had been Lauretta's. But if not, whose was it? And if it was hers, it meant that she had been alive and dancing the night away on December 15, twelve days after she'd been officially certified dead.

It could have been someone else's card. There was no name on it, since it would have hung on that silk cord around its owner's gloved wrist. But the dress was Lauretta's; it matched the Worth bills at Saltire. Everything else in the room was hers. I was very much inclined to believe the dance card was too. And if it was, and she was alive on December 15, then both the parish register and the death certificates I'd found in these trunks had to be fakes.

They were meant to deceive, to persuade whoever found them that Lauretta and her son had died together. They would have been accepted as proof. But the dance card disagreed. And it seemed clear to me that nobody would bother to forge a dance card. This insignificant little thing, a remnant of a provincial holiday party, wouldn't stand up in court.

Which made it all the more likely that it was the genuine document.

"Four more, Sarah," Gerald said, "not counting the shoes and underwear and hats. Isn't *that* pretty." He came over and lifted up the dress, pulling the train free of the trunk. "Is it her wedding dress?"

"Maybe with a different bodice. This is a little décolleté for a wedding dress," I answered automatically. I looked in the trunk, and was surprised to see a pair of shoes, matching pearl satin with lace at the instep, but marked with water and mud on the heels and soles. There was a pair of stockings, also muddied, and even a petticoat. I reached in to move them aside, and felt a corset and more soft lawn. And under them was a blanket. It was odd that the whole outfit had been put away so hastily; there was even mud on the hem of the petticoat. I shrugged, and dismissed it. I had other things to worry about.

Like why I had found those false documents. Assuming for

the moment that they were forgeries (and I was convinced of it), it followed they had been concocted to fool someone. And planted, for what was the good of a forgery if nobody found it? Who would be looking for such materials in this remote place, undisturbed as it had been for nearly a hundred years? Me. Someone had gone to great trouble to devise a fake parish register and death certificates, and to place them where I would have to discover them.

Who had known that I was going to be here nosing around at Neville Park? David—he wouldn't have forged documents that made his family illegitimate. Ludovic Walter—I couldn't imagine what his motive would be, but I somehow felt he was capable of anything. And Gerald—who had everything in the world to gain from my making this discovery.

Which was why he was hanging around this tower room with me. I had been dumb (I hoped they thought I had been dumb) enough to miss the parish register. Gerald was going to make sure I couldn't miss the death certificates, tucked in with the dresses, where I was sure to look.

The problem was, the death certificates were in my camera bag. I had already seen, digested, and decided to conceal the information in them.

My mind rushed ahead, quick to paint a worst-case scenario. We weren't going to find the death certificates. But could Gerald mention them to me? I thought not, not without giving himself away. A breezy query—"I say, you haven't found any papers in here, have you?"—would be just too obvious. So I had only to bluff out the rest of the afternoon. After all, I wouldn't *expect* to find anything in these trunks besides clothes.

I might as well know the worst, I thought. I moved over to the trunk where I had found the papers. We lifted off the moonstone-colored dress. I made Gerald hold it up, and I sketched it. A brown walking dress. A tweed suit. A riding habit. I examined them all, covertly watching Gerald. "Okay. That's it for this trunk," I said brightly, and started to fold up the tweed skirt.

"It is?" He sounded startled, and an unmistakable frown crossed his face. He looked into the trunk, where nothing greeted his eye but a thin layer of tissue paper.

"Yes, remember, most of the trunks only hold two or three outfits," I reminded him. "Would you hold this?"

He took the hem of the skirt I handed him, but he wasn't listening. And then, with a visible effort, he got hold of himself. Nothing could have proved more clearly to me that things were not going as he had planned.

He went through the rest of the trunks with a thoroughness that would have surprised me if I hadn't understood it. Having planted the papers, he expected me to find them where he'd left them. Natural enough. But when they weren't there, what could he have thought? That Walter had moved them? The glances they'd exchanged at lunch and Walter's leading questions seemed to indicate that he was in on this trickery. He certainly seemed more likely than Gerald to know how to commission a forgery. I couldn't imagine what was in it for him, but I supposed Gerald would make it worth his while.

When, at last, I took off the shawl and folded it up, Gerald looked speculatively at the trunks we'd begun with. I was sure that after I left he would come back and comb through them trying to find the papers. I was glad I'd hidden the dance card under a trunk, where he was unlikely to find it.

I was even happier that I was leaving. Gerald did walk downstairs with me, into the hall that was lit now with the harsh light of a gigantic and hideously inappropriate Venetian-glass chandelier. I thought he looked pale, but it might have been my imagination or the brightness compared with the dim room upstairs. My jacket and camera were lying on a leather chair just inside the front door. I shrugged the coat on, and turned back to Gerald (who hadn't even attempted to help me with it, so completely was his composure shattered).

"Will you still be here tomorrow?" I asked. "Where will you stay tonight?"

"I don't know. I don't suppose our host would be too happy to have me as an overnight guest, but I may try to brazen it out and shame him into inviting me."

"Well, good luck, and I'll see you tomorrow, then," I said, and walked out the door.

As I heard it shut behind me, I felt tremendous relief. The damp air seemed so clean, the wind such a token of normalcy. When I felt the rain pelting me as I stepped out from the porte cochere, it seemed cleansing, I thought a little wildly. I found my car in the dark, unlocked it, climbed in, irrationally locking the doors behind me. In a moment I was driving slowly over the unpaved drive, toward the road and Neville and Ballinasloe.

I'd had a narrow escape, I thought. I still didn't understand what was going on between Gerald and Ludovic Walter. It was certainly unscrupulous and doubtless illegal. I'd never had personal dealings with anyone who stepped outside the law. I had only the vaguest idea of how a criminal mind might react to being thwarted. I had clearly thwarted whatever plan those two had, and though I didn't think I was in any physical danger, I was sure I had avoided some unpleasantness. Raised voices, recriminations, insinuations ("Why are you so eager to protect Cousin David, then, Sarah? You were friendly enough in New York . . ."). I shuddered when I thought about what might have happened if I'd told them about the dance card. Of course, I wouldn't have. I supposed I would have flinched at their raised voices and said that I thought David should be the first to know about this family issue and I was merely trying to be discreet. I would not have raised the issue of forgery.

I contemplated the imaginary scene with near-cheerfulness. I saw myself sitting in front of them, sticking to what was actually a pretty believable story, as they stood over me and expostulated. I was glad it wasn't going to happen. It would probably take an hour to get to Ballinasloe, if I didn't get lost. I had plenty of gas, and a good map—once I got to a main road. I slowed at the end of the driveway to pull out into the road to Neville.

My engine died.

I very calmly pulled on the parking brake and shifted into neutral. The car wasn't warmed up. It hadn't stalled on me before, but maybe the wet air acted on the engine somehow. I turned the key in the ignition. The engine didn't start. There was only a whirring noise that sounded utterly hopeless.

By now my heart was pounding, but I forced myself to sit quietly for two full minutes, so as not to flood the engine. I tried the starter again. It whirred. It didn't catch.

The rain was hammering on the roof and the windshield. I felt like something in a tin can. My first impulse was to leave the car there and walk to the village of Neville, where I'd seen a gas pump. But the village was half an hour away by car, probably twelve or thirteen miles, and at least three hours' walking. . . . It wouldn't do. My suspicions about Gerald and Ludovic Walter hardly warranted my slogging along to the village in the pouring rain, rather than just going back to the house. After all, my worst-case scenario only included verbal abuse. They would think I was dumb and stubborn, but they wouldn't realize that I knew they were forgers. What could they do to me besides yell?

I had to go back. There was no choice. Before I could talk myself out of it, I opened the car door and stepped out in the rain. I left the car and started to walk up the driveway, toward the lights.

Chapter 10

Now I was scared. It was an awful feeling to be going back to the house I had just left with such relief. With every step, I tried to think of an alternative; I even considered spending the night outside, rather than knocking on the door again. But the storm was building. As I walked blindly up the drive, tripping now and then over rocks and stepping in puddles, the wind drove the rain in my face, then whipped around and pushed at my back. I was soaked before I'd gone ten paces, and I could barely keep to my feet.

My only hope was that Gerald and Walter had not yet conferred. If they hadn't spoken they might not realize that I must have found the forged certificates. But if they had . . . suddenly the scenario I had found so unthreatening loomed unpleasantly. They can't hurt you, I told myself. They can rant and rave but nothing worse than that. Ranting and raving's not the worst thing in the world.

But what if they didn't let me leave?

I stepped in a particularly deep puddle, and swore. Of course they would let me leave. They would fix my car and send me on my way, happy to see the last of me.

I was passing the stable now. Facing the drive were two large windows in what looked like an office. It looked much more utilitarian than Walter's study in the house; in fact a large console of switches and buttons was partly visible. Not unlike my fantasy about Walter's computer with the stock prices, I thought, vaguely heartened.

Just a few more yards to the porte cochere. Self-consciously, I took a deep breath and squared my shoulders and marched myself up to the front door. I rang the bell, and waited.

I could hear the sea now, when the wind came from that direction; each crash of the waves sounded forceful enough to shatter the rocks into gravel. Rain blew under the porte cochere in gusts, spattering the puddles.

The door opened about four inches. Sam stood there, looking suspicious.

"My car broke down at the end of the drive," I said. It sounded like an apology.

Wordlessly, he opened the door fully and stood aside to let me in.

"You can wait in the drawing room," he said. "But don't sit down. You're wet." He had a surprisingly light voice, but a much stronger accent than Walter's. Without even waiting to see me into the drawing room, he walked off toward the back of the house. I wondered what Walter was doing in the servants' quarters.

I'd left a little puddle where I was standing, and as I walked into the drawing room I left a trail of drops behind me. I was cold now and sorry the fireplaces weren't in use. The room was lit only in spots by the little silk-fringed lamps, so there were wells of light and larger areas of gloom. There couldn't have been a bulb in there that was stronger than forty watts, I thought with inexplicable exasperation.

Though prohibited from sitting down and soaking a crimson horsehair cushion, I propped myself against a window, where the casement ledge was just too shallow for a window seat. The rain rattled against the pane in gusts. My teeth started to chatter and I couldn't stop them. It wasn't entirely the cold; apprehension helped. Apprehension helped. I tried to imagine what Ludovic Walter would say when he walked into the room. If he had discovered the missing certificates . . .

I heard his footsteps crossing the hall. No hurry. A dignified pace. "Miss Llewellyn," he said, crossing the room toward me. "You have had a mishap?" He looked incredulous.

"My car stalled at the end of the driveway and I couldn't get it started again. It just seems to be dead. I don't know anything about cars, so I don't know what's wrong with it." I was hugging my elbows to keep from shivering but I couldn't keep my speech even.

"Ah. I will send Sam out to see about your car. You have the keys?" I handed them to him. They jingled in my shaking hand.

"Right. He won't be long." He turned to go.

"Mr. Walter," I said. He turned back to face me. "Could I possibly get out of these wet clothes? I'm afraid I'll catch cold . . ."

"Mm. I see. And it is a long drive back to Ballyhannock." I was puzzled, then remembered that I was supposed to be staying there. "But there is nothing here for you to wear."

"I could probably find something in those trunks."

"All right. If you think the Earl of Saltire won't mind," he said with what sounded like heavy sarcasm. "I will have Sam find you a towel before he goes to look at your car. Wait here."

Something else to wonder about. I was supposed to be at Ballyhannock rather than at the bed and breakfast in Neville, and why was that? Ballyhannock was so unpleasant, and so remote. Why hadn't Walter told me about the B&B in Neville?

Rapid steps approached; Sam, carrying a towel (pink, incongruously) and dressed in oilskins. "Mr. Walter says you should find what you need in the tower room and change there. What is wrong with the car?" I explained about the whirring noise and he nodded and handed me the towel. "Here. I suppose you'll need this." He left the room without waiting for me, and I walked upstairs trying not to let the towel get too close to me and get wet.

In the tower room, I stripped off my jacket and opened the trunk with the underwear in it. Chemise, petticoat, drawers. I thought I'd pass on the corset. The blue velvet tea-gown with the sable trimmings seemed likely to fit, so I pulled it on without trying anything else. To get the wet hair off the back of my neck, I twisted it up and stuck a couple of heavy hairpins in it, having found them in with the hats. The shoes were tiny, so I padded downstairs barefoot.

I went back into the long drawing room, and sat down in one of the pools of light, huddling into the upholstery of a chair. There was nothing to read in the room; nothing to do but wait, and listen to the storm and the waves.

I pulled the sable closer to my throat, trying to close up the deep décolletage. And I suddenly realized that this, perhaps, was what life at Neville Park had been like for Lauretta. I tried to look at the room through her eyes. It must have seemed as depressing to her as it did to me. Accustomed to American luxury, to plenty of warmth, to light, white-and-gold rooms in the fashionable French manner, she must have been dismayed by Neville Park. I wondered how she had passed the time alone here. Did she have visitors? Would she change into this tea-gown to receive a caller, perhaps Mrs. Pearsall from next door? Did she get fretful as she got heavier and heavier in her pregnancy? I wondered where her maternity clothes were; everything we had seen upstairs had a tiny waist, though I thought the cream-colored dress was cut larger than the rest. Of course, she'd worn it so soon after her confinement. . . .

How had those forgeries been made? I wished I had looked more closely at the parish register; had the dates simply been doctored? Or had the forgers created a whole new book? They were obviously experts. Who had paid them? Who had found them, for that matter? Not everyone knows how to get hold of

brilliant forgers. And why was Ludovic Walter playing along
with Gerald in this "rightful heir" scheme? What was in it for
him? I could understand—barely—how Gerald might cook up
a plot to make himself an earl. But Walter's role was in-
comprehensible, and all the more unnerving for that. And I'd
had a sense during lunch that it was Walter, not Gerald, who
was in charge. That mute appeal when I had mentioned the
diaries, and Walter's equally silent though equally eloquent
reprimand, made me think that Gerald was not even too sure of
his ground. Walter seemed to be calling the shots, and
Gerald—

"Sarah!" Gerald stood at the door, staring at me. "God, you
gave me a fright, sitting there. I thought you were a ghost!" He
came closer. "You're pale enough to be one, anyway."

"I'm rather cold," I said. "My car broke down at the end of
the drive and I had to walk back. I got so wet that I wanted to
get out of my clothes. Sam went to see about getting the car
going again."

Gerald sat down on the arm of my chair. "Yes, Walter told
me. Rotten luck, but I'm sure Sam will get it fixed. He looks
like the type who knows all about cars. You're shivering; shall
we huddle together for warmth?" he asked. His winsome little
smile didn't even reach his dark blue eyes. Completely pro
forma; I wondered if this was how Gerald always dealt with
women or if his charm was simply unraveling under stress.

"No, thank you. Do you have a cigarette?" I asked. I don't
smoke, but it seemed like a good diversionary tactic. He sat up
straight and fished his cigarette case from his jacket pocket and
handed me one. With a flourish, he produced his lighter and
steadied my hand with his as he lit the cigarette. The silver
cigarette case, the gold lighter. And yet Gerald didn't work,
had never had a job. Just one more thing that didn't add up.
"Do you suppose there's an ashtray in here?" I got up and
peered around. Gerald stayed still on the arm of the chair, and
stared at the empty fireplace, not answering. As if, once I was

out of his immediate range, he'd forgotten about me. I was grateful.

I had reached the far end of the room, dragging my velvet-and-satin train behind me, when Walter appeared in the door. "I am afraid Sam has not been able to get your car going," he said. "Apparently the fuel pump has given out and will have to be replaced. Unfortunately, we have only one car here, and there is not enough gas in it to get to Ballyhannock and back. Otherwise, of course, I would have Sam drive you to the inn there. So I think the best thing would be for you to spend the night here."

"There's no place I could stay in Neville?" I said hurriedly.

"You will be comfortable here, I am sure," he answered, skirting my question.

"But . . . Gerald, you drove here this morning, didn't you? What about your car?"

"I don't think I could find my way to Ballyhannock in the dark," he said, "and I certainly couldn't find my way back. And since Mr. Walter has very kindly offered to accommodate me for the night, I had planned on staying here. Why don't you want to? Are you worried about standing up a date in Bally-hannock?"

His tone was still light and flirtatious but his curiosity, I thought, was genuine. I managed a little laugh, and remembered to draw on the cigarette burning in my fingers. "No, it's just that I left some camera equipment there and the room didn't lock too well, so I was nervous about it."

"Of course. Professional concern," Walter said. "Would you like to call the inn at Ballyhannock to tell them you are staying the night here? And to check that your possessions are all in order?"

"Yes, thank you," I said, "that would put my mind to rest." I held up my cigarette. "Is there an ashtray in here?" Walter took the cigarette from my hand and rubbed it out against the inside of the fireplace.

"You may telephone from my study," he said, and led me to the round room in the bottom of the tower. He dropped the cigarette butt into a wastebasket, fastidiously. "There is the telephone; the operator will connect you," he said, and left the room.

I picked up the phone receiver and dialed O. When a woman's voice answered, I said very quietly, "The pub in Neville, please." It seemed possible that someone was listening, and it would be awkward if they found out I wasn't staying in Ballyhannock, where I was supposed to be. I left the message that I was spending the night at Neville Park and would be back the next day. I had hoped for some reaction—concern or curiosity perhaps. There was none.

When I went back into the drawing room, Sam was in front of one of the fireplaces, removing the vase of dried grass to lay a fire. Walter was gone.

Gerald, lounging in one of the chairs, said, "Don't you think it will be rather amusing to spend the night here, Sarah? I should think you'd leap at the chance. Just the kind of thing to lend reality to your research. Mr. Walter says we'll have dinner in half an hour and Sam's going to bring drinks in as soon as he gets the fire going. I think Walter's gone up to change, since you're obviously dressed for dinner."

"Sam, if you'll show me where my bedroom is, and find me some sheets, I'll make up the bed," I said to the back crouched in front of the fire.

He dusted off his hands and rose as the flame caught. "If you like," he answered.

"I just want to get myself settled for the night," I said apologetically to Gerald. "I don't like sleeping in unfamiliar beds." He raised an eyebrow, but made no comment.

Sam showed me to a room upstairs, which surprisingly had a bathroom attached, and brought me some sheets and blankets from somewhere, then left me. I fetched my wet clothes from the tower room, where I'd left them, and draped them over the carved wooden bench in my room, then began to make up the bed. The hanging sleeves of my tea-gown got in the way as I tucked in the sheets and wrestled with the horsehair mattress. But I wasn't thinking about the bed. I was thinking about why I was staying at Neville Park.

The story about having no gas was lame. I simply couldn't believe that there was only one car at Neville Park, and that Walter was so improvident that he let it run out of gas. Gerald's excuse was equally incredible. Couldn't Sam have driven *his* car to Ballyhannock and back?

I was certain that when I had reappeared at the door, Sam hoped he'd be rid of me in a few minutes. His reluctance even to let me sit down indicated that. But now Walter wanted to keep me here. Why? Did it have to do with the forgery scheme?

Suddenly I stopped unfolding a blanket and leaned against the bed, which creaked loudly. Were they going to try to force me into complicity with the forgery? How might they do that? Bribes? I thought for an instant of physical threats and told myself not to get hysterical. I had spent too much time today, I thought, trying to second-guess, imagining what they might know and what they might think I knew. I tried to persuade myself that I was inventing things.

But there were the forgeries. I had not invented the death certificates, which I knew to be false. And I had not invented the false dates in the parish register. And I had not invented Gerald Charlton's familiarity with Ludovic Walter, nor the fact that they were hiding this from me.

So why did they want to keep me here? I turned back to the bed and spread out the blanket, which smelled of mothballs. Slowly, Sarah, step by step. Say they have discovered that you found and hid the death certificates. In order to find out why you did this, they have to admit that they planted them. This would let you in on their scheme. Why should you not blow the whistle on them, exposing their scheming to the law? What could they offer to keep your mouth shut?

One answer dawned on me, improbable as it was. They could offer to make me a countess. Granted, that might not be strong motivation for everyone. But for a self-confessed Anglophile fascinated by the British nobility, it might work. And of course, Gerald could be thought of as a drawing card. I had already shown myself susceptible to his attractions, and that was before they included a coronet. What he didn't know was that since seeing him last I had fallen for his cousin David.

David, the real thing. It was hard not to think of Gerald as rather gimcrack compared to David; all that polish and charm seemed a little trumpery. It wasn't David's title that attracted me; on the contrary, I found it rather frightening. No, what I found so appealing in him was that unusual sensitivity and self-deprecating humor. It was as if he was doing his best to live up to the role of The Heir, and at the same time was amused by his efforts.

I realized suddenly that I was sitting on the side of the bed staring into space. Mooning about Lord Neville, I told myself derisively. Useless. David and Saltire were hundreds of miles away and seemed even farther. I would have plenty of time to daydream about them once I left Neville Park. But for the moment, Gerald and Ludovic Walter were waiting for me downstairs. I didn't want to make them impatient, curious, or in any way suspicious.

The drawing room looked practically cheerful with the fire going, and a completely conventional drinks tray had appeared. Gerald was seated, reading the *Times*, with a glass beside him. "What will you drink, Sarah?" he asked, leaping to his feet politely.

He poured me the whiskey I asked for, and I went to stand in front of the fire while Walter came in and poured himself a glass of soda water. "I am glad you found something to wear," he said to me. "If I may say so, it is very becoming."

"Thank you. How long do you think it will take to get my car fixed? Do you think I could take it to the gas station in Neville?"

Walter made a noncommittal gesture with his glass. "It doesn't matter. Surely you have more work that you need to do here. Didn't you originally plan to stay for three days? By that time your car should be ready."

Three days! It was true, I had originally planned that long a visit. But that was before things started to go wrong. Trying to sound calm, I said, "Yes, but it won't take me that long to get through the work there is here, and since I have such a short time in England I don't want to waste a day. Would it be possible to rent another car somewhere?"

"Don't worry about it, Sarah," Gerald said. "If your car doesn't get fixed in the next couple of days, I'll drive you back to England. In any case, there's nothing you can do about it."

Nothing I could do about it. That was precisely the point. I looked from Gerald to Ludovic Walter to Sam, who was poking the fire. It was as if a slide on a screen had suddenly clicked into focus. At one moment, they were three people whom I knew slightly, about whom I entertained certain suspicions, whom circumstances compelled me to spend more time with than I would have chosen.

The next moment, they were my captors. I was trapped there on a stormy night, miles from other people. And I didn't even have the keys to my car. Which in any case had broken down. But had it broken down of its own accord? Or had the engine been tampered with?

Paranoia, I told myself. The car had broken down, Ludovic Walter was kindly offering me a night's hospitality. But the picture didn't click back into its earlier benign focus. I felt very much in their power. Sam had stood up and for just an instant the three of them were ranged in front of the fireplace, all looking at me. Only an instant, but it lasted forever and I was sharply aware of the combined strength of three men.

Sam broke the silence by telling us that dinner was ready. Gerald and Ludovic Walter waited for me to precede them into the dining room, so I put my glass down and swept in front of them, propelled by a surge of adrenaline.

Whether or not I was paranoid, I could be careful. It was all I could do to make myself feel other than helpless. I wasn't quite sure what being careful entailed, but I planned on locking my bedroom door for starters.

Dinner was a surrealistic repetition of lunch. The dining room was so dark that I couldn't see into the corners, and the table was lit with eighteen candles in an appalling silver center-piece that owed something to Cellini and something to the local taxidermist (the candles were stuck in stags' horns) and nothing at all to taste. Sam served and poured wine from the monstrous sideboard while I tried to remember what I had read about drugging somebody. Soup was safe when ladled out of the same tureen. Individual cutlets, not such a good bet. Wine poured in front of my eyes should be drinkable.

I was too distracted to listen closely to the conversation. But as we got up from dinner to have coffee in the drawing room, Gerald put an arm around me and said, laughing, "You're worrying too much about your car."

"You're right," I answered, trying to smile bravely at him, pulling away, and moving into the drawing room.

"Would you care to pour the coffee for us, Miss Llewellyn?" Walter said majestically. I was surprised at this bit of old-world punctilio on his part, but I sat in front of the low table and picked up the silver coffeepot. I handed a full cup to Walter, standing behind me. I leaned forward to pick up another cup for Gerald. And I saw a movement out of the corner of my eye.

Seated in front of the fire, I could see our little group reflected in the leaded window. There I was presiding over the coffee tray like a dowager. And there was Gerald, standing to my right, lighting a cigarette. And behind me, Ludovic Walter was dropping something into the cup of coffee I'd handed him.

There was no pause in my movements. I poured coffee for Gerald, with my hand perfectly steady, and picked up another cup for Walter, who said, "What do you like in your coffee, Miss Llewellyn?" And bent down to the tray, holding the cup he had just doctored.

Chapter 11

"Just milk," I answered, with my eyes fixed on the cup he held. He poured in milk, stirred the liquid, and handed it to me, removing his cup from my hands.

I accepted the cup and put it down very gently on the table.

I felt frozen, like a rabbit caught in headlights. He was trying to drug me. How could I manage not to drink that coffee? I heard myself asking Gerald for a cigarette, and him answering that I was smoking a lot for someone who didn't as a rule. When he held the lighter for me, this time I steadied my hand against his. Just for the contact.

I picked up my cup and the cigarette, and strolled slowly away from the fire, along the length of the windows. I lifted the cup toward my mouth, and poured a little of the coffee onto the floor. My voice asked Walter if any of the windows had ever broken in a storm. He told me they hadn't, that they never even leaked.

I strolled back, and tapped my ash into the fire. Was Walter watching me? I went over to the window, pretending to look out. Was it possible, I asked, to see the islands on a clear day?

Walter laughed, a sharp bark. It was evident, he said, that I was new to Ireland. His reflection in the diamond-paned glass lowered itself to the couch. Gerald's reflection was staring into the fire. With a flick of my wrist I splashed the rest of the coffee down the side of my dress. I felt the warm liquid soak through the layers of lawn underwear to my skin.

I turned my back to the window, and propped myself against the embrasure. Both Gerald and Walter were turned toward me now. I lifted the cup to my mouth and swallowed my saliva. The dregs that I couldn't avoid tasted both bitter and metallic.

And now the question was, what had they drugged me with? How should I be behaving? Would whatever it was start acting right away? Was I supposed to froth at the mouth or merely drop into a stupor?

There was one way to play it safe. If I was out of Walter's sight, he couldn't keep an eye on me for symptoms.

"More coffee?" he asked as I came forward to throw away my cigarette.

"No, thank you." I put my empty cup back on the tray, and gathered the train of my dress forward, to hide the wet patch down my side. "It's been a long day, and I don't want to be kept awake by the caffeine. In fact, if you don't mind, I'll go to bed now. The rain makes me sleepy."

"Of course." Walter inclined his head. "We are not very early risers, but Sam could probably manage breakfast for you at about nine-thirty, if that's all right. And tomorrow we will see what can be done about your car."

I wanted to run once I was out of their sight, to run and slam my bedroom door behind me. But I kept to my measured pace, and shut the door gently. Only then did I collapse. I threw myself facedown on the bed, and pulled a pillow over my head. I wanted to burrow away and hide from whatever was going on downstairs. Then I jumped up again, pushing aside the pillow. I wanted to lock myself in. I opened the door again and looked at the handle.

My heart sank. I should have realized it would be a Gothic-revival latch. Instead of a knob, there was a loop of twisted iron. There was a large keyhole, and it looked as if it would activate a dead bolt. But the key was missing, and there was no way to lock the door without the key.

I shut the door and leaned against it, eyes roving around the room. There was nothing small enough to wedge under the iron loop. I tried to give the bed a push, but I couldn't move it. The bench wouldn't fit against the door, and I hadn't a prayer of shifting the paneled armoire.

So I gave up. I made one more dash, across the hall to the tower room, to get a nightgown out of the underwear trunk. By now it didn't feel at all strange to avail myself of this trove of clothes. I took the Paisley shawl, too, in case I was cold in the night, then scurried to bed. It was ten o'clock.

My bedroom faced the sea, over the drawing room. The second story was set back a bit, so that part of the ceiling of the drawing room had its own roof lined with the bifurcated battlements I had photographed earlier in the day. The area of roof might have formed a terrace if it hadn't been so far below the second-story windows. My room was at the far end, away from where the fire was lit in the drawing room, but I could see the firelight reflected in the windows. And though the rough turf and diamond panes blurred any sharp detail, I could make out a slender shadow walking back and forth along the line of arched windows, and a head, just a little knob, really, at the end toward the fire.

The knob rose and swelled. The slender shadow stopped pacing, and nodded. Both shadows moved back from the windows and disappeared, and the lights, one by one, went out.

I expected to hear steps or voices coming upstairs, but they didn't. Maybe Walter and Gerald were playing billiards. It didn't seem likely. What could they be doing? Almost anything, actually. I tried to count the hours back to New York; if the stock market was open, maybe Walter was going to do some business. Five hours' difference? The stock market was not open. And I reminded myself that the corner of machinery I'd seen in the stable didn't look like any computer I'd ever seen, and that this stock-market fantasy was something I'd fabricated as a reassurance.

Not much about the situation was reassuring. I turned off the light and spread the Paisley shawl over my shoulders and tried to think rationally.

Not a word had been spoken about the documents I'd found. Then why had they kept me here? I went over the same ground again and again: the death certificates, the parish register, Gerald, Walter, the drugged coffee. I must have sat there for an hour or more, fretting, but I could not make sense of what I knew. And finally, to my surprise, I did get sleepy. I slid down to the bottom of the bed and rolled onto my side so that I was facing the window. The storm, I noticed, had abated somewhat; though the wind still howled, there was no longer rain lashing the window panes.

I heard a creak on the staircase, and thought that Walter and Gerald must be coming to bed. But they weren't speaking to each other; I could hear no voices or even footsteps on the flagstone.

Instead, I heard my door open.

I lay completely still, grateful that my back was to the door. A flashlight flickered on the windows for an instant only. Just enough to illuminate my head. To make sure it was I.

I shifted my legs, to pretend that I was stirring in my sleep, to get them to go away. Assuming that they were going to.

The door shut. And then I heard, unmistakably, the grating of the key in the lock.

The stair creaked again. In the midst of my confusion I felt a tiny satisfaction that Ludovic Walter couldn't manage to walk down his own stairs without making a racket. It was mighty small consolation.

They had locked me in. I slipped out of bed and tested the door. The Gothic handle didn't budge. I had known it wouldn't.

There is a world of difference between locking yourself in and being locked in. Evidently the drug they'd given me was supposed to make me sleep, and the locked door was just an extra precaution to keep me out of the way. Out of the way of what?

We all have our particular fears. I don't mind heights and I don't mind speed but I hate enclosed spaces. A subway train stuck in a tunnel makes me sweaty and shaky. I avoid strange elevators. I panic when a bathroom door sticks. Logic told me—loud and clear—that if Ludovic Walter wanted to keep me out of the way, it would be in my best interest to stay out of the way. I told myself that I wouldn't know the door was locked once I was asleep.

But all the time I was giving myself good advice, I was getting dressed. Rationally speaking, I knew I should go back to bed. But a much stronger instinct moved me to pull on my clammy khakis and think about escaping. I knew it was folly. But I couldn't stop myself.

I wondered for a moment if I should wait before making my attempt. Wait for what, though? Wouldn't it make more sense to leave now, when they thought I was safely drugged and locked in?

Grateful that I'd left my bags at the Neville pub, I rifled through my purse for money and my passport. I'd need them once I got clear away. Was it worth trying to make a dummy for the bed? I thought not, remembering the flashlight. If they came back to check on me again, pillows heaped under the covers wouldn't fool them. I braided my hair, which was still damp from the storm, and pulled a strip of pale pink ribbon from the chemise I'd worn, to tie it with. I glanced once more around the room to see if there was anything else there that might help me. Nothing. I opened the casement window and looked down.

It was a long drop. I wouldn't have done it for fun. But without hesitation, I clambered into the window frame, and turned myself around, awkwardly. Feet out first. Was that the right way? Shouldn't I go frontways so that I could see where I was jumping? The forked battlements down there . . . I couldn't heave myself back in to turn around. This was it.

Damn that smooth stone! There were no footholds, not even

a roughness to stop my toes. All my weight was hanging on my hands now; the inside of the casement was bruising them and I was losing my grip.

I dropped.

The landing knocked the breath out of me, but didn't hurt. I lay for a minute in a heap, gasping and taking stock. The rain had begun again but I was sheltered in the trench created by the battlements and the wall of the house. My eyes were getting used to this darkness, even thicker than the darkness of the bedroom. To my right was the round tower that held Ludovic Walter's study and the trunk room. I knew that it was perfectly smooth on the exterior. I couldn't scale down it.

But to my left was the square tower with the mansard roof and the clock. I shut my eyes trying to remember exactly what I'd seen that morning taking pictures. As I remembered, the architecture of the square tower was a godsend. For below the mansard roof there was a double row of lancet windows that marched in a diagonal line downward. Each window had a deep exterior sill, and the last sill continued into a horizontal band around the tower. In effect, the stepped line of windowsills created a shallow flight of stairs on the exterior of the tower.

I got up and crept along the trench. When I lifted my head the rain stung my face, and I could hear the sea roaring. I hoped the water wouldn't make the steps on the tower slippery. There was the wall of the tower looming above me; there was even a clock on this side, facing the water.

I leaned over the battlements to see where the line of windows began. The upper row was just over my head. I could reach up and feel the depth of the sills, and as my fingers grasped the stone I felt enormous relief. They were wide enough. Now, how to balance myself as I clambered down to the lower set of sills? How would I launch myself over the battlements without falling to the ground?

It was all automatic. I could not, certainly, have done it on request. But as if in a dream, I calmly swung myself over the last battlement. My right foot caught the heavy molding at the top of the lower window. Then my left foot. Still holding the edge of the crenellation with my left hand, I reached down with my right. A deep molding, with rosettes studded along it. There was just room to shift my left hand so that I was crouching on the crown of the window. Left foot down, skidding along the molding, hesitating at the rosettes. And then, stretched out painfully, I had my feet on the sill.

It might not be good architecture, but it made my task a lot easier. Once I was steady on the topmost sill, I could just side-step, walk crabwise down the side of the mansarded tower. It did not, thank heaven, occur to me to wonder what would happen if someone in the tower turned on the lights and saw my figure spread-eagled across one of the narrow windows. I simply moved on, perfectly balanced, until I reached the lowest window. Another drop, only about seven feet. I landed softly on the spongy grass, falling to my hands and knees in the mud. I had managed the first stage of my escape.

My plan was to get a horse from the stable and ride to the pub at Neville. The stable was far enough from the house so that I wouldn't be heard, and it shouldn't be difficult to find a saddle and bridle. Then I would be away down the drive and the curving road to the village.

I moved quietly away from the house, doubled over instinctively, ready to flatten to the ground. My worry now was that I might get caught. Gerald and Walter could be anywhere, could spot me. There was no shelter between the house and the stable, not a wall to creep along, no bushes to hide behind. My heart hammered as I gauged the distance. Should I sprint? Would a speeding figure catch someone's eye? Instinct, again, decided for me and I ran like a hare across the lawn, with my mind belatedly telling me that the night was dark enough to hide me.

Scattered lights showed in the bulk of the big house, but none at all in the stable. I reached the nearest wall and collapsed against it, panting and trying to silence my gasps. I wondered which way to go around the building to reach the door, and remembered the window of the office. Not that way. I turned right. This was a block of stalls, probably, with small square windows high in the walls. After my dash I clung gratefully to the shelter, sliding along the wall, touching it at all times.

Ten yards along, the wall ended. The darkness suddenly seemed threatening, as if it were alive. I cowered, unable to divert my imagination from visions of men with guns trained on the corner. I would have loved to throw a pebble out, to test the reaction. Instead, after counting to ten, rocking back and forth, I peered out.

Nothing. A fence making the fourth side of a small paddock. The other sides were the bulk of the stable: the block of stalls I'd just come around, probably another of the same on the opposite side of the paddock, and perhaps a feed or storage room on the far side. No lights showing. I crouched staring into the blackness, still envisioning men with guns. It seemed so exposed to cross in front of it. I waited again, counting to twenty this time. Nothing moved. I darted across to the safety of the other block of stalls, and leaned against the wall.

My mouth was dry and my back complained after the climbing and crouching and sprinting, and I hoped I would be able to control whichever horse I chose to kidnap. I heard a muffled whicker and the stamp of a hoof in the stall next to my ear. Homely, cozy, routine. Safe. I was almost safe. In a few minutes I would be on that horse galloping up the drive.

Suddenly the unnatural calm that had carried me out my window and down the tower gave way. I had come this far in the coolest composure, as if someone far braver than I had taken over. And now, leaning against the wall of the stable, my legs buckled beneath me. All I had to do was walk calmly into a stall, saddle a horse, and leave. Yet I couldn't make myself go round the last corner.

I was sure there was something there.

I waited for several precious minutes to see if this irrational fear would pass. Maybe it was just a reaction. I'd get my nerve back.

I tried to distract myself by concocting what I'd say when I arrived at the pub in Neville after closing time, on a horse. I reached back and massaged my shoulders. I felt my pulse, which was racing. I tried to relax. I couldn't.

"Nonsense!" I whispered to myself, and leaned forward to peek around the wall. I jerked back as if I'd touched a snake.

My instinct had been correct. There *was* something alarming there. Light was streaming from a window. There was somebody in the stable after all. I couldn't just walk in and take one of the horses.

I stayed there frozen for a minute or two with my mind running ahead. I had already decided once this evening that it would take too long to reach Neville on foot. Could I risk spending four hours walking along the road? Wouldn't they come after me if they found I was gone? I wondered about the Pearsalls, the nearest neighbors. But I didn't know how near they were, or even in which direction. Was there any other way to escape? Cars? Boats? I was being ridiculous.

I couldn't go back if I wanted to; my escape route was distinctly one way. I had to go forward, and on horseback.

The realization, oddly, brought back some of my calm, and a fresh resolve. I had been watching the light from the window all this time. Nothing moved. I had heard no voices. I slithered forward on my belly.

Keeping close to the ground and to the wall, I inched along the side of the stable. I was so wet by now that the sodden ground made no difference to the state of my clothes as I dragged my legs through the mud and scrubby grass. I reached the window. Like the drawing room windows, it was formed in a broad pointed arch. The sill was only two and a half feet from the ground. Diamond-shaped panes filled the casements, and one of them was halfway open.

I got up on my knees at the side of the window. I could see in front of me an unpainted tongue-and-groove paneled wall covered with pegs, about half of which had saddles on them, dusty and in poor repair. The room seemed absolutely still. I decided to go in.

The first step was to reconnoiter. Still on my knees, I crawled closer to the center of the window, keeping my head just above the sill. The rest of the room came into sight. Hooks hanging from the ceiling, with dark old bridles draped on them. A row of dull, dented tin buckets against a wall. A small glass-fronted cupboard, with various bottles and tins dimly visible inside it. Another wall of pegs, hung with bridles and halters. Cobwebs in the corners of the ceiling. And a sturdy oak desk with a bare top. Nothing stirring. The door open to the dark beyond.

By now my heart was pounding audibly, like a drumbeat. When I climbed out of the bedroom I had been in danger of falling and hurting myself. Now I was in danger of being caught outside of the room where I had been so carefully stowed away. The risks had escalated enormously. I would have to be that much more cautious.

I planned my moves. In over the windowsill. Grab a bridle; off a peg, so that it wouldn't tangle with others. My eyes ranged over the hanging bridles and I selected one that was hanging clear of the rest and looked brighter. One of the saddles on a low peg had the same look of more recent use. I would pick up the bridle with my left hand, the saddle with my right. Then down the row of stalls to the last one, where I had heard the horse stamp.

Ready. I ran through the plan again in my mind. I'd have to be careful not to jingle the bit. Hope the floor didn't creak. Now. I got my feet underneath me. The window wasn't open wide enough, so I grasped it with both hands and pulled it toward me. There. One knee on the windowsill.

"Hey!" At the same instant that the man's voice called out, hands seized me from behind. Instinctively I struggled, pulling forward out of his grasp. But he was much stronger, and as I twisted away he caught hold of my arm. With one movement, he had it doubled behind me, with the forearm pressed upward. "Stop wriggling!" he said, and yanked the arm. The pain, sudden and sharp, flowed from my shoulder all over my body. I stood still.

He pulled me around to face him: Sam. I hadn't recognized his light voice, it was so changed by this new tone of violence. "What the *hell* are you doing?" He glared at me, with an ugly light in his pale eyes. I didn't answer.

"Hm? Spying?" He jerked on my arm, and I stumbled and almost fell; but he didn't let go, and I stayed on my feet. "You won't answer? Maybe you'll tell Ludovic, then. As long as you were going in this way, you might as well finish what you started. It's a shortcut anyway." He pushed me toward the window. I had no choice but to clamber over the sill. He followed, still holding me by the wrist, and pushed me forward. I couldn't have moved otherwise, I think. My feet stumbled at every step.

Sam shoved me through the tack room and to the right, where light showed under a door. He reached over my shoulder to knock once, as if in warning, then pushed the door open.

It was the stable office, and it was in use. Ludovic Walter sat at a computer terminal, with one hand on the keyboard, the other tracing something on the monitor screen. Gerald was leaning over a green-and-white-striped printout. They both looked up, and all three of us froze for an instant.

I must, I thought, have been quite an apparition—covered with mud, pale, bedraggled, and wide awake—when they thought I was safely locked in and asleep. Even so, Walter adjusted fastest to this new set of circumstances.

"Miss Llewellyn! I need hardly say how surprised we are to

see you here. Would you care to sit down? From the look of it you have been undergoing some physical exertion. Sam, let go of her." Walter gestured at Gerald, who had been standing openmouthed. "Gerald, a chair for your friend." He pulled himself together and pushed forward a rolling desk chair. Sam let go of me and pushed me down into the chair. I still hadn't said anything, and I began to shake.

Walter tilted his chair backward, an odd, expansive gesture for someone so controlled. "Sam?" he said.

"I found her climbing in the tack room window."

"Ah. The tack room window. Yes. It may be bolting the barn door ex post facto, but Sam, if you wouldn't mind closing that window. . . ." He rocked a bit, and smiled at me. I stared, eyes fixed. He was enjoying himself. There was a look of real relish on his face as he began to speak. "You will, I hope, forgive Sam. He gets a little nervy when the wind blows from the west. And although his methods are unrefined, his instinct, in this case, is not misplaced. Your presence here, Miss Llewellyn, is inconvenient. Perhaps you would allow me to call you Sarah? And you must call me Ludovic. One hears so often about the intimacy between prisoners and their captors; perhaps that would be putting our case a little strongly, but I would like to be correct. Gerald, you're quite a stickler. Wouldn't you say it was correct for us to be on a first-name basis?"

I couldn't help turning to look at Gerald. I was sorry I had. He was pale, and a fine sheen of sweat glossed his face. His eyes shifted around the room restlessly, avoiding me. But he stood up and pulled a jacket off a hook and put it over my shoulders. I shrugged it off.

"I think perhaps Sarah is surprised to see you here, Gerald. I might even say disappointed in your character. Perhaps she has concluded that we are not the strangers that we had appeared to be. Let me explain that Gerald and I are involved in a business venture that has reached a particularly delicate stage. It seemed important to deceive you about it."

"You didn't deceive me," I said, in an effort to salve my pride.

"Ah. And how might that be?"

"I knew that Gerald was quite at home here," I answered, looking only at Walter.

"And how did you know that? Of course, one mustn't ever ask a journalist to reveal her sources. Do you realize what this means, Gerald? We're playing a deeper game than we thought. Perhaps Miss Llewellyn—Sarah, I mean—could shed some light on the great puzzle of the Saltire earldom." Gerald had moved into my line of vision, and at this statement his eyes widened. I would almost have said he flinched.

"I imagine Gerald knows as much about the Saltire earldom as I do. If not, it's not for want of investigation. I saw you at the hunt meet, Gerald. And that was you in the dower house that night, wasn't it?" I sounded savage, but it gave me comfort, even when Gerald turned to me.

"I'm sorry, Sarah, I—"

Walter broke in. "You were at a hunt meet? Careless, wasn't it? And how did Sarah know you'd been in the dower house?"

Neither Gerald nor I told him. Walter broke the embarrassed silence. "No answer? Sarah, I can't help asking, in a purely admiring way, of course, how you got out of the house."

I looked him straight in the eye. He looked merry, appreciative. "I climbed down the outside of the tower."

"Enterprising. She climbed down the outside of the tower, Sam." He addressed himself to his henchman, who reappeared in the doorway. "And why did you feel yourself compelled to take this little climb?"

"Claustrophobia," I answered, and looked down at my hands. They were covered with mud, scraped and bruised from the climb. They throbbed.

"I see. And now there is one other thing nagging at my mind, which I neglected to ask about at dinner. Just slipped my mind; what was it? Oh, yes, I know. How do you suppose a pair of old death certificates would find their way into your camera bag? When Sam went out to look at your car the bag was open on the front seat and he couldn't help it, they caught his eye. You really couldn't say he was snooping. So odd, isn't it, how things never stay put?"

He would have gone on. He seemed to be warming up for bigger things. He had put down the legs of his chair, and edged it toward mine, until our knees were almost touching. As Walter moved forward, so did Gerald, and his hand was now on the back of my chair. But a crackling, static noise broke into the silence.

Sam moved lazily to the console behind me, which I had glimpsed from the window earlier that day. A voice came over a radio: "St. Patrick, come in, please. This is Alexander. Come in, please, St. Patrick."

Instantly the room was galvanized. Walter swore, and pushed his chair back from mine. "What time is it? They're early!"

Sam crisply flicked switches on the console. "Alexander, this is St. Patrick. We read you. Why so early?"

"Storm conditions, St. Patrick. Can't be helped. Landing estimated ten minutes from now. What are your wind conditions, please?"

"Prevailing from the west, gusting up to forty knots."

"Right. We'll come in from the east then. Over and out."

"Damn! Gerald, get something to tie Sarah with; there's bound to be a piece of rope in the tack room." Gerald didn't move for a moment, and Walter's voice dropped to a silky, odious tone. "Gerald? Mr. Charlton? Or should I say 'my lord'? If it wouldn't be too much effort?" I could feel Gerald flinging himself out of the room behind me.

In the meantime the orders continued. "Sam, the flares are right here." Walter kicked a box. "I'll bring the tractor over in a moment." It was yet another complete personality change; he was snapping out his commands, briskly moving around the room to gather a mackintosh, a pair of powerful flashlights, a ring of keys. He didn't even address me, but when Gerald came back with a length of coarse rope, he hauled me to my feet. "Let me do this." He pulled my wrists in back of me and looped the rope around them, then pulled it tight. "Look, Gerald, for future reference; make sure her fingers can't reach the rope. We'll put her in an empty stall for the moment. Go on, get the door open!"

Gerald slipped ahead of us and held the door of a box stall, which Walter shoved me into with a push between the shoulder blades. When I fell he tugged on the rope, jerking my arms back. I couldn't help crying out with the sudden pain.

"Sorry. But with your hands behind you, you couldn't break the fall. Didn't want you to bump your pretty nose on the floor." Walter's voice came from above me. As he spoke he was passing the rest of the rope around my ankles, bending my knees up so that my back was arched in a painfully tight bow. "Intelligent as you are, I'm sure you realize that you would have been a great deal more comfortable in your bed." With a final twitch on the rope, he was gone, the stall door slammed behind him. The tractor motor roared. Creaking and clattering, it left the stable. The sound receded.

Chapter 12

I sank into my pain. It was one great blur, a hot blackness. Then, gradually, I began to separate the components. My cheek against the gritty stone floor, bruised and grazed. The rope burning the skin of my wrists. The ache in my shoulders and back, the corresponding ache in my thighs. None of it, taken separately, was grave. But all of it together . . . I shut my eyes against the darkness. The fear was worse than the pain. What was going to happen when they came back?

The last item Ludovic Walter had put in his pocket was a gun.

I lay there stunned on the floor. My arms and legs were going to sleep; I wondered how long it would be before they were numb. And I wondered if it would matter. Because it seemed eminently possible that I might not last the night.

It was the first time I had allowed myself the thought. I was in the way of something. Late-night plane landings in a secluded corner of Ireland, guns and casual physical abuse: all this was a far cry from some historical research gone astray. Smuggling, in all likelihood. Ludovic Walter would not be happy to have a witness.

This was why I'd been drugged and locked in: as a precaution to keep me from finding out too much. For my own safety, if you wanted to put it that way.

I wondered if I would be in less pain in another position. My hipbones pressed awkwardly against the floor, and I wanted to get the weight off my bruised cheek. Maybe lying on my side . . . I tried to roll over; the strain pulled against the rope and sent a fresh group of twinges along my body. No good. I lapsed back and closed my eyes again. That was it. I gave up. I would lie there, wretched, until they came back. And they would do whatever it was they felt necessary.

I could hear my watch ticking in the silence of the stable. I wondered what time it was, and how long I would be lying there. I would hear the sound of them coming back: voices, the tractor's engine, the doors creaking. Did the door of this stall creak? I tried to consider this as an academic point. I thought it didn't.

And then it did. Unmistakably. My head was facing away from the door. I couldn't turn to look. This, I thought, is it. The end. I was mentally consigning myself to my fate when I heard the whisper.

"Sarah." In a moment he was next to me. "Oh, God, Sarah!"

It was David. I burst into tears.

He was busy untying the rope at my back, swearing viciously to himself. The knot at my ankles came loose, and a groan escaped me as I straightened my back. He whispered, close to my ear, "Are you all right?"

"Yes. I wasn't tied up for long."

"They didn't hurt you?"

"No." The knot was undone. Gentle hands helped me to sit up.

"You're sure you're all right? Nothing broken?" David was crouched in front of me, holding me by the shoulders. I couldn't see his expression; his eyes were just a glitter in the dark. But his voice sounded raw, anxious.

"Yes. How did you get here? How did you know?"

"My dear girl, I'm here to rescue you!" His hands moved on my shoulders, a convulsive little movement. He sounded oddly impatient, desperate, torn between anxiety, diffidence, and I didn't dare guess what else. "I can't forgive myself for letting you come here alone. I should have realized. But they're clever and I fell for it, literally." He took a deep breath. "They're smuggling. Drugs. Interpol had a raid planned for tomorrow night; a big shipment was due to come in. A friend of my father's in the CID let him know about it. But somehow Walter has found out and pushed the shipment forward to tonight, so Interpol will be too late."

"Smuggling *drugs?* In Ireland? But . . ." It seemed so unlikely. Ludovic Walter and his computer screen and Gerald, in this mad castle by the sea? I could have imagined guns, money-laundering, industrial secrets, but drugs—such an ugly trade, such a wretched, sinister, death-dealing crime!

"Let me explain from the beginning, quickly," he said. "We haven't much time. Walter has been running a drug depot here. I don't know how long. It's mostly heroin that's ready for the market, refined, cut, packaged in small amounts. They seem to think it comes from Marseilles. The drugs come in at night—the house is remote and the villagers keep to themselves. They're distributed through a network in the horse business, disguised in various ways. Interpol says they've used horse blankets, liniment bottles, that kind of thing."

I remembered the scene at the hunt—the horse vans and trunks, the nomadic population of grooms. And I also remembered the story I'd read in the newspaper on the ferry to Ireland. "There was an article in the paper yesterday," I said, "about drug distribution at race courses. Is Walter connected with that?"

David shifted his position, sitting down next to me with an arm behind me. "It seems very likely; that would be the next step of the operation. And not just race courses, where there's always a certain element of, well, raffishness. But also at hunt meets, horse shows, they said even little Pony Club organizations. Who knows, maybe that meet at Saltire the other day was just a bazaar. Currycombs hollowed out and stuffed with cocaine." His voice was bitter, and I put a hand on his arm.

"Sorry. It just incenses me to think of good people and horses being used for something so grim and—harmful. Anyway, when I started telling Walter that I wanted to come look at this place, he was alarmed. Obviously, he's not training horses here, which is what he'd told me he was doing. So he didn't want me nosing around. And he was evidently so pleased with the system he'd set up that, rather than take the cautious route of closing down operations and disappearing, he chose to put me off. Interpol seemed to find that very surprising; it seems these fellows usually make a principle of constantly shifting their locations."

David paused for a moment, as if to catch his breath. "Anyway, Walter didn't want to do that. Somehow—it must be through papers or something he found here—he discovered that there was some room for doubt about my grandfather's legitimacy. Just over a month ago we started to get anonymous letters, talking about babies having been switched, that kind of thing. Of course our first reaction was to try to find out the truth of the matter, but as you know, the facts are confusing. The letters claimed that the official death certificate was forged, for one thing." I kept silent, waiting for him to finish his story before I told him what I'd found. "In the stir of it all, naturally I put off going to Neville Park. Then I got the letter from you."

The arm behind my back stiffened almost imperceptibly. "Your coming seemed like a godsend, because you'd be doing the research anyway and would be able to interpret the documents. I'd begun to look through the trunks, of course, but hadn't got as far as finding the diaries. It was actually Henrietta's idea to have you stay, so that we'd know what you found out." I sat very straight and still, aware of every nerve of David's body, close enough so that I could feel the warmth, but not touching me.

"And then you came, and . . . you know all that bit." He rushed the last words. "It seemed like such a good idea to come here with you. So I sent off the telegram, and then I fell, out hunting. The fall was fixed. Did you know that?" He turned to look at my face, though he couldn't have seen much in the gloom.

"Yes. I unsaddled Abracadabra, remember? But David, I didn't know *what* was going on. I . . . I didn't know what to say, and then they took you off to the hospital and I didn't want to tell Henrietta. It would have worried her."

"It would have, you're right." He looked down. "The new groom told Riley later that a blond man came around the stable that morning and said he was thinking of buying 'the horse Lord Neville was riding today' and I'd sent him out to look him over. So MacIntyre obligingly let him into Abracadabra's stall and left him there. The horse had already been saddled; it couldn't have been simpler for him."

"What kind of blond man? Did he say anything else about him?" I broke in.

"MacIntyre said he was a photographer, had a couple of cameras slung around his neck."

"Gerald."

"What?"

"It was your cousin, Gerald Charlton. Go on, I'll explain when you're done."

"But how do you know. . . ? All right, I'll finish. They kept me in hospital, and when I got home you were gone and my father was there with the news from Interpol. I was . . ." he paused, "concerned about your being around these people. I couldn't think why they were letting you come here so close to when they were getting the shipment. I realized that I'd been prevented from coming here myself. So I called the Ballyhannock Inn to warn you, and you weren't there. I called a few times, quite late. They finally hung up on me," he added ruefully. "But you never got there. So I decided to come out myself and try to find you."

"But how did you get here, in the stable?"

"I called the Pearsalls, at the next house. I went straight there from Shannon this afternoon. I didn't want to let Walter know I was here, so I borrowed a horse from the Pearsalls and rode over around sunset. I saw your car, and thought I'd wait to see you leave. I left the horse in a bit of woods and came down here. I overheard some of the arrangements for tonight, and then over the radio Sam told Walter you'd come back. Walter said they'd be shorthanded tonight and they couldn't spare anyone to get you back to Ballyhannock, since there was too much to do; so they'd just have to keep you out of the way. He said it would be easy." David's tone was very even now, completely dispassionate. "He told Sam that he would give you something in your coffee and lock you in and if that didn't take care of you he could think of a lot of ways . . ." He broke off. "Then he went back to the house. I went and got the Pearsalls' horse and put it in a stall here, and waited with it until I knew they were all out of the house. Then I was going to fetch you."

"And ride off with me draped over your saddle like something in Walter Scott?" I said, aiming for lightness. He turned toward me again, and I thought he was smiling.

"Just so. But you can ride off by yourself now. You can, can't you? That *is* what you were doing in the stable, isn't it? How did you avoid being drugged?"

"Poured the coffee down my side."

"How did you know?"

"I saw Walter doctor it, reflected in the window. I'll explain, but it isn't important now and we don't have much time, do we? What do you mean about me riding off by myself?"

"I want to see what they're doing. If there isn't a witness, and they get the drugs clear, they can't be charged with anything. It will all be hearsay. But if I watch them . . ."

"David, don't," I interrupted. My hand was on his knee, as if to restrain him. "Please. Walter has a gun."

"I have to." He put a hand over mine. "You must see that."

I nodded, suddenly unable to speak, pulled my hand away

from his and covered my face. He was so damned honorable. He'd come out here to get me away from Walter, out of a feeling of responsibility. And he was going to put himself at enormous risk to stop something he hated with his whole soul—after making sure I was safely away. Here I was, millimeters away from him in the dark, aching with love and gratitude, and he was going to send me off, brave girl, with a pat on the shoulder while he did his duty.

And then, with a muffled moan—of what? anxiety? impatience?—he had his arms around me. "What is it, darling?" he whispered in my ear. And very gently he kissed me, on the cheek, on the mouth. Then less gently, as his arms tightened, and I felt a rush of warmth through my body. The desperation I had sensed in him turned into eagerness, hunger, erasing his diffidence. He kissed me like someone who had been waiting for years, bending my head back, leaning over me, pressing his body against mine. And despite my bruises, the stone floor, the danger, I met him, pulled him down next to me. For an instant we lay there, locked together, then my hands felt, under his damp shirt, some kind of bandage. I pulled away. "Your collarbone! And you rode over here?"

He leaned forward and kissed me softly again. "I don't think it hurt. I didn't notice, if it did." He brought up a hand to brush the hair from my face. "You have to go now. They'll be back soon and you must be out of sight."

"No." My arms tightened around him. "I can't. I want to stay with you."

"Sarah, you'll be safe if you get away!"

"Are you sure?" We both sat up. "I'll be so much more frightened riding off through the woods alone. I don't know the way, I don't know the horse . . ."

"You were willing to do it by yourself earlier." David, on his feet now, held out a hand to help me up.

"I had no choice."

He stood for a moment, looking down at me, holding my

hand in his, weighing the odds. "All right. We'll take the horse with us, in case we have to get away fast." He shook his head slowly. "I wish . . ." But he didn't finish the sentence. His hand came up to stroke my cheek and instinctively I turned toward him. With his good arm he pulled me closer, so that I could feel, even through our sodden clothes, the heat of his body and the urgency of his heartbeat. The mannerly self-control was gone—with a moan he moved his mouth down to kiss my jaw, my throat . . . I was clinging to him, unsteady and weak-kneed. I had forgotten everything but him, his mouth and his hands.

Breathless, he pulled away first. "We must go." He lifted one of my hands to his mouth and kissed it, then turned away to open the stall door. "I'll get Harry." His figure disappeared up the dark corridor, and returned leading a horse. "Do you know where they are?"

"They must be on the other side of the house," I said; "there's no place here where a plane could land. Probably behind that bit of woods to the right of the drive."

"Fine. We'll tether Harry to a tree then. Would you rather ride or walk?"

"I'll walk," I answered. So we set off into the night, leading Harry, a placid lop-eared chestnut. The rain had let up almost completely, but the wind blew as fiercely as ever and the noise was, if anything, worse. Before long we were beyond the shelter of the stable and the house, crossing the drive. Ahead of us was the scrubby wood.

"You'd think someone would have told the thirteenth Earl that trees don't grow very well next to the sea," David whispered as we approached the clump of scraggly hemlocks.

"They probably did. I don't imagine he paid much attention, though." We were in the undergrowth now, pushing through brambles and tall shrubs with thin, whiplike branches.

"We'd better leave Harry here, he makes so much noise." David looped the reins around the trunk of a stunted-looking cedar. "There must be a road through here somewhere if they brought the tractor, but we'll be safer in the trees." The shrubs were all soaked from the rain, and careful as David was about holding branches aside for me, I was stung repeatedly, and once my braid caught on something and yanked me back sharply. We moved slowly, trying to make as little noise as possible, though the storm whipping through the trees covered any rustlings and cracklings we made. It was so dark that I could barely see David's back in front of me.

And then, through the trees, there was light. David slowed his pace, creeping forward now as silently as possible. When we reached the edge of the wood we could see quite clearly why Walter had wanted me out of the way.

A makeshift runway had been marked out with flares in the rough grass and their pinkish glow colored the shreds of fog that flitted by on the high wind. Several large flashlights stood on a wing of the plane, the body of the tractor, the ground, to illuminate the task. It was a small aircraft; almost too small, I would have said, to carry its cargo. Which was, astonishingly, bales of hay.

They had pulled the tractor right up next to the plane, so that the flatbed trailer stood just below the door. One man pitched the bales down from the plane to the trailer where Sam and Walter wrestled them into position. Gerald just stood there, holding a flashlight.

"How many do you think there are?" I whispered to David.

"I should think there was a copilot," he answered. "With a valuable cargo they'd hardly risk something happening to the pilot and losing it all. But where is he?"

"Inside the cabin, moving the bales forward?"

"Maybe. Who's the blond?"

"Sam? The one loading?"

"No, the other one. I suppose that's my cousin Gerald. How is he involved with this?" he asked in a low voice, eyes on the scene in front of us.

"You mean you've never met him?"

"Maybe once or twice when we were children, but not recently. Doesn't look very happy, does he?"

He looked, if anything, sulky, trying to detach himself from the work at hand. "I'm not sure I understand exactly how he's involved. I met him in New York; he was at the library, researching Lauretta. And then I saw him at the hunt meet, with a camera. That must have been just after he tampered with your saddle." I turned toward him to explain. "The night I thought I heard something in the garden, remember, that was him. And the next night there was someone in the dower house when I got back there. Gerald again."

"Why didn't you tell me?" he asked sharply.

I hushed him, though Walter and his men were too far away to hear. "I was going to. But the next morning I came up to the house early to get the clothes I'd left. And I went right up to Henrietta's room to get them. They were in the closet. I wouldn't have eavesdropped on purpose," I peered at him in the darkness to see how he was taking this, "but I overheard you talking to her on the phone, and . . ." I paused, then rushed on. "It occurred to me that you might even have had something to do with the person in the dower house."

His arm came around me, brushing a shower of water from a branch. "Lord, I'm sorry you heard that. All of this uncertainty about the family hits Henrietta very hard, you know. I don't mind so much for myself, but the publicity will be particularly embarrassing for her, and possibly bad for her business as well."

"But you don't have to worry about that," I interrupted him. "It's all a fake." It was so strange to be huddled in a small wood on a windy night, watching men unloading a plane, calmly discussing the plot I had fled from in terror only an hour before. What a difference David's presence made!

"How do you know?" he was asking.

"It's very confusing. I'll explain the whole thing later, but from what you've told me, I think they must have seized on this confusion about Lauretta's death and her son's birth, and blown it up. I found a pair of death certificates in a trunk at the house that are probably forgeries, and a register in the chapel that must be, too."

"Look, they're done," he whispered. Two men jumped down from the hold of the plane and helped Walter and Gerald spread a tarpaulin over the hay bales on the trailer. "Was there anything else about Gerald?"

"Yes. I stayed in Neville two nights ago, no, last night. I heard gossip there that Gerald practically lives here. They thought he was Walter's lover."

"Is he?"

"Unlikely," I said dryly. "But what's curious is that when he showed up today, he pretended to be dropping in for the first time, and Walter pretended that he was annoyed."

"For your benefit? Watch it, get down!" He pulled me to the ground as Gerald swung his flashlight idly toward the woods.

"Yes," I whispered.

"Why?"

"I think they had much the same idea that you did, of letting me do the research and make the discoveries. But where you wanted to prove your grandfather's legitimacy, they wanted me to discover the opposite. Gerald would have the title, then, wouldn't he? So if I made this startling revelation, he could just step gracefully into your father's shoes without seeming to have wanted to. And since he's working with Walter, maybe he'd let this business continue here." I gestured at the plane and the tractor, whose engine we could hear roaring over the storm.

"It sounds likely, at least. Here they go. We'd better get back to Harry and away, before they find you're gone." He stood up and held a hand out to me, looking over his shoulder through the screen of trees. The tractor trundled toward the house with Walter, incongruously, at the wheel. The two men were in the plane with the hatches shut, and the propellers were whirling slowly, then faster. Sam had taken up a pair of flares and began to signal with them while Gerald stood, arms crossed on his chest, watching. The wind from the storm and from the propellers blew his hair around, but he was still as a statue.

"Why do you suppose he did it?" David said, as if reading my thoughts. "Money, maybe. As Henrietta said, he's never been able to make a living. He's loaned his name—our name—to some pretty unsavory investment schemes, and he came very close to bankruptcy not long ago. Our solicitor has kept a casual eye on him to warn us what to expect next. What a scandal this is going to make!" He shrugged, and turned. "Come on. I think Harry can manage both of us as far as Neville. It's closer than the Pearsalls'. Fortunately Walter et al don't know I was here at all, let alone with a horse, so if they look for you it will be on foot."

The rain had begun again, but more softly this time. I brushed by a hemlock branch and was drenched, as if by a giant paintbrush. Over the wind we could hear the crescendo of the plane's engine as it taxied down the makeshift runway and took off, with the wind to help it. It flew right over us, very low, and I wondered momentarily about the cottagers in its flight path. Flying low to avoid radar, I thought. A stone moved under my foot and I recalled that I needed to concentrate on moving quietly. As David held a nasty switch of witch hazel aside for me, my hand touched his. It gave me such comfort. Very soon we would be on poor old Harry's back, riding down the drive, invisible in the darkness. And we would be safe. Ahead of me, David stepped on a branch that broke with a loud snap. It sounded like a cannon to me. He froze, and so did I.

And Harry neighed, a long, loud whinny.

The only immediate answer came from the wind. It rose to a howl, tossing the trees about as if they were ferns. I could hear nothing over the rushing, keening sound. But David gripped my arm hard, and though I couldn't see his face clearly, I knew he was alarmed.

"I'll lead them away," he said urgently in my ear. On one level I was aware of his breath on my cheek and my urge to lean against him into a kiss. But more than that, I was angry, furious that we had been so close to safety. Above all, I was afraid again. And even while I was clutching his arm, unwilling to leave him, I could see David's logic.

"They don't know you're out, so they'll just be looking for the horse," he went on. "I'll come back for you as soon as I've got rid of them. Can you climb one of the trees?"

I looked up at the hemlocks dubiously, but nodded.

"Okay. Up you go then. Do you have a watch?" I nodded. He put both hands on my shoulders, and I could feel, rather than see, his sense of imminent danger. "Sarah, if I'm not back in three hours, go to Neville and rouse the police." I nodded. There was nothing to say.

He kissed me, quickly and hard, then broke away, looking upward. "This one looks steadiest," he said, stepping over to the largest tree. "Let me give you a leg up."

He laced his fingers together and stooped next to the trunk. Far off, we heard a shout as the wind suddenly dropped. I put my foot in his hands and reached for a branch over my head. "Ready?" I nodded. He straightened, throwing me upward. I scrambled onto a sturdy branch and looked down. He was already gone, not even a shadow between the trees.

I could feel tears starting hot in my eyes as I looked upward to choose my path. The branches all slanted unpleasantly downward, but they were evenly placed and strong. Numbly, sobbing, I started to climb. The bark was prickly and tore at my hands but I was happy to have them torn, and threw myself savagely against the branches. How could David possibly get away from them? One man, unarmed, against three with at least one gun? He had said he would come back for me, but how could he? I paused, leaning my face against the trunk of the tree, and shut my eyes. Why go on? Why not just walk out of the woods with my hands up? Why allow myself to be found, treed ignominiously like an animal? Why not try to salvage at least my dignity out of this?

Then I heard a branch break somewhere below me. Without thought I clambered farther upward, until the branches were thinner and started to sag under my weight. They met the trunk at such an acute angle that I couldn't sit, but had to stand, with my feet right next to the trunk. How long, I wondered, would I be able to stay here?

In a sudden gust the tree rocked, and my foot slipped, dislodging a bit of bark. I watched it fall but lost sight of it long before it reached the ground. The gust was followed by silence, and now, to my terror, I could hear footsteps. He wasn't even trying to be quiet. He was just searching, very carefully. And he had a light.

I could see it now, below me, flickering here and there. Was I high enough from the ground? Would the branches hide me? I was grateful that my khaki trousers were so covered with dirt that they were black; at least no unlikely patch of paleness would give me away.

"Sarah? Sarah, it's Gerald." He knew that it was me he was looking for. Did that mean Walter had already been back to the stable, and found me missing? Or—worse by far—that they already had David?

The flashlight beam was leaping up the sides of trees now. I couldn't look away. It was powerful, powerful enough to reach . . . as high as my perch?

"Don't worry, Sarah, I swear I won't hurt you," he said softly. The wind now seemed to have died completely, and the trees were so still that I could hear water dripping from them. Gerald was breathing hard. I could hear that too.

My hands, clinging to the branches over my head, were tingling, but I didn't dare move the fingers for fear that the movement might catch his eye.

The column of light compressed itself to a short beam at the foot of a tree, then sprang out again, this time along the ground. It probed here and there—bushes, shrubs, the ground. Gerald had not come near my tree, and he seemed to be moving away.

Then the beam extended to its full length, and halted as if caught on something. I couldn't see what it was trained on, but Gerald moved forward. I craned my head, stooped a little to see. What was he looking at?

I could see his hand reaching out. His movements were as measured as if he were sleepwalking. He pulled something off a branch. I squinted, trying to see what it was.

I gasped. My hand flew to my hair, loose on my back. The pink ribbon.

The ribbon I had pulled from one of Lauretta's chemises, and used to tie my braid. Gerald had certainly seen it when Sam dragged me into the stable office. I remembered the tug on my hair when David and I had come through here. The ribbon had been left hanging there, to give me away.

Chapter 13

He turned around. Now he knew I had been here, without much time to get away. He began to retrace his steps, but more carefully. Much more carefully.

And, what was worse, systematically. I could see how he was doing it. He was searching in circles from the shrub where he'd found the ribbon. Widening circles. He scuffed up the pine needles on the ground, peered into the very middle of bushes, and sent the beam up to the top of every tree. Stood right under the tree, and looked straight up.

He couldn't possibly miss me.

He was talking again, almost pleading now. "I know what you must think of me but, really, it's not that bad. I know you're here. I wish you'd trust me." As he looked up the trunk of the tree next to mine, the flashlight lit his face from below. He looked haggard, and worried. But even the harsh brightness of the beam flattered him. The fine line of his jaw as he stretched to look up the tree; the dramatically dark shadows from his brow and cheekbones; the blond hair, still lying smooth and elegant against his skull—a completely detached part of my mind was admiring them.

Until he shone the light in my eyes.

"There you are!" he exclaimed. "I've been looking for you all over. Obviously." He ran a hand over his face, and looked back up at me. "I have to explain. It's not . . ." He took a deep breath. "It's not what it looks like." He was standing now at the foot of my tree. "Come down, Sarah. There isn't any point in your trying to get away, and you can't be comfortable up there."

I wanted to point out that I hadn't been comfortable tied up in the stall, either, but I couldn't say anything.

"Come down, Sarah," he repeated. "I can't stand here shouting up a tree at you." His voice was ragged.

"Why not? There's nobody to hear except me, and I don't mind." The annoyance I felt gave me a little spurt of energy. I flexed my hands and wiggled my arms one at a time.

"I can explain everything," he said again, almost desperately.

"I'm sure," I said, but I don't think he heard. My control snapped. "I couldn't care less about anything you have to say, you cheap little sneak!" I shouted down at him. It was a mistake. Gerald practically flinched. He reached for something beneath his oilskin, and held it up to me with the flashlight trained on it.

My heart jumped with fear, and all the anger drained out of me. Gerald had a gun, and he was pointing it at me.

"I won't shoot you, but I could shoot the branch under your feet, Sarah. I'm quite accurate with a gun." I believed him. There was a flat matter-of-factness in his voice that gave weight to his threats.

I turned my face to the trunk of the tree and leaned my forehead against the bark. Why had I let myself bait Gerald? I would have been better off trying to cajole him into letting me escape. It might not have worked, but insulting him was idiotic. Now he was angry. David had surely been caught. The situation was hopeless. I started to feel for the next branch down. Might as well go quietly.

I was hanging by my hands from the lowest branch, ready to drop to the ground, when Gerald's hands closed around my rib cage. I wondered where the gun was. Would this be the end?

Was he going to shoot me in the back, at point-blank range, as I climbed down from a hemlock tree?

No. He caught me as I dropped, set me down firmly, and let me go. The flashlight, stuck in the branches of a sturdy bush, gave a ghastly artificial illumination to the scene.

"You have no need to run away from us, Sarah. We wouldn't hurt you. We just wanted to keep you out of the way while we got some business taken care of. You must believe that."

"Then what is the gun for? And what was the business? What could possibly be so urgent that it has to be carried out in the middle of a storm, miles from nowhere?" I could hear my voice rising, and wondered if I was getting hysterical. "Gerald, what is in those bales of hay?"

"That's what I'm trying to tell you," he almost shouted at me. "Look, sit down. There, there's a tree trunk. You sit on that."

It was surreal. Here we were in the middle of the dripping woods, and Gerald was brushing off the tree trunk for me. But he didn't sit himself. Instead he stood in front of me. He wasn't actually pointing the gun at me. But it was in his hand. And his index finger never strayed too far from the trigger. I wondered if the safety catch was on. He was so distraught that I was afraid he'd forget he was holding a weapon.

"Granted, it's not legal," he began. "But all Walter is doing here is trying to get around a punitive wealth tax. I don't know how much you know about taxation in Great Britain, Sarah, but it's appalling, and Walter is simply a businessman trying to maximize his profits." I watched him, and listened. He began practically reciting chapter and verse of the tax code. Reciting it like someone reciting a spell whose potency he no longer believed in.

I let him talk. There was a vein throbbing in his temple, and his face was wet. With sweat, I thought, rather than rain. He paced back and forth in front of me, scuffing up the fallen hemlock needles, and constantly glancing out into the darkness.

He didn't look at me. Nor did he mention the bales of hay. He started by saying that Walter had offered him "a business opportunity."

"If you knew, Sarah." He rubbed his face again. "I've had such bad luck; one thing after another falls apart. I've tried, God knows. I have good ideas, but you can't get anywhere without capital. Walter may not be the kind of man one would choose to work with, in fact he's . . ." He paused and shook his head. "But I had no choice. I don't want to disgrace the family name, you know. Particularly when . . ." He looked down at me, meeting my eyes for the first time. "Did you understand what those death certificates meant? I am the real Earl of Salt-ire!" For just a moment, an expression of pure happiness erased his drawn look. "Of course there will be some procedure in the College of Heralds, but if you *knew* . . . if you only knew what it was like to see Saltire, and those cousins of mine, and to think that only an accident of fate put them there, while I've had to cobble together schemes to live decently. But you see with Walter, my luck has turned. And if only I can stick it out . . ." He closed his eyes for a moment.

"Gerald." My voice brought him back. "What about the hay bales?"

His eyes shifted again. "Even I don't know exactly. Walter has never told me outright, but it's currency. It has to be. Large amounts of currency." He nodded as he said it, affirming the statement.

He wanted so badly to believe it, and he was so afraid it wasn't true.

"I see. Have you got a cigarette?" I asked idly. I wanted to keep him talking, but I was afraid I couldn't hide my disbelief from him. And I thought it might be unwise, if not downright dangerous, to force him to face what he'd been involved in.

"Yes, just a moment," Gerald answered, abstractedly. He reached into the left-hand pocket of his mackintosh, but the cigarettes weren't there. Without thinking, I stood up, with my hand out, as if to receive the cigarette. He reached across his body, but couldn't reach the right-hand pocket with his left hand. So he took the gun in his left hand, and put it in that pocket. And, with both his hands, prepared to light a cigarette for me. I found just a moment to think that it did him credit; his good manners went far deeper than any violent instinct. Then I lunged for the gun.

I didn't get it; but my hand was in the pocket before he caught on and grabbed my forearm. I could feel, against my fingers, the cold metal sliding against the rough fabric. But I couldn't quite get a grip, and now Gerald had my other arm twisted up behind me. He was pulling on both of my arms, and at the same time forcing me backward. I tried to butt his chest with my head, but it was useless. He was stronger than I was.

And then I heard the shout. Not very far off. Gerald raised his head and called out, "Sam! Here!" In that instant's break in his concentration, I kicked him. And got the gun.

It was in my right hand, pointing at him. My forefinger was on the trigger. We faced each other warily, with our eyes locked together. We must have been close to the flashlight, for his face was brightly lit and he had to squint. Dimly I heard branches snapping and rustling a few yards off. Gerald feinted with his right hand, making as if to grab the gun. I flinched away from him.

Then he stepped forward. And everything happened at once. Involuntarily, I stepped back, but there was no steady ground under my left foot; it was some kind of animal hole. As I lost my balance I must have squeezed the trigger, for my right hand leapt and I heard a sharp crack. I grabbed at the branches over my head and the flashlight tumbled from its perch. It landed facing upward, making a tall shaft of light among the tree trunks. An easy way for Sam to spot us, as if the gunshot weren't enough.

And Sam's arrival was going to be disaster, since Gerald had caught hold of me by the ankles, and snatched up the gun that I dropped when I tried to break my fall.

He helped me up with a polite hand under the elbow. "That really wasn't necessary," he said. "There's nothing to be afraid of."

But I was scared. Even more so when Sam crossed over the column of light, carrying a shotgun. Including Walter's, that meant there were three guns. And the bad guys had them all.

Chapter 14

"Well done," Sam said to Gerald. "Ludovic's looking for the horse. Let's get her back to the house so we can give him a hand. In fact, why don't you get one of those brutes from the stable and start searching? I'll tie her up."

They marched me off between them, each holding an arm. A few bruises more or less, I thought, could hardly matter. Still, Sam was rough, rougher than he needed to be.

We came out of the woods onto the grass. I was surprised at how still the night was, and how loud the water sounded. The waves, I supposed, would stay angry for a while, even though the storm was over. The fog had thickened since the landing of the plane; the lights of the house and the stable glowed in aureoles. I was glad to think that the visibility would be worse. It was a stroke of luck for David.

As we crossed the drive Gerald let go of me, and turned toward the stable, while Sam and I walked up toward the house. Once I tripped. He yanked me up. He was carrying his shotgun over the arm away from me, broken, like a country gentleman out for a stroll. Pretty cocky, I thought.

And with reason. I certainly wasn't going to make a fuss at this point. The man meant business.

He wasted no time on ceremony, either. Once we were inside, he dragged me into Walter's study. He sat me in the desk chair, tied me to it with a length of nylon rope he pulled from his pocket, and tied my feet to the brass rail around the fireplace. He looked once around the room, swept the paper knife and ruler into a desk drawer, and locked it. Then he shut the door and locked me in.

They had at least learned their lesson, I reflected. No windows I could climb out of in this room. I was not even uncomfortable. Without the ropes, I could have been curled up in my chair next to the fireplace, taking a little nap. Killing time.

Waiting to see what happened next.

My mind, by then, was numb. I couldn't see my watch, and though I spent some time trying to hear it tick, that amusement wore out rather quickly. I just sat there. My chin sank onto my chest.

I don't know how much time passed that way. My mind was far away when the key sounded in the door, and Ludovic Walter walked in.

He took the "tut tut, this is all a mistake, Sam has been much too enthusiastic" approach. Bustled around, untied me, poured me a glass of brandy, lit the fire in the fireplace. "Please, Sarah, accept my apologies and let me explain myself." He was incredibly smarmy.

Having placed me in a wing chair by the fireplace (drinking the brandy, and gratefully at that), he sat in his desk chair facing me. "I can see that we underestimated your intelligence, Sarah. We should never have tried to deceive you in the first place. But, you see, we were under some pressure ourselves, and it is so easy to make a faulty judgment. You probably wonder why we have to go to such extraordinary lengths to receive a shipment of hay. You may have considered the possibility that, in fact, those were not bales of hay." He looked at me beadily, to see how I was taking this. "If that did cross your mind, you were right." He put his feet up on the desk, a big mahogany partner's desk with a red leather top. "I don't know how much you know about the tax situation in England." Was I going to get another lecture on British tax law? "Suffice it to say that taxes are very high. I have a number of business interests in England and much of that business is done in cash. What I've done here is certainly illegal. But, on balance, I do not think it unethical. I've simply removed some of my cash, and in its current disguise it will leave the country."

It didn't seem worth arguing. And besides, I didn't want to make him any more suspicious with a show of skepticism. It was easy enough, certainly, to simply look at him blankly.

"Now, you have certainly received terrible treatment at our hands. But you can see, can't you, how we might be suspicious of you? Especially when you got out of your bedroom."

I shrugged. I was so tired. It wasn't just that I was having trouble keeping my eyes open. I could barely follow what he was saying.

"And now that you've gotten free again, we have to be more suspicious, because you couldn't have done it alone. I tied those knots. I know you couldn't have untied them yourself." His voice changed suddenly. "Who untied you?"

Numbly, I told him I didn't know.

He rolled his eyes, as if to say, "God give me patience with this woman." "How can you not know?" he demanded.

I was staring numbly into the fireplace. It seemed as if the only part of my body that was still working was my brain, and that at only half capacity. "I didn't see him. Romantic, isn't it? I was lying on the floor, on my face, where you left me, and somebody sneaked in and untied me, and by the time I rolled over and got up, he was gone." I was rather pleased with the story. I didn't think he'd believe it, but I could stick to it, thereby protecting David, and just possibly giving him more time to get away.

Out of the corner of my eye, I was aware of Walter getting out of his chair. He began to pace back and forth across the room. "Don't you think that's just a little bit implausible? A damsel in distress rescued by an unknown cavalier?"

"No more implausible than being drugged and locked into my bedroom," I pointed out.

"Ah. Perhaps you have a point there," he conceded. "Then no doubt you are curious as to the identity of your rescuer?"

"I have a number of other things on my mind, but if you want to tell me who he was, feel free," I answered.

My rudeness didn't disturb him. "I think it must have been Lord Neville."

Although I didn't move by a millimeter, my stillness hardened into stiffness. I could feel the muscles in my face tighten. I hoped he couldn't see them. "But he's in the hospital, back in England," I said. "He fell out hunting and got hurt."

"Nonetheless. Who else knows where you are?"

"I made some friends in Neville last night," I told him. "I didn't stay in Ballyhannock but in the pub in the village. The men in the pub all knew I was coming here. And they have their doubts about you, what with all the late-night airplane landings. Maybe when I called to say I wouldn't be back, they got suspicious."

"I doubt it. I very much doubt it. No, this has all the marks of a true romantic rescue." Walter's pacing had brought him to my chair, where he stopped. "I think, to be blunt, that you have in mind to be a countess. What's more, you have grasped that the future Earl of Saltire may be one of two people, and you've been clever enough to beguile both of them." I didn't move, but kept staring into the fire. "Look at me when I talk to you!" he suddenly shouted. With his foot he kicked my chair around to face him. "Why did you steal those death certificates?"

I looked up at him. "I wanted to think about what they meant."

"No you didn't. You've been careful enough to play both Neville and Gerald along until now, and I have no doubt that if Gerald turned out to be the real earl you'd drop Neville like a hot potato. But you like Neville a little better, don't you? So you'd be willing to suppress proof that Gerald's the earl. In fact, you've really fallen for Neville, and Gerald is nothing more than a life preserver! You're just using the poor bastard!"

"*I'm* just using him? What the hell are *you* doing? How did you get hold of him anyway?"

"The little charade you saw earlier today was based on Gerald's original visit to Neville Park. He waltzed in just like that, and owing to, perhaps I should say his charm, we became fast friends."

"And you've been using him ever since! Did you cook up this claim to the earldom together, or was that all your idea? I know it was to keep David from coming round and seeing what was going on here." I was working myself up into real anger now. All the tension, the fear of the evening—and my despair about its outcome—had somehow translated themselves into this incautious rage. I stood up, and faced Walter. "Obviously you told Gerald the lie you just told me, about laundering money. He doesn't have a clue, does he, that those hay bales are actually full of drugs? And he seems to think those death certificates are genuine, that he's really the Earl of Saltire. What's going to happen to him when you leave this setup? This must be your last shipment coming in here; it has to be getting too dangerous for you. So what's going to happen to poor Gerald?"

I was so wrapped up in my tirade that I didn't think about Walter's reaction. In fact, there wasn't much of one; he stood in front of me, completely still, silent, looking at me. His eyes strayed once or twice to look behind me, and as I stopped speaking I noticed they were fixed on something. I turned to look.

Gerald was standing in the doorway. All the color was drained from his face, making his gold hair look jarringly yellow. His eyes were empty. I wondered how much he heard.

"Is that true?" His voice was thin, pinched, completely uninflected.

"What?" Walter asked, looking him straight in the eye. I thought he was trying to stare Gerald down.

"All of it. About the drugs. And the death certificates. They're forged, aren't they? When I came here the first time, you said there was no key to the chapel. Then you found it, and there was the parish register. And then when I came back from America, you'd suddenly found the key to the tower room and I found the death certificates in the trunk. Was that all faked?"

"Of course it was," Walter answered dismissively. "You even gave me the idea for the parish register, the way you went on about it. There wasn't one in the chapel, so we made it up."

"And the death certificates?"

"You wanted more proof. So we made more proof." Walter shrugged.

"And what about the drugs? Is that true too?"

"Sarah's imagination is overheated," Walter said casually, stepping toward the desk. He pulled on the drawer that Sam had locked, then reached in his pocket for a bunch of keys and unlocked it.

"It's not," I said to Gerald, pulling my eyes away from whatever Walter was doing. "He's shipping drugs, and Interpol found out. That's why he changed the shipment to tonight, and it will be the last time he uses Neville Park. I'll bet he even has plans to disappear. You might think of asking, Gerald, if he has plans for you. You've been very useful for maintaining his cover so far, but your usefulness has probably run out. . . ."

"Shut up," Walter said quietly. "If you're so smart, you might think about my plans for you."

I turned back to him. What I saw jolted me into silence and sent my blood pumping full of adrenaline again. For in one hand he held a small gun. Its barrel was pointing directly at me.

In his other hand he had a hypodermic needle.

I know I gasped and backed up, out of reflex. He moved

toward me. I took another step back. I couldn't take my eyes off the needle. It looked enormous, large enough for a horse. Glistening at the tip was a drop of some clear liquid. I inched farther back. I should have learned, from the woods, to look behind me, for the chair hit me in the back of the knees. Awkwardly, I sat.

Walter stepped forward again, and placed the gun deliberately on the desk. I glanced toward Gerald at the door. A look convinced me it was useless to hope for help from that direction. He was staring openmouthed at the two of us, but I don't think he even saw.

In which case he wouldn't have seen Walter seize my left arm and push up the sleeve. Even I didn't see the needle go in. I shut my eyes. I screamed, as loud as I could. And I kept screaming as the coldness rushed in on me, until everything went black.

Chapter 15

I was sore, and very cold. Somehow my right arm was folded under me, numb. My mouth tasted dry. I twisted to straighten my arm. The floor was uneven. I could see only blackness, and hear roaring. Maybe I didn't have my eyes open. Maybe the roaring was inside my head. There was a bump in the floor under my shoulder. The roaring swelled and receded. I fell back into unconsciousness. Time passed.

Why was the stable floor so bumpy? How had the ropes been untied? I tentatively moved my ankles before I opened my eyes. There were no ropes, but one of them throbbed. Why?

Because I tripped on a root in the woods. When was that? When was I in the woods? With David. But David untied me. So I wasn't on the stable floor anymore.

And what was that roaring?

For just another moment I kept my eyes shut. Gathered all the resources of my mind. Did an inventory; all my limbs were there, were whole. Fingers moved. Feet moved. Toes wiggled. Aches and pains: headache, throbbing ankle, stinging cheek. But I was all in one piece.

I opened my eyes. And what I saw frightened me more than anything, out of this whole nightmare, had frightened me yet.

Water. Gray, choppy water. About a foot away.

I scrambled into a sitting position, regardless of the pain that felt as if it would split my head open. And the following facts became plain to me.

The sun was rising. I had no idea what time it was and my watch had stopped, but the sky was light.

I was perched on top of the large rock in the cove near the chapel. I had no clue as to how I'd gotten there.

The water was close, and the high waves from the night's storm had not subsided. They were huge, streaked with brownish foam, and kept rolling toward the shore, thudding against the low bluff. Every now and then a few drops splashed me. But discomfort was the least of it. I put a cold palm against my forehead to soothe the headache. I was sitting on barnacles, with which the entire surface of the rock was covered. I remembered standing on the shore and concluding that when the tide was high, this rock would be completely submerged. Since my clothes were relatively dry, the tide must be coming in, not receding.

Sooner or later, my seat, however uncomfortable, was going to disappear. The question was, how long did I have? When I had looked at this boulder yesterday with the evil-looking cormorant standing on it, the water was close to its base. That was at midday. But was that the low ebb of the tide? I didn't know.

A particularly large wave slapped the rock and spray hit my face. I pulled my legs a little closer to my body and carefully, consciously swallowed my panic. Was I sitting on the highest part of the rock? I turned around to see, and for a moment my gaze was arrested. The horizon was filled with water, wave upon wave. All of them advancing smoothly. Helpless to look away, I watched as one enormous swell traveled toward me. Two, three, five smaller waves hit my rock. I braced myself. The big one was next. *Smack!* Water lapped to within an inch of me, murky water clouded with sand and seaweed and the miscellaneous residue of the storm.

The tide was coming in, and fast. There was a little knob of stone just slightly higher than the rest of the boulder. I pulled myself onto it. Huddled there, with my legs coiled around me like a mermaid's tail, I had a safety margin of a foot all around me. A foot of rock that was not, so far, under water. But wet. Already wet.

I caught sight of another giant swell coming. Was it true that they came in sevens? That each seventh wave was outsize? I watched it surge toward me, inexorable. It was big. Much taller than the rest. Involuntarily, I stiffened myself for the impact. No spray this time. Just water at my feet.

Better to turn my back on the waves. I could very easily go crazy watching them, waiting for the large ones, counting, anticipating. I could end up screaming my head off in panic. Which would do me exactly no good at all.

I twisted myself around and faced the shore. Even that was not an altogether reassuring sight. It was gray, and gloomy, and deserted. I couldn't see the house; in fact, all I could see of civilization was the steeple on the little church. And, now that I looked for it, the path down the cliff.

For a moment, my spirits brightened. Hadn't I surmised that the thirteenth Earl had used the little cove for swimming? The distance to the path was not so great; a distance of a few hundred feet, no more. But something told me that the thirteenth Earl had not made a habit of swimming after storms, in early March.

The waves hit the cliff hard, and shattered. I tried to imagine what it would be like to arrive at the shore with one of those waves. Painful. And there was a great sucking undertow. You'd be flung at the rocks, pulled back beneath the oncoming wave—and swallowed.

Of course I was going to be swallowed anyway. Sooner or later I was going to get washed off my rock and carried shoreward. I could not stop my imagination from showing me the sight: myself, a bloody rag doll, smashed against the cliff. I flinched. Maybe the cold would get to me first.

Or maybe I could drown myself first. It was strange, heaven knows, to be sitting there trying to calculate just how I was going to meet my death. But I am such a coward about pain, and the idea of my poor arms and legs battered against the rocks of the shore, bones broken, teeth knocked out . . . It was the only choice I had left. Maybe I could spare myself that.

I turned back to the waves. Could I fight them, swim far enough out to drown before they washed me back to the shore? Was I strong enough? Or would I be carried instantly toward the cliff? I raised my arms over my head, stretching them this way and that. I was already stiff from the climb down the tower—or it might have been the ropes, or Sam's rough handling, or even a bruise from Walter's needle. I stared at the swells, calculating. Each one rose at least three feet; the big ones, probably six and a half feet. Doing a breast stroke, I could probably manage to stay above them. But for how long?

Another big wave hit the rock, and this time my feet got wet. The water was very cold. That was another possibility: maybe I could die of cold? I remembered from reading, it was a painless way to go. You just fell asleep, and never woke up. But it took a long time, I thought. What was the right name for it? Hypothermia? Your whole body had to reach a low temperature, very low. Cold as the Atlantic might be in March, I didn't think it would dispatch me fast enough.

I would swim for it. Drowning, I had read somewhere else, was also a painful death. But it seemed better than being hurled against a cliff and broken to pieces and *then* drowned.

I wondered what had happened to David. He probably hadn't gotten away, with three men looking for him. I allowed myself a moment's softening. I remembered that one instant in the stable, when we had kissed, when the whole patina of a civilized man had fallen away, showing me the raw desire underneath. Even in retrospect, it warmed me. I summoned up his picture in my mind's eye, David as I had first seen him, the English country gentleman at his desk—gold-rimmed glasses and baggy corduroys, slow, measured movements, and deep voice. A little sigh escaped me and I felt my eyes filling with tears.

I tried to blink them back. I tried to control myself. A sense of unreality had cocooned me as I made my little calculations about the waves. And I wanted it back. I wanted to scramble off that rock into the water without any sense of what I was doing. I didn't want to be aware that I was dying.

All of this flashed through my mind as I tried to stop crying. Went through my mind very quickly, without effect. And reality thrust itself in on me. I was going to die.

My control broke. I screamed, I started to wail, to bellow, to rage. I lifted my face to the gray clouds and keened, mourning not my death but the life I would miss. I thought of my parents, shocked and anguished. I thought, oddly, of my belongings at Neville Park and at Saltire. Who would have the task of collecting them? My book would never be finished; Lauretta's diaries would be forgotten. Poor David was probably dead, too; his great-grandmother's story wouldn't matter to him any more.

My mind was still dwelling on that fact when I forced myself to stand up. I had nothing to gain from waiting any longer. If I went into the water at an angle, I wouldn't be tossed right back onto the rock. I bent down to untie my shoes and placed them carefully together at the top of the rock. And before I lost my courage, I dove into the water.

I am a strong swimmer, at home in the ocean. I aimed my dive into the bottom of a big wave, where I would be least disturbed by the movement of the crest. All the same, I came up gasping. And very frightened.

I was being carried right back beyond my rock. The waves and the tide were much stronger than I was.

I tried. I made an enormous effort to swim forward. I lifted my head over the crest of a wave, slid down into the trough, breasted the next wave. I stroked as powerfully as I could, and kicked with all my strength. The cold had shocked me, made me shiver all over. The water was very salty and I was swallowing lots of it.

At the crest of a wave, I could see another big wave coming. For all my efforts, I was barely keeping level with the rock. Like the Red Queen, I thought, running to keep in place.

But after all, it didn't matter where I drowned. As long as I was unconscious by the time I hit the cliff. That was all I wanted; the only thing I asked from life. What there was left of it.

The big wave was towering over me. I ducked my head and swam through it, flinching when my hand touched something in the water. A piece of wood, a dead fish, what did it matter? I came up for air.

I was tiring already. Each stroke was a fight. I could see a series of lower swells coming. Maybe, if I could make some progress over them, I would be able to take a little rest, tread water for a while. Summoning every reserve of strength I had, I pushed forward. My hands were getting numb now, and my lips felt rubbery and chapped from the salt. I started counting. One, two, three, four, pause. One, two, three, four, pause. A little longer pause. My arms were so heavy. One, two, three, four. I was drifting backward. Must kick, push forward. As I lifted my head for a breath, water slapped my face and I choked, gasped, and sank. Maybe this was it.

I bobbed again to the surface. Not yet. Amazing how the body floats. Must go a little farther. Just a little, before I let go. Another big wave coming. Maybe I would let it carry me. No, I should choose a smaller wave, less impact. One, two, three.

Very big wave. Funny shape, too. Little pointed things on top. One, two. Flotsam and jetsam. But moving. Another wave in the face. Down, down. Out of breath. Bursting. This is drowning. Bursting. No. Surface. Gasp for air. Facing wrong way now. Swimming toward shore, silly. Wrong idea. Ugh, dead fish. Brush it off. Doesn't matter now.

But it wouldn't brush off. It caught my hand. And it wasn't dead, or cold.

It was a human hand, holding mine. I was turned around now. And I could see that what I thought was a big wave was a boat. The two pointed things were men. And the hand holding mine was David's.

Chapter 16

It was actually very hard to get into the boat. David's broken collarbone prevented him from either hauling me out of the water or rowing to keep the boat from being carried to shore. Finally, the oarsman maneuvered over to my rock. It was almost covered with water, so I had to make very little effort to scramble on top of it. And from there over the gunwale was relatively simple.

My legs collapsed and I tumbled into a heap in the bottom of the boat. I was shivering terribly, my teeth chattering. But David produced a blanket, which he tucked around me. I wanted to look at him to ask what had happened, but I didn't have the strength. I lay there with my hand in his, only barely conscious. The little craft pitched and tossed through the waves, landing sometimes with a jolt that set every ache in my body throbbing. Nobody spoke.

At last, the pitching lessened, then stopped altogether. David stirred as if to lift me off his lap, and I sat up groggily, clutching the blanket. Our boat was moored in a rocky cove like the one we'd just left. But it was much more enclosed, and a jetty had been built out from shore, so the water was calm enough to launch a boat. I didn't conclude all of this then. I merely peered around, grateful to be near land.

The oarsman, having made fast the boat and disappeared for a moment, came back into sight leading a donkey cart. Before I could make any protest he lifted me out of the boat and onto the seat of the cart. David climbed up next to me. "Lean against me, and go to sleep if you like. We'll be at the house in about twenty minutes."

"What about Walter?" I asked, to be sure.

"Don't worry about him."

So I went to sleep. I do remember arriving at the house, with the donkey cart halted under the grandiose porte cochere. I was carried upstairs and my wet clothes were taken off. Then I was put to bed, and slept. I woke once or twice, aware of light coming in from the window or the door opening. But each time I remembered luxuriously that I was safe and so was David, and I went back to sleep.

Finally, I drifted toward consciousness again, and woke completely, clearheaded and even anticipatory, like a child on its birthday. There was something to look forward to: David. Incautiously, I tried to sweep back the covers. The first movement of my arm flattened me with its ache. I lay back for a moment. Of course, I must be fairly bruised. And stiff from all that swimming and clambering down castles and up trees. I wriggled a leg, which sent back only minor twinges. So I would slide out of bed and try not to use my arms.

I shoved my legs toward the edge of the bed and, preparing for the complaints from my shoulders, thrust myself into a sitting position. I took stock. A bath first; I had been put to bed all salty, and my skin was beginning to itch. Not to mention what my hair must look like. I shook my head and received a vague sensation of a clotted mass.

But could I bathe myself? My hands, lying in my lap, looked ghastly, covered with cuts and scrapes, swollen, bruised. And I was not even sure I could stand, for my ankle was still throbbing and I could see now that it was puffed to double its size.

The door opened slowly, and I looked up from contemplation of my foot. Standing in the doorway, as much of a vision as ever, was Henrietta, neatly dressed in russet tweed and holding a tin tray. "Henrietta! What are you doing here?"

"I brought you some tea," she said, not really answering my question. "You must be famished. How long have you been awake?"

"I just woke up," I answered, looking with interest at the plate of cookies on the tray she had brought in. "I am hungry, but you know what's worse is that I itch. I'd rather wash before food."

"You itch? Oh, the salt water. Don't tell me they put you to bed without a bath!"

"I was probably a dead weight," I said. "I don't think they had much choice. How did you get here?"

"Such a tale! Can you walk?" Henrietta put the tray on the bureau and held out an elbow to me. "I'll help you bathe and tell you the whole story. There are some very senior police downstairs waiting for Sleeping Beauty to wake up, so we'd best make it brisk."

I stood up and managed to hobble to the bathroom, leaning heavily on Henrietta's arm. While I had a rather chilly bath— the plumbing was not up to the standard of Saltire—she explained.

When David first reached the Pearsalls' house, he had asked them to call his father if he didn't return in a few hours. So the Earl had been alerted, just before retiring, that his son might be in danger from drug-runners.

"He was furious, of course; David hadn't said he was coming here, and Papa would have tried to talk him out of it. So he called Sir Giles at the CID and they decided to send in a couple of men very quietly to make sure everything was all right. Then he decided to come here himself. If you lean back a little more, I'll wash your hair. It needs it."

"I'm sure it does. There's probably seaweed and pine needles in it," I answered. "So, did you talk your father into letting you come too?"

"Not strictly speaking. He got into the car to go to the air-port and there I was. It's all been frightfully exciting. David said you climbed down the side of the tower. What a hideous place this is!" She wrapped a towel around my hair. "I would have brought some of your clothes if I'd known, but we thought you'd have them here. David didn't know where you'd left them."

"They're at the pub in Neville, I hope. Maybe someone could go pick them up?" I pulled myself out of the tub, feeling like I had a new skin. "I have to put something on, though, if all those people are waiting downstairs. We might as well get something from Lauretta's trunks. I'll look peculiar but I don't suppose that matters."

We limped back to my bedroom, and Henrietta peered out the window. "Is this where you climbed out? Good heavens, Sarah!"

I hopped over, out of curiosity, and leaned down. "It was dark," I said. "I couldn't see much." The ground was very far away, and craning to look at the tower, I could see how shallow the ledges were that I had climbed down. "It all looks much more frightening in daylight."

"Let me pour you some tea, and I'll go find some clothes for you. Where are they?"

"In the tower room down the hall. One of the tea-gowns would be the best bet, since anything else would be too small."

She was back in a few moments, arms full. "Here's some underwear, and this is reasonably conventional-looking." She held up a pale apricot brocade gown with heavy lace trimming. "Like a rather lavish bathrobe. And I couldn't resist bringing this to try on myself." It was the bright green ribbon-patterned Worth dress that had been on top of one of the trunks. "We'll get you downstairs first, though."

And finally, we did. Henrietta pinned up my hair and found a tapestry slipper for my good foot. "I wish there were something we could do about your poor hands," she said as she did the fastenings of the tea-gown. "But we'll try to get some bandages in Neville for the worst bits." Finally, she produced a silver-handled cane.

As we hobbled downstairs I heard the voices in the drawing room, a rumble of masculine discussion. But the men must have heard our steps, for in an instant David was in the hall, looking up at us.

You hear about time standing still, and you hear about the feeling that you're the only two people in the room. You hear about hearts turning over. Like so many clichés, they're all true. I know that for a long moment everything in me was concentrated on David's face, on the expression in his brown eyes. I could not begin to describe it, but the shyness I had begun to feel dropped away, and I was sure of him. Though we had to say it all again later, that one look between us made everything clear.

David rushed up the stairs and took my arm, removing the cane from my hand. He didn't say anything, but he didn't need to. So the three of us stumbled into the drawing room.

Three men stood up, and now I was embarrassed at being the center of attention and appearing so melodramatically. The tall, thin man standing by the fire was obviously the Earl, and as he spoke I could hear the same hesitating hint of a stutter that David had. "Miss Llewellyn, we have been hearing great tales of your bravery," he said, very seriously. I blushed, feeling the heat rush into my face, and said something trite. I had not been particularly brave. "David," he went on, "perhaps you would pull up a footstool for Miss Llewellyn. Henrietta, do you suppose there might possibly be any ice in the kitchen for a compress?" So I was seated in front of the fire, David produced a footstool, Henrietta went off to the kitchen. I was surprised to note that the drawing room looked brighter, somehow more lived-in. The light of another gloomy day was just leaving the sky, but the lamps were already on, a silver tea-tray stood in front of the fire, the strict geometric arrangement of the furniture had been shuffled about.

"Would you care for a cup of tea? Or perhaps some sherry?" Lord Saltire offered. "There are a number of questions we would like to ask, but only if you're strong enough."

Henrietta came back with a pudding-basin and some linen towels. "Sarah should eat something. David, give her a piece of that cake. You'd better cut it up for her because of her hands." She sat on the floor and began to arrange an ice pack around my ankle while the conversation went on. It felt a bit uncomfortable to have people fussing over me so much.

As David obligingly cut a slab of cake into sections, his father said, "No doubt Miss Llewellyn would like to know how we got here and what happened to David. Why don't you tell her quickly. . . ."

David handed me the plate and sat on the couch beside me. In a gesture that I found absurdly appealing, he put on his glasses. "Let's see. I left you in the woods and went back to get that beast that gave us away. I thought my best plan would be to try to draw off as many of them as possible. So I made a lot of noise, and rode toward the stable to be sure they saw me. Then I headed over to the wall at the edge of the property, toward the Pearsalls'. As the animal jumped the wall, I popped off and hid in the bushes, and when the fellow who was following me came along, I grabbed him and got his gun from him. I hobbled him and left him there, and the police have him now. That was Sam." He took my empty plate and began to cut up another slice of the cake. I was embarrassed to eat so much but I was starving. "I went back to the tree to find you, but you were gone. Then I went to the house, rather foolishly thinking that everyone would be in the stable. Walter caught me in his study, where I was trying to phone. Stupid to get caught in a room with only one exit. Anyway, he got our disreputable cousin Gerald to tie me up, and explained in the most unctuous way possible how sorry he was that he was going to have to put me out of the way. He wouldn't tell me where you were, but he hinted that you were dead." David handed the plate back to me, and though his voice was steady, he paused and took a deep breath.

"He got rather abusive. It was unnerving to watch, almost like wax melting; his accent got thicker and thicker and he began to rant and rave about the English, and the English upper classes in particular, how snobbish and shiftless and heartless they are, and how criminally stupid, and so on. And he began making fun of poor Gerald, talking about how he'd been so gullible, and how the public school system trained people to be credulous but Gerald was unbelievably naive. He was extraordinarily vicious.

"Anyway, in the middle of this . . . I don't know how to say it except bluntly. Gerald had been getting restive. You know, at first he looked shocked, then enraged; then he very calmly took out his gun and aimed it at Walter, who wasn't even looking at him. And shot him, right in the chest." He looked to see how I was taking this. I thought of how Gerald had talked to me in the woods, and how desperate he had seemed. Walter had pushed him too far, and Gerald's tenuous self-control had finally snapped. I wasn't surprised. Nor was I very sorry.

David went on. "Gerald apologized profusely, but he left me tied up, in fact added a few knots. Then he told me how they had killed you. He was honestly upset by that. He said Walter had knocked you out with a hypodermic full of something, and Sam had rowed out to dump your body on a rock in the bay, where it would get swept away by the tide. Gerald kept saying how horrified he was. Then he left. And I sat there in the study with the late Mr. Walter until these gentlemen came and undid the knots."

"But how did you find me?" I asked.

To my delight, he flushed and looked down. "I was . . ." he glanced sideways at me, "a bit upset. Remember, Gerald had told me you were *dead*. So I tore down to the water to see the rock in the bay he'd talked about. I thought there might be some chance . . . and I was looking at it, thinking what a funny shape it was. Or what a funny blob of seaweed, like an enormous strand of kelp, was draped on top of it." Now he was smiling a little. "You did look exactly like a piece of kelp, just the same color, all sorts of golden browns."

"I felt just about like one, too," I said tartly. "When did you realize I was not an extra-giant-size specimen of ocean flora?"

"Well, I was wondering idly if these weren't rather cold waters for kelp beds when you moved—you stirred a bit and then were still again. Though I was naturally inclined to identify you as a mermaid, it was obvious you were you. I called out but I don't think you heard. I saw the tide was coming in, and the current looks very fierce there, so clearly there wasn't much time. The Pearsalls have a tenant, Niall, who's very good at handling a currach. So we came to get you. When we rounded the headland into the cove and you weren't there . . ." This time he barely paused and he was very earnest. "Had you decided to swim for it?"

I glanced around the room at the five people listening. For an instant, I allowed myself to remember the water and the cliff, and the only choice I thought I had. I didn't want to remember it again, and we had all had enough melodrama. "Yes," I said blandly, "I thought I could make it but I didn't realize how strong the current was."

"Very good. And now, could we ask a few questions?" Lord Saltire said. "We are aware of the broad outlines of Walter's criminal activities. The shipment of hay he received last night is actually a rather large quantity of cocaine, well disguised. I am told it would have left Neville in a horse van perfectly innocently, and been distributed to lower-level dealers in the horse world. From sources in the village we understand that this is the sixth or seventh such shipment. What we do not understand is the role Gerald Charlton played in this, and why the succession to the title had to be dragged into it."

One of the other men, looking rather out of place in his blue chalk-striped suit, said, "Can you tell us whether or not those claims about the earldom are true?"

"I'm sorry, Miss Llewellyn, let me introduce Sir Giles Newell-Layton, who is a friend of the family's as well as being professionally involved in this case. And this is Inspector Oliver Gregson," indicating a man so nondescript that I couldn't remember what he looked like after he left.

"They aren't true. There are two forged death certificates here—at least, I found them in one of the trunks upstairs. I'm afraid I more or less stole them, and put them in my camera bag. That was on the front seat of my car." I looked at Henrietta and David. "Have you seen it? I left the car at the top of the drive, and Sam had the keys."

Sir Giles answered, "We pushed the car back down the drive, since we couldn't start it. I believe that your camera bag was examined, principally for identification. No death certificates were found in it."

"Well, they were for Lauretta and her son. And there's a parish register in the chapel that lists their burials and the baptism of another baby boy, which must be forged as well. They went to a lot of trouble."

"There was a great deal at stake, and Walter wanted to avoid interference from the Charltons. The scheme was complex, but I suppose it started off simply enough," suggested Sir Giles.

"Yes. I think it must have." I paused, trying to decide where to begin. "David wrote to Walter saying that his lease would soon be up, and could David please come out to look over Neville Park to make plans for a stud. When was that?"

"A bit more than a month ago," David answered.

"I think Gerald must already have turned up here. He apparently just waltzed in one day, told Walter that he was a relation of the family, and probably Walter grasped very quickly that Gerald could be useful. Evidently he presented this operation to Gerald as a fairly innocent business scheme." I looked down at my apricot-brocade lap and paused. "Gerald probably can't be excused. But you can understand, I think, how he got involved; he was so obsessed by the family, and so jealous of the two of you." I looked at Henrietta and David. "And desperate for money."

I noticed Sir Giles nodding at this. "There were considerable debts," he said.

"When he got your letter, David, Walter had to find a way to keep you from coming here. He hit on using Gerald as a tool. They probably knew enough about the family history to realize that there was this one slightly murky moment that nobody knew much about. Gerald nosed about a bit and realized that, if indeed Lauretta had died without giving birth, or if her son had died, he was the earl."

I sighed and wondered how much to explain. "There was enough evidence to make that just possible; for instance, when he was in New York, he found out that Lauretta's money would revert back to her father if she died without children. Her husband didn't get to keep it, and since he'd married her for her money in the first place, that would be a tragedy. So he had a great interest in her producing an heir. Anyway, that's a refinement. The point is that Walter had the parish register forged and planted it where Gerald would find it. So Gerald suddenly thinks he is the true earl. Then, according to Walter, he started agitating about more proof, and the death certificates appear in the trunks."

"Amazing to be able to get things forged just like that," Henrietta said. "Do you suppose you have someone on tap and you just place your order, two death certificates circa 1899, like ordering a pair of lamb chops?"

"A bit," Sir Giles said. "Walter's had a number of identities, all of which require papers, so he would have capable contacts."

"But why was no formal claim lodged with the College of

Heralds if Gerald was so sure of his ground?" Lord Saltire interjected.

"Well, you started getting anonymous letters, didn't you? David first, then Henrietta? Hinting that there was something wrong?" They all nodded.

"I think that Walter's idea was that Gerald make the claim through the usual channels," I went on. "But maybe Gerald found that unappealing. Rather than make a vulgar fuss, he'd rather stir things up, let you all investigate the legitimacy of the claim, and then step gracefully into the title when the dust settled. Without having looked pushy."

"The frightening thing about the letters," Henrietta said, "was that they were so exact. He seemed to know so much about us now and about the family history."

"I think for a long time he had made a cult of you. He *was* very well-informed. And I'm afraid I helped him out a bit when I met him in New York."

"You did?" Henrietta looked up in surprise. "How did you meet him?"

"At the library. We were using some of the same books, and he asked for my help."

"So that is how you got involved with these people," Sir Giles said.

"Yes. Gerald asked if I was coming here, and I think he had roughly the same idea that you did," I addressed David. "I was going to do the research, and find out that he was the true earl."

"Like our plan for you," David said, with a glance at Henrietta. She got up and left the room, saying something about dinner.

"Yes. The documents were placed where I'd be sure to find them. And Gerald had also been prowling around Saltire to see what I'd discovered there."

"Miss Llewellyn," Sir Giles interrupted, "what about last night? According to what you've told us, you should have been able to do your research and leave, though I can't say that taking the death certificates with you was wise. Obviously you had trouble with your car. But how did you know the documents were forgeries?"

I was getting tired of concentrating, and a little foggy-minded. I rubbed my red, raw hands over my face. "Could I just tell you everything that happened? It would be easier."

"Of course."

I began to explain about my arrival at Ballyhannock, and my impulsive drive to Neville Park, where I'd seen Gerald. I got as far as repeating the pub gossip about the Neville Park goings-on when David interrupted.

"Why did you come here then? Why not just go back to London?" he asked. "You were suspicious of me, and you knew my fall had been fixed. Why wasn't that enough of a warning?"

I looked sheepishly at him. "I thought I was being hysterical and paranoid, and that any brave journalist wouldn't pass up such a great research opportunity."

Sir Giles interrupted. "So you were vaguely suspicious when you arrived. Then?"

"Walter showed me the church and the tower room, and left me to my own devices," I went on. I remembered my Alice-in-Wonderland feeling that nothing was what it looked like as I told them about finding the forged documents, and Gerald's appearance at lunchtime.

"Then after lunch, Gerald came upstairs, ostensibly to help me look at dresses; obviously what he really wanted was to make sure I'd found the death certificates. But I'd already hidden them." I chuckled. "He was very funny when we got to the trunk where they should have been; like a dog when you've hidden his bone. But then I discovered something they hadn't seen which disproved all their forgeries." Forgivably, I think, I paused.

On cue, Lord Saltire said, "And what was that?"

"There's a dress Lauretta bought in Paris that she couldn't

have worn during her pregnancy. But it has been worn, and when I shook it out, a dance card dropped out of the folds. It was all filled in, and dated the fifteenth of December. Evidently there was a dance at the Pearsalls' and Lauretta went and danced every dance. Gerald and Walter couldn't have known about it."

I hadn't noticed Henrietta, standing in the doorway, wearing the green dress. It looked splendid on her. "I've thrown together what I found in the kitchen and we can have dinner anytime. Don't you think this dress is superb? And I can't tell you how glad I am, Sarah, that Papa is still Papa."

There was a momentary buzz of excitement as Henrietta kissed her father and settled herself on the other side of me, carefully arranging the heavy folds of the emerald-patterned brocade.

"Netta, you look tremendously fetching, but aren't you a little chilly?" David asked.

"No chillier than Lauretta would have been," Henrietta answered, with some asperity.

"If I might continue," Sir Giles broke in determinedly, "I think we are close to the end of Miss Llewellyn's story, and then I will leave you all to your own devices." Henrietta glanced mischievously at David. "You discovered a dance card that proved the death certificates to be forgeries. What did you do then?"

"I hid it under one of the trunks, and tried to leave, but my car broke down, as you saw. Walter wasn't too happy to have me back, but pretended nobody had enough gas to take me to Ballyhannock. I thought that a bit odd, and that it might have something to do with the forgeries, and I was getting very worried. Then after dinner I saw Walter put something in my coffee, which I didn't drink; then they locked me in my bedroom. That was why I climbed out the window. I guess I panicked."

"And actually they were probably just trying to keep you out of the way," David said, "while they received the shipment of coke. Protective custody, so to speak."

"I guess so. If I'd known they were running drugs, my God, I'd never have come near them, let alone try to get out of my bedroom."

Finally, Sir Giles seemed satisfied, and he and the inspector prepared to go back to the pub in Neville. It wasn't until they were in the hall putting on their coats that I remembered my question. Ignoring Henrietta's protests, I picked up the cane and limped out of the drawing room to ask, "What about Gerald?"

Sir Giles turned to me. "He has disappeared. If he has got safely out of Britain, it will be harder to find him. But there is a murder charge against him." He nodded, and followed the inspector out the door.

David was at my elbow. "Do you mind what happens to him?" he asked, looking intently at me.

I sighed, thinking. "I'd hate to see him in jail. I think he was an unwilling accessory to most of Walter's activities. He's obviously feckless, but I wouldn't have said really harmful. Still, murder . . ." I shrugged. "I suppose what I feel for him is pity."

"Come and have dinner, you two," Henrietta said, from the door of the dining room. "I think I've done us rather well, considering."

And she had. Miraculously, it was a wonderful meal. The four of us sat at one end of the table, far away from the huge silver centerpiece. Henrietta had come up with a box of candles and lit all of them, and Lord Saltire had found some wonderful wine. I mostly listened and looked, admiring the way the green dress set off the pale skin of Henrietta's shoulders, noticing how her father enjoyed her teasing, smiling quietly when she called him "stuffy." He had the same kind of charm as David, I thought; a similar reserve and keen perceptiveness, overlaid with an air of confidence, even command. I caught him, once or twice, glance speculatively from David to me; and the second time, when he met my gaze, he smiled very slightly.

As we all got up to leave the table, Henrietta announced that she and her father would do the dishes. "It will be a novel experience for you, Papa," she said, handing him a stack of plates.

"Nonsense, my dear, I have washed my share of dishes in the army," he answered, obediently heading toward the kitchen.

"That was much too long ago to count," retorted Henrietta, gathering up our glasses. "And Sarah, I think David must be eager to see that dance card that proves he is Lord Neville." She grinned at us, and made a shooing motion with the glasses. "Go on. You can't do dishes anyway, Sarah, you'd bleed all over them."

"Gruesome but true," David said as he took my elbow. "We'll take you to a doctor tomorrow."

"If there is one," I answered, suddenly nervous. For the first time, I felt uneasy, self-conscious with David. As we went up the stairs I glanced sideways at him; he seemed unperturbed.

"Now where did you hide this dance card, whatever that might be?" he asked, turning on the light in the tower room.

"It's here, under this trunk," I said, pointing with the cane.

He bent down and lifted one of the handles of the trunk, and as he did I heard a distinct sliding and a thump. As if something heavy in the trunk had moved. He picked up the little pasteboard square with its silk tassel. "Ah," he said, turning it over in his hand. "This is the positive proof of my rightful claim to be the next Earl of Saltire." He looked at me quizzically. "Do we think it would stand up in a court of law?"

"Wait," I said, "open the trunk. Something slid around in it when you moved it."

He gave me the dance card, and lifted the lid of the trunk.

"Under that dress," I said. "And under the petticoats and the shoes and that blanket. I think there must be something else."

David was carefully draping the dress over the top of another trunk. "I must say, that *is* beautiful," he said seriously, and he looked back at me with an odd expression before leaning over to remove the underwear and the blanket.

Then he reached back into the trunk, and smiled. "Is this what you were looking for?" he asked. And held up a heavy book. He put it in my lap, and I read the gilt letters on the cover: "Diary." The missing volume.

I opened the book and turned to the end, to December. On December 4, the entry began, "I have a baby boy." David, on his knees next to me, craned to read, but I flipped over more pages, skimming for more references to the child. "Neville is doing well, he gets stronger every day," I read. I flipped more pages, until I got to the entry for December 15. "I am going to the Pearsalls' tonight. Mrs. Party says I must not, for the weather is fierce, and she thinks I am not yet strong enough. But W. will be there, and indeed I am longing to be up and to see company. I shall wear the white brocade from Worth, for the first time."

"Who is W?" David asked.

I looked at the dance card. "William Pearsall," I read. "They danced three times. Practically cause for scandal in that era. It's nice to think she had an admirer." I looked over at the dress. "I wonder what happened; all of those things thrown in together, maybe in a hurry . . . she must have been taken ill that night, after the dance."

David got up from his knees, and picked up the dress. "Very possible. Perhaps . . ." He looked at me, and the air of calm I'd noticed in him had disappeared. He paused, looking down at the white brocade. And, flushed, he said, "Perhaps you'd like to wear it as your wedding dress?"

I stared. "What?" I said. My mind seemed to have stopped working.

In a swift movement, David tossed the dress back into the trunk and came over to me.

"This is probably better, on my knees, like a proper suitor," he said hurriedly. "Sarah, I so hope you'll marry me. Will you?"

The only answer I could think of was, "Of course."

I did wear Lauretta's white dress, with the neckline altered to make it more modest. Henrietta wore the green, as my bridesmaid. David told me later that his brother Hugh, who married us, thought we were overdressed; but Hugh is, as Gerald had told me, awfully stuffy. Lately he has expressed disapproval of my traveling to promote my book, which I managed to finish before we got married. Hugh thinks it unbecoming that David's wife (my maiden name is on the book, but Hugh ignores that fact) "traipses all over the States to drag our name into the newspapers." He mutters darkly about Antonia Fraser.

For the moment we divide our time between the dower house and Neville Park. David has put a lot of work into the stud but we won't know for several years whether or not it's going to pay. There's a caretaker living there full-time and he says that even now he gets occasional visitors asking odd questions about certain brands of liniment or horse blankets.

The police haven't found Gerald. I actually hope he is safe in Kenya or someplace like that.

For all of Hugh's mutterings, I did ask the publicity department to leave off the press releases the fact that David and I had married. I was afraid talk-show hosts would insist on discussing what it was like for an American girl to marry into the English aristocracy not a hundred years ago, but now.